They weren't in the Deathlands anymore

Sixty feet and maybe more below, an emerald green ocean lapped at the bottom of the terra firma they found themselves on. There was no indication of land mixed in with the accumulated snow and fresh layers of ice. Out ahead, scattered across the wide expanse of the sea, were hundreds of ice floes. Nearly all of them were smaller than the one they were encased in.

Mildred stepped up beside Ryan to look out over the ocean. "We're in a damn ice cube floating in the middle of the goddamn ocean!"

And that, Ryan figured, just about summed it up.

JAMES AXLER

DEATH LANDS®

Way of the Wolf

A GOLD EAGLE BOOK FROM

WORLDWIDE®

TORONTO • NEW YORK • LONDON
AMSTERDAM • PARIS • SYDNEY • HAMBURG
STOCKHOLM • ATHENS • TOKYO • MILAN
MADRID • WARSAW • BUDAPEST • AUCKLAND

First edition July 1998

ISBN 0-373-62542-1

WAY OF THE WOLF

Song of the Wolf

Silent, sleek, savagely swift
on the watchful hunt.
Locking eyes with the chosen one
to see who yields to the final call.
While the stars wheel on their course
we are at one with that primal force.

O Pure Brothers, a sacrifice
to the gods of survival.

THE DEATHLANDS SAGA

This world is their legacy, a world born in the violent nuclear spasm of 2001 that was the bitter outcome of a struggle for global dominance.

There is no real escape from this shockscape where life always hangs in the balance, vulnerable to newly demonic nature, barbarism, lawlessness.

But they are the warrior survivalists, and they endure—in the way of the lion, the hawk and the tiger, true to nature's heart despite its ruination.

Ryan Cawdor: The privileged son of an East Coast baron. Acquainted with betrayal from a tender age, he is a master of the hard realities.

Krysty Wroth: Harmony ville's own Titian-haired beauty, a woman with the strength of tempered steel. Her premonitions and Gaia powers have been fostered by her Mother Sonja.

J. B. Dix, the Armorer: Weapons master and Ryan's close ally, he, too, honed his skills traversing the Deathlands with the legendary Trader.

Doctor Theophilus Tanner: Torn from his family and a gentler life in 1896, Doc has been thrown into a future he couldn't have imagined.

Dr. Mildred Wyeth: Her father was killed by the Ku Klux Klan, but her fate is not much lighter. Restored from predark cryogenic suspension, she brings twentieth-century healing skills to a nightmare.

Jak Lauren: A true child of the wastelands, reared on adversity, loss and danger, the albino teenager is a fierce fighter and loyal friend.

Dean Cawdor: Ryan's young son by Sharona accepts the only world he knows, and yet he is the seedling bearing the promise of tomorrow.

In a world where all was lost, they are humanity's last hope....

Chapter One

"What the hell are you doing out here?"

Ryan Cawdor shifted casually in the long shadows of morning, a flexing of muscles that most people might have missed, bringing himself around to face the coming trouble squarely. But several of the men among the twenty-six coldhearts, who were gathered in front of Doc and him, took notice. Their hands dropped to their weapons.

Ryan's own hand touched the butt of the SIG-Sauer P-226 holstered on his right hip. He was tense, knowing what he and his companions faced, and knowing they had a slim chance of walking through the coming fire unscathed. They were all on triple red: Krysty Wroth, J. B. Dix, Jak Lauren, Mildred Wyeth and Ryan's son, Dean, who hid in the forest beyond the clearing, watching over them.

Of course, Ryan had made sure the odds were tilted in their favor as best he could. He was a brave man, a man who'd faced some of the worst Deathlands could offer and walked away a winner by simply surviving the encounter, but he was no greenie stupe when it came to trapping and being trapped. This day he was the trapper, but he'd had to step into the lion's den to get it done.

The clearing under the tall trees held the promise

of defensible positions, but only if Ryan and his companions didn't get cut down before they could make a move toward the enemy.

Rough-hewn, and stamped by violent events as a true son of Deathlands often was, Ryan stood over six feet tall and went over two hundred pounds, all of it rolling muscle from living hard. His curly black hair framed a sun-bronzed face, but the dark color was picked up again in the weathered patch that covered his left eye. He carried the SIG-Sauer pistol in a worn, serviceable holster at his right hip, and held the Steyr bolt-action sniper rifle in his right hand. His finger rested inside the rifle's trigger guard, the safety off.

"Why, my dear fellow," Doc said congenially, addressing the man who'd spoken to him and spreading his hands to indicate the small packages spread across the rough woolen blanket before him. "I came here to conduct a little free enterprise."

"Trading?" the lead rider asked.

"The very thing." Doc grinned, showing his unnaturally perfect white teeth.

The gang members were mostly young, Ryan noted, but they had all the moves down. It wasn't anything military or a result of organized drills. They ranged the way a pack of natural predators moved against a possible enemy—or a potential victim.

Dr. Theophilus Algernon Tanner gave them the impression of a victim, which was why Ryan had delegated him spokesman. Doc was nearly six feet three inches in his stocking feet, but built as gangly as a stork. Silvery white hair framed his face, blowing in the gentle wind that came at them from the east, making it brush his shoulders. He'd washed his clothes in a small stream the group had camped by overnight. The dress shirt hadn't come entirely white, and wouldn't without some strong detergent and bleach. Still, it looked presentable with the black string tie and the Victorian black frock coat that held a greenish hue and luster that time had ground into the garment. Black pants and cracked leather knee boots completed the look. The lion's-head walking stick—really a sword stick—was an affectation of Doc's, not a necessity.

"Could of done your trading in town," the stranger said. He was a big man, broad across the shoulder and narrow at the hip, almost looking too large for the dappled gray mare beneath him. Like the other men, he wore chaps over denim jeans and a sheepskin coat with the sleeves roughly hacked off. A violet-and-white-striped bandanna circled his head. Blue tattoos of knives and naked women and impossible monsters marked his arms and face, making him one with the rest of the group.

Ryan knew the purpose of the tattooing was to bind the group together. Once marked, there was nowhere the recipient could go without his history catching up to him. It tied him to the band forever.

"I could have," Doc agreed, "but the forest is my theater, and here I owe no man." He looked pointedly beyond the speaker to the man at the center of the group. "I had been told that any business conducted within the ville had to pay a tariff to the sec chief.''

Ryan and his companions knew the ''sec chief'' from an earlier recce. They'd come out of a mat-trans unit in what used to be southern Kentucky early the previous day, worn and lathered from the events at the mall. The jump had been a hard one, and Doc had slept most of the preceding twenty-four hours recovering from the effects.

Living off the land in the Berland Mountains region was easy pickings for the survivalist group. What wasn't so easy was finding ammo for their weapons. All of them were running low after the last bit of killing, and the redoubt they'd arrived in had contained no ammunition, but did yield many items they could trade for what they needed. Then Ryan had heard about Hazard, the nearest ville, from a hunter he'd met in the deep woods the previous evening, when he and Jak had been tracking mule deer.

According to the hunter, the sec chief's name was Liberty, and he ran Hazard's buffer zone, keeping the area clear of muties. The people put up with the band of coldhearts as long as no violence was directed at any of the citizens. Now Liberty sat in a horse-drawn buggy that had once been an old Ford convertible sedan from predark times. The front end had been cut out, leaving the steering intact. Two horses stood in traces before the vehicle.

Lean, his face clean shaved but shadowed by tat-toos, his hair cut short enough to show more tattoos on his scalp, the man sat impassively with his legs in the rear seat and his butt on the trunk. A Winchester lever-action rifle leaned against the seat at his side.

A dwarf in silver-and-blue livery occupied a makeshift bench seat across the empty space where the engine had been. A wriggled scar pulled his mouth out of line as he gazed at Ryan. There weren't as many tattoos on the little man, but they were there just the same. The dwarf adjusted the traces.

"So you're out here trying to avoid the tax," the rider stated.

"Yes," Doc admitted. "Being a free man, I have no love for most barons. They are generally only tyrants with self-aggrandized titles."

The coldhearts broke into sudden laughter, the noise startling their horses. The sounds of leather creaking and the stamping of restless hooves filled the small area under the canopy of branches.

Ryan knew he was drawing more stares than Doc. The gang had already written off the old man as harmless. Him, they recognized as danger. But Ryan had counted on that. The riders didn't know about the big Le Mat blaster Doc had hidden behind a nearby tree.

"If you're gonna do business in these parts," the rider said, "you're gonna pay a tax."

"I thought the wares I am exhibiting might preclude any such taxation without representation," Doc replied.

The rider looked uncertain, obviously not following all of the words the old man used. He peered over his shoulder, back at the Hazard ville sec chief.

"What he's saying, Philox," Liberty said in a quiet baritone voice, "is that he thinks the stuff he's got is worth so much that he ain't gonna have to pay a tax 'cause we're gonna like it so much."

Philox swiveled his head back to Doc. "Mister, I ain't seen nothing we couldn't live without. And if I did, I'd take it anyway."

"Always happy to see a confirmed consumer." Doc nodded happily. He looked beyond Philox. "Mayhap I could have your name, sir, since it appears I am going to be conducting my business with you instead of your associate."

Anger deepened Philox's coarse features. He put spurs to the mare and started forward.

Doc stood his ground, both hands resting lightly on the lion's-head sword stick. "I warrant, young man, that you should remember what was said about respecting one's elders." The good-natured grin never left the old man's face.

Philox grinned, and the expression was one of the purest expressions of evil Ryan had ever seen. "If I get a hankering, I'll beat you to death, gray hair." He urged his horse forward, straight into Doc.

Instead of stepping aside, Doc reached out and seized the horse's reins. He yanked them roughly, twisting the bit in the animal's mouth and causing the horse to rear in pain and surprise.

Philox bellowed and grabbed for his saddle pommel, but missed. He landed hard on the ground and came up roaring, pushing away from the rearing horse. The sec man pulled his pistol, fisting it in one beefy hand while he tried to hold on to the horse's reins with the other.

For a moment Ryan thought he was going to have to chill the coldheart right then and there, and open the ball on the rest of it. Then Liberty's voice roared.

"Philox, you pull up right now or I'll chill you myself!"

The big man froze into place, shooting the sec chief a glare that told Ryan he was contemplating disobeying the order. Ryan closed his hand around the SIG-Sauer's butt.

Liberty pulled up the Winchester and levered a round into the breech with a metallic rachet. "I said pull up, you stupe bastard!" The rifle barrel pointed straight at Philox.

"This what it's gonna come to, Liberty?" Philox demanded. "We start protecting some bastard ville, tying ourselves down like nurse-mommas, then we're gonna start taking guff from a near-deader?"

Liberty kept the rifle pointed. "We're gonna do what I say we're gonna do. *That* ain't gonna change. Ever. You don't like how I call the shots, you're free to pull up stakes and ride on."

Ryan's respect for Liberty rose. The one-eyed man had ridden as lieutenant for the Trader in years gone by. Keeping the crew of War Wag One in line had been demanding, and a weak man or one hesitant to chill someone who spoke out against him wouldn't have lasted a tick of a chron.

Philox's displeasure with the harsh words from his commander showed in the dark blood that filled his face. He shoved his pistol back into his holster and gathered his horse's reins. He mounted and rode to the back of the band. They parted and let him through. As he passed, another man pulled out of the crowd and rode with Philox.

"What about you, One-Eye?" Liberty demanded. "You got a name?"

"Is it important?" Ryan asked. "Man you're going to be dealing with is standing there in front of you."

Several of the gang turned to look at their leader. Liberty kept the rifle draped across his thighs. His thin smile remained in place. "Like to know who I'm dealing with."

"This is Doc Tanner," Ryan said, nodding at Doc. "He's the man you're dealing with."

Liberty turned his attention to Doc. "Who's your friend, Doc?"

"My boon companion," he replied easily. "A man I'd travel the river with, no matter where it took me or how treacherous it became."

"He got a name?"

"Indeed he does. There are some who call him Noman."

"Noman?" someone repeated. "What the fuck kinda name is that?"

"A proud one, sir, with a long lineage. In histories past, even long before skydark set in and swept the old world away with nuclear winter and cataclysmic contortions of the earth, Noman was renowned as a giant-killer."

"A giant-killer?" a gang member asked. "Seen

some bastard big muties, but none I'd rightly call a giant.''

"In those days," Doc said in a voice measured for drama, "giants roamed the earth."

"He's talking about *The Odyssey*," the dwarf said. He craned his head and looked back over his shoulder at Liberty. "It's from an old book that was ancient like he said. Man in there was named Odysseus. Had a big war, then he was trying to get home, only he kept having these adventures that kept getting in the way. Odysseus used the name Noman to kill a giant without the other giants knowing he was there."

"Ah," Doc said in obvious delight, gazing at the little man. "Someone who knows literature."

"I was a teacher," the dwarf stated with a trace of pride.

"You've fallen on hard times, my friend," Doc said sympathetically.

"He's alive," Liberty replied in a harsh voice, "and he's got a job. A lot of men can't say that. Ain't that right, Albert?"

The dwarf gave a short nod, clearly not happy about his present situation.

Ryan's attention centered on Philox. At the end of the band, a third man fell in beside him. Ryan reached up and touched the corner of his eye patch, as if he were scratching a small itch. The prearranged signal would alert Jak Lauren and send the albino teen into motion. Evidently Liberty had done some thinking about his overconfidence in riding up to face the two lone men in the forest.

"Now, let's talk about what you got," Liberty said, "and what you want for it."

Doc grabbed the lapels of his frock coat, the sword stick casually tucked up under his left arm. He put on a smile and an appearance of merriment. Ryan had long ago decided Doc was a born huckster. With the love of words and all the tangled histories that threaded through Doc's mind, J.B. was certain the man could talk a cannibalistic stickie nine days from its last lunch out of its next meal. Sometimes mat-trans jumps left the old man's brain addled for days, but the effects of the previous day's jump had already left his system.

The line of men moved around, coming naturally into a half moon in front of the woolen blanket. The move also developed a scrimmage line of sorts.

Ryan noted with satisfaction that the men lined up much in the positions that he'd planned for. He maintained his ground.

Albert, the dwarf, shook out his traces and clucked the horses to pull the wag in closer to inspect Doc's wares. The wooden wheels rolled smoothly over the ground. Liberty maintained his seat in the back of the convertible, the long blaster resting easily across his knees. He pinned Ryan with his gaze. "What about you, One-Eye? You gonna take a look, too?"

"I've already seen it," Ryan replied.

"I guess it must have took you twice as long as most people."

Ryan remained silent.

"I get the feeling you don't exactly trust me," the man said.

"Like a good hunting knife, trust cuts both ways," Ryan replied. It was a saying the Trader had often used. He looked past the sec chief, but he could no longer see Philox or the men who rode with him.

Liberty bared his teeth.

Ryan quietly hoped none of the gang looked up. The ropes above had been impossible to completely hide among the branches, and white scarring showed where limbs had been hacked away. The skin around the scar on his face tightened as the final cards were about to be played. He had seven rounds for the Steyr, and a full clip plus three for the SIG-Sauer.

Usually the companions didn't get so low on ammo. There were places to trade, and there were the redoubts that they had access to that sometimes hadn't been opened in a hundred years. Pressing on past Hazard didn't make any kind of sense unless they were better armed. And if it had been possible to trade without getting their throats cut, Ryan would have been all for it. Only Liberty and his band didn't have a reputation for dealing from the top of the deck.

In quick succession, Doc unveiled the denim shirts and pants in neat stacks on the woolen blanket. From there he moved on to the dozen packs of manufactured playing cards they'd raided from personnel lockers in the redoubt. Deathlands had their own pasteboards, many of them crude and hand-drawn,

In some areas, a deck of predark playing cards brought top jack.

"Let me see that deck," Liberty demanded.

Doc reached down for the cards. Ryan remembered the deck, remembered talking to J.B. about it, both of them agreeing that it would capture the eyes of most of the gang. The cards held pictures of creamy female beauties from a bygone era, clothed rather than naked like some of the decks, and oozing a sexuality that had affected Ryan, as well, as he'd looked at them.

The box said they had been drawn by someone named Gillette Elvgren, some time in the 1940s. The pictures seemed subtly more provocative than many of the sexually explicit ones Ryan had seen. Nudity was commonplace in Deathlands, but the flirty near innocence exhibited in the drawings of the women on the cards was something seldom seen.

"Ah, a connoisseur of fair feminine beauty," Doc said, handing over the deck. "Do be careful with it. They are quite valuable."

Liberty took the box and opened it. He fanned a number of the cards, some of the mounted men crowding in close to him to get a better look.

Ryan gazed in the direction Philox and his men had gone, guessing he'd never see the men. Nor would he see Jak, because the albino was one of the deadliest killers around.

The sec chief shoved the cards back together and reverently placed them within the cardboard box. "What else do you have?" He made no effort to hand the cards back, and a handful of the men around him cast covetous eyes on the prize their leader had selected.

"A few knives," Doc said. "Military blades with a sheen and a luster not seen often in these times." He unfolded another section of the blanket to reveal a half-dozen sheathed combat knives. One of the gang asked to see a blade that could have doubled as a small machete. Doc passed over the weapon.

The man drew the blade from the leather sheath. The keen edge splintered the weak sunlight that penetrated the tree canopy. Murmurs of appreciation followed the knife as the man whisked it through the air. He shaved the back of an arm with it, startled by the bright line of blood that followed one of his passes that had pressed too hard.

"Show the rest of it," Liberty ordered.

Ryan knew the gang leader was only buying time. The deal had been closed with the deck of cards, and the larceny in Liberty's warped soul wouldn't let him settle for anything less than all of the prizes displayed on the blanket. Trader had a saying: before a man learned to recognize honest emotion in a lover's eyes, he had to learn to spot greed in the eyes of a man waiting to cut a deal.

The one-eyed warrior saw greed all over Liberty. The sec chief wasn't used to playing his cards close to the vest. Most people he dealt with saw it coming.

"I have salves and ointments," Doc said, "antibacterial lotions for preventing infections, and antibiotics for inflammations and diseases that do occur in spite of the best efforts." The tubes and vials lay spread out across the blanket, each clearly marked by the Red Cross emblem and military markings. Doc held up a short, wide-mouthed blue jar. "There is even some topical anesthetic, good for dental problems, as well as limited invasive surgeries." He turned to face Liberty again. "As you can see, sir, I have quite a selection of valuable merchandise."

"Stuff you got," Liberty admitted, "is worth a lot of jack."

Doc grinned, but Ryan felt like a fist was squeezing his insides. His breath came shorter and clearer, the adrenaline pumping through his system. It was coming down to it.

"A man in my position," Doc said, "likes to hear that as an opening comment from a potential buyer."

"Where did you get this stuff?" Liberty demanded.

"Scavenging," Doc replied. "This area is still rocked by the occasional quake." The companions knew that from an earlier jump to the region. "My friend and I stumbled across a subterranean site that must have been heretofore undiscovered, possibly covered over, then pushed to the surface by tremors like a boiling pocket of pus."

"And you got lucky enough to find it?"

"My dear sir," Doc said, "it was bound to be found by someone."

Liberty shifted his attention to Ryan. "That the way you're gonna tell it, One-Eye?"

"Mebbe." Ryan faced the man directly. "If I was of a mind to tell it." He knew the gang leader didn't believe him. A larcenous gleam colored the man's eyes. "I came here to deal, not dicker. If you're not interested enough, reckon we'll push on."

"I'm interested," Liberty said. "I'd be more interested in knowing where you got this."

"That would be stupe," Ryan said. "If we told you where, you could go get your own. You wouldn't need to buy what we got to offer."

Liberty waved a hand toward the covered blanket. "So if I buy this, you'd tell me where you found it?"

Ryan shook his head slowly. "I'd sell you the location."

Liberty laughed. "You saying there's more?"

"Mebbe."

"And how am I supposed to trust you?"

"I think that was *my* question just a short time back," Ryan said. "We're here. We could have let your people ride on past us."

"Wrong. We cut your sign almost two hours ago. Trailed you here."

"If you'd have followed it back instead of following us," Ryan said, "you'd have found that trail dropped off into the edge of nowhere in one of the streams through this area. Look all you want. You won't find where we came from." Jak had seen to that, then made sure the other companions had arrived in the present location without leaving a trail, as well.

"You think you're a canny son of a bitch, don't you?" Liberty asked.

"I'm a man," Ryan replied, "still standing in my own boots and making my own way."

"A bullet changes all of that," Liberty replied.

"Changes it for any man," Ryan countered easily. "I've spent a few cartridges myself, permanently changing the thinking of some folks."

"What do you want for this, old man?" Liberty directed his question at Doc, but he didn't take his attention from Ryan.

"How much of it?" Doc asked.

"All," Liberty said. "All of it."

"We want some ammo as an exchange," Doc answered.

And Ryan knew things were about to go down now from the slight shifting Liberty exhibited, from the way the younger man's eyes narrowed. Perhaps if Liberty had been a little older, more experienced than just killing muties, he would have settled for trading. But Liberty wasn't going to play it that way.

"Ammo?" A crooked grin lighted the man's face. He smoothly raised the Winchester from his knees and aimed it at Ryan. "Goodbye, One-Eye."

Chapter Two

Jak knew death as an intimate experience. It measured in heartbeats, from the last one to the next one that didn't come. A man trained in killing knew which heartbeat to act on. He waited patiently.

Breathing easily, he ran a hand down the front of his camo vest. His fingertips avoided the sharp bits of metal sewn into the cloth to prevent man or beast from wanting to get too close to him. More metal bits studded his pants, providing an offense, as well as a defense.

He stood slightly below five and a half feet tall, wiry and whipcord lean. His skin held the pallor of a corpse, mirrored by the shock of white hair on top of his head. Bone white and savagely scarred, as still as death, his face looked like a mask. Only the burning heat of his ruby red eyes showed life as he watched the men before him.

Philox and the two men who rode with him dismounted from their horses a few yards back of the clearing where Doc and Ryan conducted their business. They unsheathed their long blasters and crept forward, never knowing that death dogged their heels.

Lush forest growth, overgrown for decades, provided cover for Jak. He remained behind the men as they went forward. Their attention stayed on the events spinning out in the clearing. The albino teen left his .357 Magnum Colt Python in its holster, filling his hands with the leaf-bladed throwing knives he made himself and kept secreted on his body and in his clothing.

Seated atop an outcrop thrusting from the uneven ground less than ten feet from the three men he followed, Jak saw Liberty make his move against Ryan. The Winchester came up blasting as the gang leader levered round after round into the breech and fired away. Doc scattered to the left, just as they'd planned, making his way toward the huge Le Mat blaster.

"Keep the old man alive, you stupe bastards!" Liberty yelled above the sudden din.

Philox and his two partners raised their long blasters to their shoulders, taking aim.

Both hands flashing, Jak threw the leaf-bladed knives, then leaped from his vantage point. The three men howled in pain, hands reaching over shoulders to try to grasp the knives that sank deep into their backs. One of the men turned as Jak landed, alerted by the noise even over the crash of gunfire.

The man yelled out a warning as he brought up his weapon.

Jak whipped back a hand and released another throwing knife as he spun and ducked into cover behind a thick bole of an oak.

The knife sank deep into his victim's throat, the man gagging instantly on his own blood. He dropped to his knees, firing his blaster into the ground.

Hand dropping to the butt of the .357 Magnum revolver, Jak ripped the big weapon free of leather. Following his momentum around the tree bole, the albino brought up the blaster in a two-handed grip, rolling the hammer back with his thumb for a quick snap shot. He punched a round through Philox's forehead. The man's head jerked backward as the bullet emptied his brain pan across the brush behind him. He went wide-eyed, face first into the dirt.

"Fucking ghost!" The third man panicked, trying in vain to find cover.

Jak relentlessly pursued, bringing up the .357 pistol again. The front sight fell over the back of his target's skull, then a full-metal-jacketed hollowpoint caved it in. The albino recovered Philox's long blaster, scooping it from the ground in a quick, practiced movement. He recognized the weapon as he brought it to his shoulder—a Marlin bolt-action .30-.30 with a 5-round clip.

Squinting through the telescopic sights, he tracked across the clearing where Doc and Ryan scrambled for their lives. The gang poured a constant barrage of fire, fighting against their struggling mounts.

Jak slipped his finger inside the rifle's trigger guard and took up the slack, knowing the lives of his friends existed only one heartbeat to the next, with no guarantees.

RYAN MOVED in a smooth uncoiling of muscles, not bothering with a feint. Liberty struck like a snake, with no warning and without hesitation.

Diving to the right of the clearing, Ryan knew he pulled most of the gang's guns in his direction. He broke his fall with his left arm as he kept hold on the Steyr with his right hand. He rolled, keeping the long blaster tight against his body.

"Get him!" Liberty yelled. "Get the bastard now!"

Long blasters and pistols broke the stillness under the leafy canopy behind Ryan as he came to his feet behind a three-foot-high shelf of rock the brush covered from casual view. He misjudged his roll and smacked his right cheek against it. Blood wept warmly down the side of his face. He pulled himself into position behind the rock and raised the Steyr. The weapon's butt pressed into the side of his face against whatever injury he had taken. The abraded flesh stung at the touch, but parts of his face where the old scars were didn't have any feeling at all.

Thrusting the Steyr's barrel through the underbrush, he noted that Doc was safely out of harm's way. The gang members milled around in the clearing, not yet in complete control of their mounts.

"Philox!" Liberty roared, twisting his head to the right as he reached under the wag's seat and came away with an ammo belt.

Ryan put the Steyr's crosshairs over Liberty's face, leading the man slightly as the gang leader moved across the wag. He squeezed the trigger, spotting the horse and rider that reared in the way only a chron tick before the big sniper weapon crashed into his shoulder.

The 7.62 mm round cored through the horse's neck, cutting through the jugular and unleashing a torrent of blood. It whinnied in pain and fear, fighting harder than ever against the commands of its rider.

"Fireblast!" Ryan snarled, chambering another round. He looked for Liberty again, but there was too much confusion in the clearing.

Some of the gang members took advantage of the situation to start raiding the supplies spread out on the blanket. They remained in position, though. Ryan peered through the scope. A slight squeeze of the trigger, and one of the riders sprawled to the ground, kicking through the last reflexive movements his nervous system allowed.

Bullets smacked into the shelf of rock before Ryan, driving him back. He found another target, so close he didn't even need the Steyr's scope. He trusted his instincts and experience with the weapon. His finger stroked the trigger, putting a bullet into the center of the man's chest and bursting his heart.

Three bullets gone and two men down. It wasn't enough, and fighting a protracted engagement wasn't something the companions could afford to do.

Ryan raised his voice as he swapped shots with another gang member, neither of them hitting anything. "Krysty, do it now!"

TITIAN-HAIRED Krysty Wroth moved from hiding and made for the tree along the uneven rock face

where she had taken up a position. She raised her
.38-caliber Smith & Wesson Model 640 and ripped
off two shots at a man closing in on Doc. Both shots
went wide of their mark, but they came close enough
to send the man diving for cover.

"Down, Krysty!" Mildred Wyeth yelled behind
her.

Krysty dived at once, splaying flat on hands and
knees. Still, she kept moving forward. Bullets
pocked the rock face above her, showering rock
splinters that stung her back and legs.

She heard the distinctive detonation of Mildred's
.38-caliber ZKR 551 target pistol banging behind
her. Men yelled and cursed in pain. A shootist in
the last-ever Olympic games, Mildred was hell on
wheels with a pistol.

Krysty threw herself the last few feet to her goal:
the old gnarled oak tree that held the rope to spring
the trap Ryan had set up for the encounter. She
ripped Ryan's panga from her hand-stitched cowboy
boot and rose with the knife in her hand.

The rope snaked around the oak tree, safely hidden from most casual inspections.

A man erupted from the ground in front of Krysty,
rising up out of the brush. The maniacal face was
limned in blood, and there was no way to tell if it
was his or someone else's.

"Goddamn bitch!" the man snarled. He raised a
double-bitted ax that had been cut down to a hand
weapon and looped around his wrist by a leather
thong. "Going to cut you a little now, cut you
deeper later." He swung the blade.

A little under six feet tall and graced by nature and hard living with a strength that surprised most people, Krysty met the man's attack head-on. She lifted the panga and turned the sweep of the ax head enough to miss her. Then she brought around the panga, the razor edge neatly slicing off two of the man's fingers. The wounds spurted blood as the digits dropped to the ground.

The man shouted in pain.

Krysty rammed the .38 into his face and pulled the trigger twice. The first bullet kicked the man's head back, and the second turned it sideways.

As the dying man dropped to the ground, Krysty turned and swung the panga at the rope coiled around the tree. The keen-edged steel sliced through the rope as if it were wet paper.

Sheared of its moorings, the rope slithered through the tree branches. As she watched it, Krysty sent a small prayer to Gaia, the Earth Mother, to watch over her companions and keep all safe from harm.

She took up cover behind the oak tree as she listened to the crash and thunder of heavy objects smashing through the trees overhead. She barely made out the thick tree trunk that swept down at the gang still trying to steal their trade goods.

Then it was among them, over a ton of falling wood that Ryan had selected from farther up the hill. Steel cable had been easy enough to come by in the redoubt, and Ryan, Dean and Jak had returned for it after the one-eyed man had picked the ambush spot and made his plans.

Short loops of the steel cable jutted from the underside of the huge tree trunk. The loops folded out big enough to catch a man's arm, hand or foot, and it was thin enough with the force coming up with it to slice right through skin, flesh and bone as it passed.

It was also in a man's instinct to lift a hand to defend himself against something he thought was falling on him. Ryan had counted on that.

Krysty watched the tree trunk arc through the trees, staying less than two feet above the ground just as Ryan and Doc had planned on. Three or maybe four men lost their lives when the tree trunk smashed into them. At least that many lost hands and arms in the vicious coils of steel cable.

A head spun free of one man's body, scissored off by the cable before he could escape. The sound of dying men multiplied below.

Krysty extended her arm and fired her remaining two shots at a man rushing the last position she'd seen Ryan in. The man went down. Ducking behind the tree, she broke open her weapon and shook the brass loose. Her fingers moved smoothly as she refilled the cylinder. After those rounds were fired, she had only four more in her shirt pocket.

She shifted around the tree, finding a new position that offered a less constricted view of the clearing below. They were down to all or nothing.

RYAN SHOVED HIMSELF to his feet as the tree trunk suspended from steel cables swung back in its trajectory. The huge block of wood slammed into two other men who'd been missed the first time. They flew almost thirty feet with the impact, and didn't move again after that.

Doc came up with the Le Mat blaster and fired a round of scattergun pellets that knocked a handful of men reeling. Then he went to cover.

On the second time through, the trailing coils of steel cable caught more hands and arms. It also smashed into the converted horse-drawn wag. A horse whinnied in pain and terror as it struggled to get up.

Standing beside a tree, Ryan picked his targets coolly and fired with rapid accuracy, choosing the biggest part of the men's bodies to hit. The gang members went down in succession.

When he'd fired the Steyr empty, Ryan left it by the tree. If he survived, he could get the long blaster later. He drew the SIG-Sauer P-226 and rushed forward, gaining ground and assuming a new position that caught the gang unaware.

Rising to one knee, he fired three times and cut a man down in midstride. His combat senses caught some movement to his left. He pulled around as a line of bullets chopped into the ground where he had been.

Liberty stood beside a tree and levered another shell, then fired again. "You're a dead man, One-Eye!"

Ryan shoved the SIG-Sauer forward, facing the .30-.30's barrel as it swung toward him. There was no time to move, and he knew Liberty had him dead in his sights. He squeezed the trigger, expecting to feel a bullet hit him in the next heartbeat.

Instead, Liberty's head snapped back, his skull opening up and loosing brain matter over the trees behind him. The corpse dropped in an uncoordinated tangle of limbs.

Turning back to the clearing, Ryan saw one of the gang members spin away from Doc. A load of buckshot had taken the man's face from him, along with his life.

Nothing moved out in the clearing.

Ryan lifted his voice. "Jak!"

"Done," the albino called back, letting them know the three men who had disappeared from sight no longer mattered.

"J.B.?" Ryan wiped perspiration from his forehead before it had a chance to drip down into the open socket behind the eye patch and burn.

"I think we got them all," the Armorer replied.

Ryan took a fresh magazine for the SIG-Sauer and changed it with the partially depleted one. "Cover me."

"Give me plenty of room to shoot around."

Ryan stood and moved from behind concealment. He kept the 9 mm blaster in front of him and moved slowly. The muzzle tracked across the scattered dead men, looking for signs of life among the mangled bodies.

Ryan only found two men alive. One of them still

had the breath to beg for his life. Ryan didn't waste a bullet on either of them, instead taking a knife from a nearby corpse and slitting their throats. He intended to take his group into Hazard, and he didn't mean to leave a chance of any vengeance coming up from behind them.

The converted wag rattled from a faint movement. At first Ryan thought it was the only surviving horse feebly kicking out its life. The wag had turned over, coming to a rest across the horse's legs. But when he looked into the horse's eyes and saw only death reflected there, he knew something else caused the motion.

"I got somebody still alive in the wag," Ryan called back to J.B.

"I can put a few rounds into it," the Armorer offered.

Ryan directed his voice at the wag. "Is that what it's going to take?"

"Don't kill me," a voice said. "Mebbe I can help you."

"Looking around at things," Ryan replied, "I don't get the feeling we're in a spot to need a lot of help."

"Are you planning on going into Hazard?"

Ryan crouched and looked under the overturned wag. The dwarf, Albert, stared back at him, eyes wide and frightened. "And if we are?" Ryan asked.

"The folks in the ville are going to wonder what happened to Liberty and his bunch. They might not like it if you just come strolling into the ville. But if I go with you, I can tell them Liberty said it was okay.''

"The way I hear it," Ryan said, "the people of Hazard have been letting Liberty do their chilling for a while now. Could be there's not many in the ville who'd care to stand up against us.''

The dwarf licked his lips, laying his final ace on the line where they could both get a good look at it. "You want to take that chance when you could take me with you and be sure?''

Ryan grinned in spite of the situation. The little man had a lot of nerve. "How do I know you and Liberty weren't related or something? Mebbe you'll try to stick a knife in my guts as soon as you get the chance.''

"Me and Liberty related?'' The dwarf had to strain to make a rude noise, but he succeeded after a dry-lipped moment. "And I got all the looks. He kept me around to torment, mister. A few miles to the north, there was another ville just setting up. I was part of that ville. Some of us had a disagreement with a local baron, so we pulled up stakes and tried to make it on our own. Except we hadn't counted on Hazard being so territorial. Twenty miles away, we were, and the ville elders decided we were still too close. They were afraid we were going to overhunt the game in this area.''

Ryan knew that was a serious worry for a ville like Hazard, which was still living off the land.

"They warned us to move away last year, but by

then winter was coming on," the dwarf continued. "We asked them to give us till the spring. Instead, they sent Liberty and his bunch of coldhearts to burn down our tents and the two permanent buildings we'd started before we talked to them. When they rode out of the ville, not many people were left alive. I don't think the ones that escaped survived. Winter hit the next week, and the land around here can be bastard inhospitable during those times. Thirty-seven people, and all of them wiped out. No, sir, I don't have any love for the folk of that ville."

Ryan stood, not presenting his back to the dwarf in case Albert tried for a last-minute escape. He spotted Krysty coming down from the hill.

"I believe him, lover," she said.

Ryan nodded. "Might be an idea to have a guide in the ville." He took the panga from her. "Least until we get situated and figure out where we're going from here."

"Personally, my dear Ryan," Doc said as he walked over and dusted off the tails of his frock coat, "I think we could all enjoy a few hours respite after our trip to North Carolina."

"Yeah." The one-eyed man turned to the up-ended wag. "Come on out of there."

After a brief hesitation, Albert clambered out from under the wag. He made certain to keep his hands in view, his stubby arms not allowing him to shove his fingertips much up past his head. "You won't regret this."

"I don't have much in the way of regrets," Ryan said. "And I aim to keep it that way." He scanned the corpses. "Okay, let's see what we can salvage."

Chapter Three

The companions took their time, and the warm air in the clearing filled with the stench of the corpses. J.B. and Jak set up security along the perimeter on Ryan's orders.

When it came to scavenging, Albert proved invaluable. The little man had ridden with the gang long enough that he knew the hiding places most of the dead men had in their clothing.

Albert paused beside a fat man with half his face missing. "This is Gustuvson," the dwarf said, grimacing. "I know for a fact he keeps a pouch with gold teeth shoved up his ass. He steals them from corpses they've found in areas around Hazard. Liberty was always one to poke and prod in new areas, and they found a few places back up in some caves that nobody's been to before."

"How do you know about the pouch?" Dean asked. The boy's dark hair and burning blue gaze clearly marked him as Ryan's son. He ran his hands along the dead man he was searching, his nimble fingers plucking away loose cartridges, as well as an oilskin containing tobacco leaves.

"I was with Liberty's group a couple months back when they found a new pocket in the mountains they were searching," Albert replied. "Quakes run through this area pretty regularly, and they shove up new stuff to the surface all the time. He took a couple teeth from a dead woman in that building, knocked them out with a rock because he was in a hurry, and stuck them in that pouch he's so proud of. What he didn't know was there was some residual radiation in that gold. By the time he found out, he had running sores in his asshole. He didn't get any slack from the rest of the group for being so stupe.''

Dean grinned, thinking how stupe the man had really been. Nobody with any sense at all had anything to do with metals in a rad-hot area because they picked up radiation first and held on to it longest. Especially the precious metals, like gold. "Hey, Dad.''

Ryan looked up from the man he searched. "Yeah.''

"Do you think Albert ought to cut those gold teeth out of that dead man's ass?'' Dean opened the oilskin of tobacco and inhaled the deep, heady scent of it.

"No.''

The dwarf sighed in relief, then released the fat man. He pushed up, then walked to the next corpse.

"Doc,'' Dean called, "I got some tobacco here.''

"Ah, lad, you are a prince,'' the old man replied.

Dean tossed the oilskin to him, then turned his attention back to the man, who had carried a nearly full box of 9 mm shells that Dean knew would fit his father's pistol, J.B.'s Uzi and his own Browning

Hi-Power. It wasn't enough, but it was a start. He kept searching.

RYAN SURVEYED the gear they'd taken from the corpses. Spread out on the blanket Doc had used, it didn't look like much. But Ryan knew they were in a lot better shape than they'd been in after returning to the mat-trans unit under the hospital in North Carolina.

"Didn't get any shells for the M-4000," J.B. announced. He squatted next to Ryan with the shotgun across his knees. He was a wiry man scarcely more than five and a half feet tall. He kept his hair cut short and wore a battered fedora.

"They didn't seem to favor shotguns," Ryan said.

"Our bad luck." J.B. removed his steel-rimmed glasses and wiped them clean on his shirt. "Hey, Albert."

The dwarf looked up, still nervous in spite of the fact that the companions had let him live for the past forty minutes. "Yeah."

"Hazard got anything in the way of an armory?" J.B. asked.

"They got Tinker Phillips and his boys," Albert replied.

"What kind of hardware do they deal in?"

"He kept Liberty and his group supplied. Tinker's pretty good with most weapons. He's got a shop hooked up next to the blacksmith's. His brother runs that, but they share the forge. Out here in this country, a man needs a blaster and a horse."

Ryan silently agreed with that. He'd watched over the nearby surroundings since the ambush and had seen no signs of any interest.

"We can go back to the redoubt, lover," Krysty said. She stood on the other side of Ryan. Dean and Mildred were taking care of security for the moment. "Mebbe make another jump and take our chances there. Or we can avoid Hazard altogether and live off the land."

"With either of those choices," Ryan said, "we need to be better equipped than we are now to handle ourselves. The ville's the only sure way to get the things we need to restock. We're almost flat out of self-heats and ring-pulls, and if we can't eat and drink when we need to travel light and quiet for a while, we're in trouble."

"I know."

"Ville's best bet," Jak agreed. He sifted through the assortment of knives the gang had carried. Most he threw away, but some of them he saved.

Ryan knew from experience that the albino was interested only in the blades he could break apart and use to make more of the leaf-bladed throwing knives he'd lost in North Carolina. There wasn't always time to recover them during the heat of battle.

He pushed himself to his feet as a dark shadow skated across the ground in front of him. When he looked up, he saw another crow had joined the ones that patiently waited in the trees above.

He checked the sun. After the jump into Kentucky, he'd adjusted his chron according to darkfall the first night, but he didn't know how accurate the time was. "Let's finish it, get something to eat and get on the road."

He raised his voice. "Albert."

"Yeah," the dwarf replied.

"The way I got it figured, the ville's about a couple hours away on foot."

"Mebbe a little less if you really stretch your legs."

"How do they feel about people coming into the ville at night?"

"As long as you're with me," the little man said, "I reckon you'll be fine."

"Then that's what we'll do." Ryan took up a portion of the gear they'd salvaged and hid it away in his clothing. He'd filled his extra magazines with the 9 mm ammo they'd found, as had Dean and the Armorer. The .38 Special ammo used in Krysty's and Mildred's weapons had proved plentiful, and J.B. had been the first to point out the cartridges had been reloads. Even before Albert had told them about the gunshop in the ville, they'd had an idea. There hadn't been too many .357 cartridges for Jak's blaster, but the cylinder easily accepted the .38 cartridges. They just packed less bite for the change.

They left the dead where they lay and went up on the hill. Crows dropped on the bodies before the companions even made it out of the clearing.

"Sure made a hell of a mess in these trees," J.B. commented as they hunkered down at the crest. He gazed at the broken branches left by the tree trunk they'd hidden for their trap.

Ryan sat on his haunches and took a ring-pull

from his pack. He pulled it open and drank half the contents, then passed it over to Krysty. "Main thing is it worked."

At the foot of the hill, scattered around the huge tree trunk that had killed a number of the enemy, the bodies resembled dolls—until the crows climbed on them and began their work.

DOC SHOULDERED his pack and easily matched the stride set by the others. He'd filled his pipe with the wondrous blend of tobacco Dean had found, and his head was wreathed with smoke.

Jak and Dean ran point up ahead as they followed along the faint trail that wound through the hilly country back to Hazard. Or from Hazard, Doc reflected, depending on one's perspective. J.B. covered the back with Mildred to keep him company.

Ahead, Ryan walked with Krysty, and they talked quietly among themselves.

A feeling of contentment filled Doc. He breathed expansively, the morning's killing already fading in his mind.

"You enjoy that pipe," Albert said at his side.

Doc looked down at the dwarf. Ryan had given the little man a pair of snub-nosed .38s that had been reclaimed from the gang. Albert had displayed a flair for working with leather and had arranged a pair of holsters for himself to carry the weapons. Even though they were short barreled, the blasters still ran down his thighs nearly to his knees.

"Yes," Doc said. "Yes, I do." He found an odd quote floating around in his head.

"Tobacco, divine, rare, superexcellent tobacco, which goes far beyond all the panaceas, potable gold, and philosophers' stones, a sovereign remedy to all diseases..."

He stopped, not quite able to remember the rest of it.

The dwarf was slightly out of breath from trying to keep up with the companions. His legs weren't made for rapid movement, and stride for stride, he definitely came up short. "That's quoted from something?"

"A work by Robert Burton, unless I misremember."

"If you'll pardon my saying so, you seem very well educated to be traveling with your current company."

"Well," Doc said with a smile, "I guess that depends on one's line of thinking. Myself I consider to be almost vastly undereducated when it comes to the art of survival. But that man up there that I consider to be a friend, is a true artiste. Until today you evidently thought no one could destroy the men you traveled with."

"That was not by choice."

"And my statement was not an accusation," Doc returned gently.

The dwarf was silent for a time. "His name is Ryan."

"Yes."

"Does he have a last name?"

"Cawdor."

Albert looked up, eyes widening in surprise. "*That* Ryan Cawdor? The one whose father was a baron in the Shens? The Ryan Cawdor who rode with the Trader on War Wag One?"

"Yes," Doc said. "I see you have heard of him."

"In this part of Deathlands, who hasn't?" Albert stared at Ryan with increased curiosity. "I thought somehow he would be bigger."

"Any man would be hard-pressed to fill that man's boots," Doc replied.

"If you have time in Hazard," the dwarf said, "I'd like to stand you to a drink at Cobb's. He's got a line of homemade wines that are among the best I've ever had the chance to sample."

"Well, my small friend, an opportunity to lose one's melancholy in a bit of the grape is always a fine thing."

"Cobb's doesn't just serve liquor," Albert stated. "There's books there. Dozens of them. I'd like to hear what you have to say about them. And I know Cobb would, too."

"I shall look forward to that." Doc glanced at the dwarf again. "I have a suggestion to make, if I might."

"What?"

"Mayhap I could give you a few moments of respite by offering you my back for a time." Doc hurried on before the little man could object. "In return for the consideration you'll be showing me."

The dwarf looked away, mopping at his sweating forehead with a handkerchief. "I don't like feeling I owe anyone."

"Nonsense. You are going to be showing me an establishment that I might not find on my own."

Albert was silent, then said, "Cobb's can be hard to find if you don't know what you're looking for."

"Then I take it we have a deal?" Doc stopped and thrust out his hand.

Hesitantly the little man put his hand out, as well. Doc knelt in front of him and let him climb on. With his short arms, Albert had difficulty holding on. Finally Doc shoved him up onto his shoulders, and Albert sat there like a child.

The comparison cut Doc through to the quick. A memory, blunt as a ghost in a Shakespearean play and as cutting as ridicule in Louis XIV's courts, drifted into his mind. He had carried another small person like this in the past. A name filtered through to his mind. "Rachel," he groaned, almost seeing the little girl in his mind. Emily and Jolyon were there as well. In that moment Doc's heart turned to lead, weighing him down.

"Dr. Tanner?" Albert asked in concern.

Doc ignored the tears that trickled down his face. They would fade soon enough, just as all the others had. "I am all right, my diminutive companion. But please, honor me and entertain me with a discourse you have read, heard about or imagined. Something that would keep my mind occupied as I walk this winding path. And please call me Doc."

"A learned discourse, eh?" Albert asked. His voice brightened. "Do you know Percy Shelley and Lord Byron?"

"The authors of *Prometheus Unbound* and *Childe*

Harold's Pilgrimage, to name but a couple of their major works?'' Doc asked. ''By the Three Kennedys, I would be remiss not having read their works, even more so not having heard of them.''

''Those are the two.''

Doc felt better already. Both poets were personal favorites of his. ''Then pray tell me.''

''Okay,'' Albert said, ''Shelley and Lord Byron go into this bar, see...''

RYAN CROUCHED at the top of the hill that led down to Hazard. The ville was less than a quarter of a mile distant now. He surveyed it through his field glasses.

Krysty knelt at his side, her hand resting casually on his thigh. ''Look at the houses, lover,'' she said wistfully. ''All painted white and looking brand-new.''

''From here,'' Ryan said. ''You get closer up, you'll see where the whitewash didn't quite cover.''

''Still, it's a pleasant thought. What about the big building in the center? It looks like a hotel.''

''It is,'' Ryan replied. The building was three stories tall, bigger than any other in the ville, and only the church steeple was taller. Pink-flowered green curtains filled the windows. A sign ran along the side of the building's second floor, reading Hazard Royale Inn.

''A bed would be nice, wouldn't it?'' Krysty asked. ''For a night or two.''

''Mebbe,'' Ryan said. He shifted the binoculars, taking in more of the ville. Despite the ville's peaceful appearance, he didn't trust it. Memory of the thirty-seven people who'd been butchered by Liberty and his band at the bequest of the ville's elders stuck out in his mind.

No wag tracks showed in the beaten earth of the roads marked out in straight lines through the ville. Evidently it had rained lately, because great washouts still showed mud in the center of the streets. A few children played in the ville square under an old, tattered flag of the United States of America. A Civil War cannon, grimed over with rust that hadn't been removed despite a dogged attempt sat in the square atop a small, shaped hill partially covered by a carpet of yellow-and-white daisies. More daisies thrust out from the cannon's mouth.

Women talked in front of a two-story laundry that had a generous wooden porch and hand-lettered windows. Men sat and whittled on the benches in front of the laundry, while the women stood with baskets of clothes on their hips.

It looked idyllic, but the men wore weapons and so did some of the women. The ville wasn't a place that took kindly to strangers.

Ryan knew they needed a story. And the trading one sounded as good as any. "Albert."

The dwarf turned from where he'd been talking to Doc. "Yes, Mr. Cawdor."

"Just call me Ryan," the one-eyed man said. Too many people in the area might have heard the name, and Harvey Cawdor had given it a large disservice. "Does the ville have a healer?"

"Yes. Doc Kirkland."

"How's he fixed for medicines?"

"Most of what he uses are herbs that we grow around the ville," Albert replied. "The stuff you had to offer Liberty, the anesthetic and such, he'll be interested in."

"Figuring on doing some trading?" J.B. asked.

"Gives us as likely an excuse as any," Ryan said. "We show up at the ville, people are going to be talking. When you go see the gunsmith, make sure you keep those reloads out of sight. Man will probably know his own work and wonder how we came by those shells."

"Already figured it."

Ryan put his field glasses away. There wasn't anything else to do but the doing of it. "Let's move out."

Chapter Four

"You folks want to hold up there for a minute?"

Ryan stared at the lean, hard man that stepped off the porch near the laundry. He held up a hand and stopped the companions. The six members of his group, Dean included, spread out into a skirmish line.

"Something wrong?" Ryan challenged, shifting his grip on the Steyr. But he watched the way a handful of men spread out across both sides of the street behind the man that braced them.

"Just want to ask you a few questions is all," the man said. He was dressed in denim jeans and a green shirt that somebody had minded with care so that the fit was like a glove. Salt-and-pepper hair lay down neat and proper under a faded baseball cap advertising something called NASCAR. A hammered copper star on his chest read Sheriff.

"Sure," Ryan responded. "Day's not been so busy that I can't answer a question or two."

The man stopped ten feet in front of Ryan, his right hand on his hip just above the Colt .45 automatic on his hip. The restraining thong had already been slipped, hanging like a silent warning from the holster. "Name's Dodge," the man said. "I'm sheriff of this ville." He gave an easy, affable smile.

Ryan waited, not making it easy for the man. Dusk was starting to settle around the ville, drawing long shadows through the streets. A number of people in houses on either side of the street peered through their windows. "Okay."

"I need to ask you what you're doing here, son."

"Came to do some trading," Ryan answered.

The sheriff shook his head. "I'm sorry to tell you this, but you probably come to the wrong place. Hazard's got most everything it needs. We try to be a self-sufficient community."

Ryan nodded. "That's what we heard when we started out this way. We didn't come with empty hands, Sheriff Dodge." He beckoned Mildred forward.

Mildred drew a lot of attention from the ville. Ryan had noticed only a handful of black people during his earlier observation, and none of them sported the colored beaded plaits woven into her hair.

She opened her pack under the sheriff's supervision, bringing out a jar of the topical anesthesia. The soft blue of the jellylike substance looked clear and clean against the glass walls of the jar.

"What's that?" Dodge asked.

"Topical anesthesia," Mildred answered. "If you got a healer in the ville, you can bet your ass that he'll be interested in this."

"If that's not enough," Ryan added, "we've got some jack to spend, too. Hazard may have all it needs, but we're running low on some staples."

"We don't run a charity here, mister," Dodge

said flatly. "Nor do we cotton much to outlanders. We got our lives pretty much set, and don't like folks butting in."

"That's what we heard," Ryan agreed. He kept the edge of anger out of his voice with effort. "But we've been scavenging, came up with this topical anesthesia and thought mebbe a place getting as civilized as Hazard would want something this good."

"Do you know what a topical anesthetic is?" Mildred demanded.

"No."

"I do." The voice belonged to a man in a white blazer and wire-rimmed glasses. He had a bull's neck and his body was big to match. He stepped out of a small building called the Bottlefly Emporium, leaving the bat-wing doors swinging behind him. "I am Dr. Neil Kirkland, healer in these parts."

Dodge touched the bill of his baseball cap respectfully. "Guess you'd know about such things, Doc."

"If they have topical anesthesia from the predark days," Kirkland said as he approached, "these people shouldn't just be allowed to trade in our ville, Sheriff Dodge. They should be our honored guests." He stopped in front of Mildred. "Madam, if I may?"

"Of course." Mildred unscrewed the lid and removed it from the container, showing that the seal hadn't been broken.

Kirkland's furry eyebrows lifted in surprise. Despite the fact that he shaved his head, he sported a goatee and sideburns of fiery red hair. "Unopened?"

"Found it that way," Mildred answered. "Had no reason to open it so far."

"Are there more of these where you found this one?" Kirkland asked.

Ryan regarded the man coolly. "We're talking about this one."

The healer raised a curious eyebrow, but evidently didn't take any offense. "I see. May I open it, then?"

"Are we going to be allowed in to trade?" Ryan asked, pushing his advantage.

Kirkland glanced at Dodge. "Sheriff, you may not realize it, but this is an absolute treasure."

Reluctantly Dodge nodded. From the way the sheriff acted, Ryan knew the healer carried a lot of authority in the ville. "I'll take your word for it," Dodge said.

"You don't have to take my word for it," Kirkland said. He looked back at Ryan. "Sir, whatever you want for this—within reason—in this ville will be yours. I do all the surgery in Hazard. If I can't get whatever you want for you myself, I can work out a deal with anyone in this ville. These hands are surgeon's hands, only one step removed from Saint Elvis's himself, may his voice never be silenced."

"You got yourself a deal," Ryan said.

Kirkland gave an expansive smile. Delicately his fingers ripped the aluminum-foil seal from the topical anesthesia. He smelled the stringent odor and smiled again. "Fabulous."

"You'll want to be cautious with that," Mildred said. "It'll go a long way because of the cocaine-type base."

Kirkland raised his eyebrows in surprise. "You know about such things?"

"I've done some cutting and stitching myself," Mildred acknowledged.

"Then I'd like your company for lunch or dinner sometime before you leave Hazard. My housekeeper prepares a fine table."

"If we can work it out," Mildred answered.

Ryan knew Mildred was only acting compliant. She wasn't going anywhere away from the companions until they were all sure everything was safe. The only security they had was with one another. And if the chance did present itself where she did accompany the man for a meal, she would also be in a position to ask questions they might need answers to themselves.

Kirkland dipped the corner of a handkerchief into the anesthesia, then handed the container back to Mildred and turned to the sheriff. "Remember a few months back when I had to pull that bad tooth of yours?"

Unconsciously Dodge rubbed his jaw. "Can't say that I'm going to forget anytime too soon. Meaning no disrespect."

"None taken. That *was* a frightful piece of business, and if I hadn't scraped the bone as well as I had, gangrene might well have set in, taking your life. And there's another tooth or two in that head of yours that I'm going to have to go in after one day soon. I'm sure you're not looking forward to that.''

"No."

Ryan watched the men behind the sheriff. Most of them had stood down where they were, getting relaxed now. It took some of the edge off of the situation. He caught Krysty's eye, looking a question at her.

The redhead shook her head slightly, letting him know she was getting no negative feelings. Her mutie ability of precognition had pulled them through hard times before. There were times that Krysty had known the lies they were being told as soon as they were uttered. Evidently Kirkland was being totally honest.

The healer opened the sheriff's mouth and scrubbed the dampened corner of the handkerchief across the inside of Dodge's lower lip.

The sheriff stepped back and spit. "Now, that's some bastard vile tasting—" He stopped, then touched his lip, looking surprised. "Hey, I can't feel my lip!"

"Exactly," Kirkland said, motioning for Mildred to close up the anesthesia. "And for your consideration in this matter about letting these people into our ville, your dental work will be on me."

"As long as you do it with that stuff," Dodge conceded, touching his lip, "you got yourself a deal."

"You have my word on it," Kirkland said. He reached for the anesthesia.

Mildred kept the jar back. "We haven't talked trade yet."

Kirkland's forehead furrowed then it was gone. "Madam, I've given you my word that anything you want within reason is yours. What is it you would wish?"

"Rooms at the hotel for starters," Krysty spoke up.

Ryan nodded. "We'll dicker from there."

"As you wish." Kirkland glanced at Dodge. "Sheriff, make it so. And anything else they want, pass the word around to the rest of the ville that I'll be indebted to them."

Dodge inclined his head. "Sure, but they got Albert with them."

The doctor glanced at the dwarf for a moment in perplexed annoyance. "You've already met young Liberty, I gather?" Kirkland asked.

"Yeah," Ryan said. "We settled up with Liberty, then he sent the little man on with us. Said that way you'd know we'd already been through him."

"He's demanded his tribute, I take it?"

Ryan knew from the man's gaze that Kirkland was fantasizing about what Liberty had taken. "And gotten it. We had some playing cards and some knives, some self-heats he said he'd never seen before. I figure he got mebbe a little more than was fair. He didn't understand about the anesthesia."

"And you didn't further his elucidation?"

"Not when a man's already committing highway robbery on me," Ryan said.

"I'm surprised that he didn't follow you in."

"Didn't say he always did," Ryan stated. "Mebbe he'll be along."

"He's looking for the stickie tribe that's come down from the north," Albert said. "They cut sign on them a few days back."

"Hopefully he'll get them all." Kirkland took the topical anesthesia when Mildred offered it. "At any rate, I leave you in the sheriff's capable hands." He turned and walked back to the emporium.

Dodge waved two fingers. Two young men that favored him greatly came from the porch behind him. One of them carried a sawed-off double-barreled shotgun.

When he saw the weapon, Ryan figured J.B. was feeling better already.

"These here are my sons," Dodge said. "Ira and Tucker. They'll show you around the ville. When you go to bed at night, as long as you're in Hazard, one of them will be down in the hotel lobby. When you get up in the morning, one of them will be down in the hotel lobby. You get out of the hotel without them seeing you, could be I'll feel a little unfavorable about that."

"Sure," Ryan said easily. "But what if we don't plan on staying together?"

"Oh," Dodge said with a smile, "I got plenty more deputies."

Chapter Five

"Here are your rooms." The maid paused at the top of the stairs leading to the third floor of the Hazard Royale Inn and gestured toward a line of doors. She held out metal keys on circular plastic chips with numbers on them. "If there's anything else I can get for you, Aunt Maim said to let me know and I'll get it for you straight away."

"Are there bathtubs in the rooms?" Krysty asked, taking one of the keys from the girl.

The maid didn't look a day over fifteen. A mop of brown hair nearly hid her eyes, and every now and then a bit of a blue tattoo showed on the rounded cleavage she was showing above the unbuttoned green blouse. Her attitude about her job definitely wasn't enthusiastic.

"Yes, ma'am," the maid replied.

Ryan glanced at the hallway, getting its layout in his mind. It would be dark soon, and there was no guarantee they'd live through the night. A ville's hospitality generally extended only as long as their guests' usefulness remained. Even when there were signs of civilization in some locale of Deathlands, it tended to be superficial. Then again, Kirkland was a greedy man and might be wondering how to coax more anesthetic from them.

Clean and neat, the hallway formed a T at the top of the stairs. Six rooms lined the wall, promising small quarters, but at least the hint of privacy. Pictures covered the walls, set apart in hand-crafted frames. Upon closer inspection, Ryan saw that they were pages torn from a magazine. All of the pictures on the pages featured beautiful old wags that Ryan had seen in magazines himself. The two nearest him were of a bright red Corvette and a black Viper.

"Is it running water?" Krysty asked, getting impatient with the girl's reticence.

"No, ma'am. We'll have to bring it up in buckets."

Ryan faced the girl. "Are baths extra?"

"No, sir. Aunt Maim said to give you whatever you needed."

"We'll have a bath, then," Krysty said. "And I want hot water. A lot of it."

"Yes, ma'am." The maid dipped her head and gave Ryan the rest of the keys, then fled back down the steps.

"Enjoying your newfound wealth?" Ryan asked with a grin.

"It's not often we're given the run of an entire ville, lover." Krysty put her key in the lock and turned it. The mechanism opened after a slight hesitation.

Ryan's hand strayed to the butt of the SIG-Sauer as he peered over Krysty's shoulder. But the small room beyond was clear. A bed filled the center of the room, with a small table and a chest of drawers the only other furniture. A glass door led out onto a small balcony that fronted Hazard's main street. The sun in the west was an hour or so from disappearing behind the hills.

"I want to enjoy myself for the few days this lasts," Krysty said, entering the room and looking around.

Ryan glanced at J.B., trading looks with his old friend. While they'd been with the Trader, they'd sometimes enjoyed the hospitality of a ville. But often that hospitality had come with a price. Like the Trader had always said, sugar-coated shit was still shit.

"Do a changeover at two in the morning," J.B. said. "Give you a knock on the wall, let you know."

Ryan nodded. "I'll take first watch. We'll sleep in when morning comes. Mildred and Krysty can keep an eye on things until we catch up on our sleep."

"I watch," Jak volunteered, knowing from experience that Ryan and J.B. were dividing up the time between them. "Not too tired."

"Figured you weren't," Ryan said. "Thought mebbe you could drift through the ville after dark for a while. Get the fastest way out of here mapped. Just in case."

The albino nodded, understanding.

"What about me, Dad?" Dean asked.

Ryan looked at his son. Since his return from the Nicholas Brody School and the experiences they'd been through of late, Dean appeared steadier, more mature. "Feel up to a little recce?"

Dean smiled. "Sure."

"Jak?" Ryan asked, shifting his gaze to the teenager. "Your call."

The albino looked at Dean. "You listen? Move when say move? Quiet when say quiet?"

"Yeah."

Jak turned back to Ryan and nodded. "Look for anything special?"

"Horses," Ryan answered, "in case we have to leave quick. Any gear we might need in a hurry if we don't have to dicker for it. Self-heats, ring-pulls, road rations." He flicked his eye over to J.B. "You going to take a look at the gunsmith's?"

"When we finish up here," J.B. replied, "I planned on that being the next place we go. If it's open, I'll give it a look, see what's what. You going to be around?"

"Somewhere. I'll be close." Ryan tossed the Armorer a key. J.B. caught it with a quick flick of his hand, then opened the door and guided Mildred into the room they were going to share. "Jak, you and Dean okay with a room to yourselves?"

The albino nodded, and caught the key Ryan threw him. "We go in, get settled. Get gone soon."

"Hey, Dad," Dean said, "what if I find something I want?"

"Come talk to me. Mebbe we'll figure something out."

Ryan turned to Doc. "You and Albert feel okay about bunking up?"

"Verily, my dear Ryan," Doc responded, "I find I enjoy my small companion's versatility for conversation. Our companionship for the nonce will be quite pleasant.''

"I'll take your word for it." Ryan tossed the old man a key. "You going to be around?"

"In the ville," Doc replied, "there's a place called Cobb's that has a reputation for good literature and fine wine."

"Keep your ass covered."

"Tighter than the proverbial duck's," Doc said.

Ryan followed Krysty into the room. She sat on the bed, pulling off the second of her stitched blue cowboy boots. She wiggled her toes luxuriously.

"We've got to see if they have something that passes for a general store in the ville, lover," she said with a grimace after she examined her boots. "And mebbe get a new pair of heels. These are tore all to pieces."

Ryan nodded and crossed the room. He moved the curtain from the window overlooking the balcony. The air inside the room was thick and unmoving. He opened the balcony door and felt the circulation improve almost immediately.

A horse-drawn wag parked out on the street in front of a building with a sign that read Mercantile. The driver tied up his reins and climbed out of the wag, walking across the uneven wooden boardwalk. Three boys joined him, walking just behind him.

Ryan shifted his gaze, taking in as much of the ville as he could.

"What's on your mind?" Krysty asked.

"Trader always had a saying," Ryan said, "about how calm water covered everything. Even a man drowning in it.'' He nodded at the ville. ''I look out there, all I see is calm water when things should be muddied up some. Kirkland calls the tune in this ville, and everybody else seems to dance. Me, I'd kind of like to know what the piper's got under his sleeve.''

Krysty joined Ryan at the window. She ran her fingers across his hard, flat stomach. Ryan liked the feel of her, and liked thinking about the clean bed and the possibility of a bath and whatever came after. He took her hand in his, splaying his fingers between hers and holding tight.

''Mebbe it's only calm water out there,'' she suggested.

''Mebbe,'' Ryan agreed. But the uniform calmness about the ville unnerved him. Liberty had been a cunning, heartless bastard. It gave a man pause for some reflection thinking about what tied a man like Kirkland to Liberty. And he wasn't going to forget Albert's story about the wholesale slaughter anytime soon.

A discreet knock sounded at the door.

Krysty disengaged from Ryan. ''Yes,'' she called.

Ryan glanced at the young maid standing in the doorway. The girl's eyes were brazen and bold, meeting his own with no shyness.

''I've got your water on the way up, ma'am,'' the maid said. ''Aunt Maim asked me to tell you and your man that she'd enjoy your company for supper tonight. She said to tell you that she understood it was short notice and everything.''

''When?'' Ryan asked.

"At eight o'clock," the maid replied. "After the evening church services."

"Sure," Ryan said. He glanced at his chron. "How long is that from now?"

"A couple hours." The maid covered a faked cough, then trailed her fingers down the gap in her blouse. Another button had evidently come loose on her trip down and back up the stairs. "She has some clothing you can borrow for tonight. She likes to have something of a formal dinner. Gussied up and all."

"Tell her we'll accept," Krysty said. "Have you got a kitchen available?"

"Yes, ma'am. Cook is one of the best in these parts. Aunt Maim wouldn't have no other. A lot of people in the ville set store by her larder and the meals we serve out each day."

"What have you got in the way of fresh fruit and cheeses?"

"Apples and pears," the maid replied. "And we've got a half dozen different cheeses."

"I'd like a plate sent up shortly after the bath-water," Krysty said.

"Yes, ma'am. Aunt Maim said to tell you she had some rhubarb wine if you've a mind to sample some. She said you might be hungry from your trip, too. But she said to save some space for dinner because she's having Cook do some special dishes."

"Tell her thank you for us," Krysty said.

The maid nodded, her eyes still focused entirely on Ryan. "It's Chastity," she stated.

"What?" Ryan asked.

"My name," the maid replied. "It's Chastity."

"I'll remember that."

"You do it," she said without hesitation. "I'll see to it you get anything you want. Aunt Maim told me to make sure your stay at the inn was a good one. Told me to see to it personal."

Krysty crossed the room and closed the door in the maid's face. She turned back to Ryan, her face reflecting her amusement. "Guess we don't have to wonder where she's coming from."

"No," Ryan agreed. The girl's attentions didn't affect him. A strong man in Deathlands brought out the sexuality in a woman looking for somebody to protect her when she knew she couldn't do the job herself. She was only reacting the way she'd trained herself to react. "Guess she outgrew her name some time ago."

"Doubt if she remembers the passage."

"Be interesting to find out if any of the others got the same invitation we got."

Krysty nodded. "If you run into little Miss Big Eyes outside—"

"I'll tell her she's late with the hot water."

"You do that."

Ryan grinned, then let himself into the hallway, relieved when he saw the maid was nowhere around. He knocked on J.B.'s door.

"Who's knocking?" the Armorer called out.

"Me," Ryan replied.

"Come ahead."

Ryan opened the door carefully. J.B. wasn't a man to creep up on.

The Armorer stood in the center of the room on the table. A bed slat blocked the balcony door from sliding open. J.B. worked the curtain cord through a bent nail sticking out from the ceiling. The nail was obviously in a new position.

"Redecorating?" Ryan asked.

J.B. shot him a wry glance. "We walked into this whitewashed ville, doesn't mean angels live here. I'm just taking a few precautions to make sure we get to walk back out of here."

Mildred came back out of the bathroom. "Running water would help things, but sleeping high and dry is a good enough thought for the moment. They got a pitcher of fresh water in there if you're dry, John." She nodded at Ryan. "Making a social call?"

"Krysty and me got invited to dinner tonight. Wondered if you'd been treated to the same invitation."

J.B. shook his head. "I got plans to see the gunsmith. Mildred and I will figure something out for ourselves."

"Probably wouldn't be a problem to set an extra plate or two."

"I kind of like the idea of spreading ourselves out a little more," the Armorer said. "Get what we need as fast as we can, get ourselves set up to leave if trouble comes along." He stepped off the table and grabbed the curtain cord. Then he took up the M-4000.

"Dinner's at eight. To be sociable, we'll probably hang around until ten and talk. We get any later than that, come looking. If you're not in by then, I'll do the same.''

''Sounds good.'' J.B. sat the straight-backed, wooden chair on the table. He cradled the shotgun across it, pointing at the door. A couple lashes of another piece of the curtain cord secured it into place. Then he threaded the long cord through the nail and through the trigger guard, as well, fixing it so a drawer from the chest of drawers worked as a counterweight to pull the trigger. He attached the cord to the doorknob.

Ryan observed the setup. It wasn't anything fancy or elaborate, just deadly. And that was all it had to be. When the door was opened by anyone who didn't know the shotgun was in place, they'd get blasted stepping into the room.

''If you come by later,'' J.B. said meaningfully, ''you want to make sure you knock.''

Chapter Six

"Those guys still following us?"

Jak glanced over at Dean, as if he were talking to the boy, but actually he used the reflection in the glass of a leather worker's shop on the other side to check on the three men trailing them. There was no sign of the deputy that had first trailed them from the inn. "How many you find?"

"Three," Dean answered.

"Three's right." Jak ran a hand across his clothing, touching the hafts of his hidden knives. "Now, which three?"

"A test?" Dean grinned at his companion.

"Mebbe. Good to know if we agree on targets."

Some of the smile left Dean's face. "You think they're going to try to brace us? Wouldn't that be bastard stupe after what Kirkland and the sheriff said?"

"Stupe to ignore possibility," Jak argued. "Mebbe these friends with Liberty. Mebbe found after we get here."

Dean nodded. "Guy behind us on the right side of the street. Got a limp in his left leg. Man directly behind us. I keep track of him by that stinking cigar he's smoking. And the guy up ahead of us carrying the bull-snake whip with the silver handle. Mighty stupe to carry something that lights up so well after dark.''

"Those are three," Jak said. "Good eye. See deputy anywhere?"

Dean shook his head.

"Got ask where he is."

"The sheriff did make a big deal out of the fact that we were going to be followed everywhere, didn't he?"

"Yeah."

"Not likely that he lost us in all this rush of folks out this late at night, is it?"

Jak looked at the empty streets. A few of the windows spilled warm yellow light out onto the wooden boardwalks. The sound of music came from up ahead, punctuated by the roar of drunken voices and ragged cheers. "Not likely," he agreed.

"It's going to be hard to get away from these guys and get a look at those stables," Dean said.

Jak knew that. He was already working on resolving the problem. If it had been just him, he probably could have melted into one of the shadows getting fat between the buildings. And maybe Dean was even good enough to avoid detection the same way, if they'd been out in the rough, in the trees and underbrush that were a lot more forgiving of a wrong move than the straight lines and angles of a villescape.

"Mebbe not," the albino said. "Want look at girls?" He pointed his chin toward the gaudy house in front of them. The open door spewed the piano music and bawdy talk out onto the street.

Dean tried to keep a smile from his face. "Okay." He struggled to sound complacent, but Jak could hear the excitement in the younger boy's voice.

"Like girls, Dean?" Jak asked.

"Sure. I mean, who wouldn't?"

"Girls can be rattlesnake mean," the albino warned.

"Guys can be a lot meaner."

"Yeah." Jak nodded. "But not matter how pretty guy is, if you not turned that way. Think wrong about girl, your head all stupe inside. Think so much, forget rattlesnake mean. Till wake up, find dick laying on chest."

"Don't have to be like that. You had Christina for a while."

Jak closed off the pain he still felt from his wife's and daughter's deaths. Even his acceptance that such things happened didn't let him completely forget. He was strong enough to move on afterward, and strong enough every now and then to spend quiet moments thinking about them, wondering how his life might have been different. "Not always like that," he admitted. "Enough like that, don't let many close."

"I understand that." Dean paused at the doorway, peering in over the bat-wing doors.

A big man with a shaved head and a huge walrus mustache graying at the ends stepped forward through the bat-wing doors. He wore a leather vest with fringe and had incredibly hairy shoulders. He carried a billy club in one hand, waving it slightly like he was really looking forward to using it. "Something I can do for you two?" he asked.

"We come to see the show," Dean said. His eyes were locked on the naked dancer twirling around a brass pole mounted on the center stage inside the small, low-ceilinged room.

The bald man studied them in an exaggerated fashion, then kept his eyes on Dean. "You look a little young for the Brass Ass, boys."

Jak lowered his hand to the butt of the .357 pistol. "Used to going my own way."

A distasteful look covered the bald man's face. "No reason to go getting all heated up."

"Standing in doorway. Cover charge fine. You making decision not."

"I'm not looking for any trouble, friend," the bald man said.

"Me, neither," Jak replied. "Looking kill time, not man."

"Fuck! It don't take much to put you on the prod, does it?" The big man took a step back.

"No." Jak took the step forward. His hand never left the Magnum blaster. Ryan didn't want any trouble in the ville until they figured out the way of it, but the albino wasn't used to walking away from trouble. "Got cover charge?"

"Cost you some jack."

"Know Dr. Kirkland?" Jak asked.

"Yeah, sure." The big man jerked a thumb over his shoulder. "The doc's inside. He's a regular. Everybody knows him."

"Kirkland paying."

The big man looked like he didn't believe it. "Mebbe we ought to go ask the doc."

Jak nodded. "Go with you."

Unhappily the big man led the way into the building. Smoke wreathed the room, tainting the smell of everything. The albino's nose wrinkled in protest at the stink of soured sweat and stale beer, and he could already feel the acrid stench of the smoke burning at his nasal passages. He stayed close to the big man, watching as he signaled two other men who approached quickly.

The room was laid out in an H, and the crossbar of the letter pattern was the runway jutting from the center of the curtained stage. As with every other building in the ville, this one had been cobbled together from bits and pieces of other buildings and houses. The pieces fit well together, though.

With the low ceiling, everything in the room seemed closer, including the naked girl on the runway. Her skin resembled warm, burnished butter with the glow of oil lanterns flooding over it. The shadows battled the light, even the glow of the lanterns hanging from the semicircle in front of the stage, and clung to the girl. The effect made her even more erotic in appearance.

She was in her late teens, baby fat still clinging to her hips, thighs and breasts. Her dark brown hair was razored close, cut just above her eyebrows and flowing down even with the line of her jaw. She wore only an orange bikini bottom, leaving her full breasts swinging free. As she swung to the music played by the pianist in the far corner of the room, she hooked her fingers in the bikini straps and tugged them up, offering momentary glimpses of the fleecy down barely covered by the material. Her smile was plastic, and the bumps and grinds she offered were for the jack only.

Dean's steps became a little awkward as they made their way through the mazes of tables and chairs. Invective followed them as they blocked the views of the onlookers.

Jak's hand closed around his blaster's butt. Gunplay wasn't on his agenda, but he wasn't going to be manhandled, either. He locked eyes with the bald man. "Kirkland," the albino reminded him. "Somebody draws on me, you first die. Won't miss."

For a moment the bald man hesitated, swallowing hard. He waved to the two approaching men again, keeping them back. He resumed his path through the tables.

Kirkland sat up front in a private booth. The doctor, now in dark pants and an open-throated shirt, sat alone in the booth. His attention was focused entirely on the dancing girl, only diverting momentarily to the glass in front of him.

The bald man approached Kirkland and leaned down to whisper into his ear.

Jak glanced around the room, knowing he and Dean were drawing more than their share of attention. A look back at the doorway confirmed the three men had followed them in from the street. He rested his gaze on Dean for a moment.

All of Dean's attention was riveted on the dancer, who was almost peeling the bikini bottom, one hand disappearing into her pants in a frenzy of suggestive movement. The girl's face wrinkled up in a pantomime of lust.

"You like the girls?" Jak asked.

"Oh, yeah," Dean answered.

"Never showed much interest before. What teach at school?"

"Didn't get to this part," Dean replied.

Jak studied the younger boy, getting a flash of insight the way he sometimes did. "Was girl at school?"

Dean shook his head. "Not rightly."

From the way Dean answered, Jak knew he wasn't getting all the story. Dean sometimes talked with Ryan and Krysty about things that had happened at the school, and even went over some of the schoolwork he'd learned with Doc, which led to long conversations that Dean seemed more interested in than he'd showed before.

Kirkland looked up at Jak and Dean, then waved them over with a smile on his face. The bald man held up a hand, stopping the approach of the other men.

Jak led the way to the table, aware that he was drawing attention from the other men in the room. He sat in one of the proffered chairs across from Kirkland. Dean took another.

"Had no idea you boys would like looking at the girls," Kirkland said, waving to a young waitress wearing only cutoff jeans, "or I'd have extended an invitation." She came over at once and put a fresh glass in front of the doctor. "Would you like something to drink?"

"Water," Jak replied.

"What have you got?" Dean asked.

"Homemade ale and an assortment of wines. There's a watermelon flavor that turned out exceptionally well. If I might be bold enough, I'd recommend that."

"Sure," Dean said.

Kirkland nodded to the waitress, and she walked away. "I don't see your father here."

"Not father," Jak said. He jerked a thumb at Dean. "His father. My friend."

"I see. And would your father approve of your being here, lad?" Kirkland asked Dean.

"I've seen naked women before," Dean replied. "And I've drank."

"Your father seems to be quite liberal in his views," Kirkland replied. "Here in Hazard, we take a more conservative view. Children are kept away from such things as this."

"Mebbe," Dean said. "But I learned how to kill a man before I had any real interest in girls." His voice was flat, matter-of-fact. "I guess I'm not like most of the kids you got in this ville."

Jak grinned only slightly, feeling the scars on his bone white face tighten. But it wasn't an expression he knew Kirkland would recognize. He felt a little prideful at Dean's reply; it was something a man would have said to draw the line and gather some respect from another man on the verge of stepping over that line. And the albino could hear Ryan Cawdor's tone in Dean's voice.

He glanced back and saw that the three men had stationed themselves along the free-standing bar. All of them wore weapons that looked like they'd seen a lot of use. Two of them, Jak noticed, had tattoos on their faces, identifying them as probable members of Liberty's gang. It felt comforting to know who the hunters were.

"Mebbe you'd like to do more than look at the girls," Kirkland offered. "All of these ladies are willing to be more—companionable—for the right price."

"No," Dean said. "Looking's fine. I figure buying it only puts me mebbe a step ahead of selling it. And I don't sell myself. My dad taught me that."

"Your father sounds like a smart man." Kirkland leaned back in his chair as the piano number ended. The dancer picked up the clothing she'd discarded during her performance, moving back toward the curtained area of the stage, her hips undulating and sending the onlookers into a faked frenzy of lust.

A man jumped onto the runway and dropped his pants, doing a jiggling dance and yelling at her. Before he could yank his pants back up, a woman ran from behind the curtains with a wet mop in her hands.

Jak appreciated the economy of motion the woman used in bringing the mop across to connect with the man on the stage. The wet mass of strands slammed into the guy's head and released a flood of water that drenched some of the men seated close around the runway.

"Goddamn it, Suzie," one of the men yelled in protest. "Sykes was just having a little fun. Letting off a little steam."

The comment drew a chorus of laughter from the onlookers. But the closer ones grabbed their drinks and headed back from the runway. Sykes, tripped by his pants and propelled by the wet mop, hit the runway hard. The woman was a loose scarecrow of beauty. Her bra and panties fit her, but the hard planes of her breasts, stomach and thighs showed a lot of hard usage.

"So let him cool off! Stupe fucker's not gonna put a show on while he's on my stage," Suzie shouted in righteous indignation. "I got working girls here who got to feed their families. They're gonna get some respect if I have to beat it into you bastard sons of bitches myself." She brought the mop over her shoulder again, putting all of her weight into it.

The mop handle cracked against the back of Sykes's head. His face bounced off the runway floor, then blood pooled under him. He gave up trying to pull his pants up and worked on just sliding off the runway. His hand slid across the pool of blood as he crabbed his way toward escape, and his face thudded against the wooden platform again.

The laughter this time was at Sykes's expense. A couple men grabbed him by the legs and dragged him from the runway. Nearly unconscious, the man dropped to the floor. The onlookers ignored him and set to cleaning their tables and chairs.

"Okay, Suzie," one of the men said. "Stage's all yours again. Let's get the show back on the road."

"No one touches one of my girls," Suzie told them. "Less they pay for the privilege. Next man gets himself a load on and figures his thundering little dinky is so great he's got to show it, he's gonna go home with it floating in the bottom of a bottle of whiskey." She wiped the floor clean, then stalked back to the curtained area. "Tickle them ivories, Amadeus."

The piano player tossed her a salute that turned into a single finger when her back was turned. Then he grabbed the half-empty bottle from the top of the piano and took a deep draft. Finished with the bottle, he set it back on top and lit up a fresh cigarette. He cracked his knuckles, then began a raucous tune.

Another girl came from behind the curtains. This one wore a green Mohawk that had to have been eight inches tall. A brief, loose loincloth covered her sex and her behind, but gave fleeting glimpses of both as she strutted and shimmied. Mirror sunglasses covered her eyes, and she used her arms to keep her breasts hidden for a time.

"So what are you boys doing out tonight?" Kirkland asked. "Besides bar crawling?"

"Used living out in open," Jak said. "Hard get used being in four walls."

"I can well imagine." Kirkland nodded and sipped his drink.

Jak drank his water, finding it had a metallic taste, but no odor and no aftertaste. It didn't matter, because he wasn't stupe enough to drink a quantity that would hurt him. He watched Dean sample his wine, noticing the way the boy tried to hide his grimace.

The girl with the tall green Mohawk dropped her loincloth and swivel-hipped around the stage. The audience roared its appreciation. A small, genuine smile played across the woman's cold features.

"New talent," Kirkland said. "She still enjoys what she does. That attitude is what sets her apart from the other women, and it's what makes the other women hate her."

Even Jak, as interested as he was in finding out the information Ryan had sent him for, was hypnotized for a time by the woman's unleashed sexuality.

Kirkland leaned a little closer. "Konikka's a lot more expensive than the other women," he said. "But I can still make it happen. She still owes me from her last abortion. She tried to do it herself with a coat hanger and ended up nearly killing herself. I had to do a lot of repairs, still nearly lost her."

"Why do that for us?" Jak asked.

"Because I want some more of that anesthetic," Kirkland said. "If I can't cut the deal with the others of your group, mebbe I can cut it with you."

Jak regarded him with a cold look. "I'll think about it."

Kirkland's face froze for just a moment, and Jak sensed the doctor was struggling internally to maintain control. "You drive a hard bargain. Tell you what, I'll give Konikka to you and your young friend for the evening and give you even more to think about.''

"I pass," Jak answered.

The doctor nodded slowly, then looked back at Dean. "What about you, boy?"

"No."

Kirkland heaved a loud sigh, then laughed as if in disbelief. But the effort was strained and didn't come off as natural. "You boys really don't know what you're passing up."

"Mebbe," Jak said. "But walking in today, got different impression of ville. White wash buildings. Church. Figured something like this wouldn't exist."

"Every ville has its dark underbelly," Kirkland replied. "Hell, after skydark most of what was left was dark underbelly. You expect good people to survive something like that, come clawing back from radiated lands and near Stone Age conditions?" The doctor laughed and belched. "I'll tell you what doesn't fit here is that white wash look. Those people are delusional if they think a pedestrian society can exist anywhere right now."

"Must think so."

"Only because I allow them to believe in that delusion. I keep Hazard well stocked in weak people, make no mistake about that. But they serve my purpose. And I don't give a damn about any of them." Kirkland laughed. "But you try and get one of them on the street to believe that. I allow them to raise their families here. Protect the weak ones from stickies. And they labor in my ville, stocking my larder and providing me with amusement.''

Jak kept his face immobile, proud of the way Dean did the same. The companions had seen some hard times, dealt with some harsh barons, but Kirkland promised to be one of the most inherently evil.

''I'll talk to you boys tomorrow,'' the doctor said as he stood. He glanced toward the curtained stage, then waved. Konikka came out a moment later, sashaying across the runway with less enthusiasm than she'd carried before. The mood in the room darkened immediately as the men stared after her with greedy lust.

Jak figured it was a good thing the girl's eyes were covered by the mirror lenses, because he didn't think she'd be able to hide the reluctance in her gaze that she tried so hard to hide from her moves. The girl linked her arm in the doctor's.

Kirkland looked at Jak. ''If you should decide to change your mind on my offer, let me know.''

The albino teen watched the man leave the room, noticing how the other men gave him a wide berth. The three men at the bar averted their faces, but Kirkland noticed them anyway. He didn't stop or acknowledge them, though.

''He's gone,'' Dean said after the man left, ''and I'm glad to be rid of him. I'm beginning to think the worst thing we could've done was come here.''

''For him or us,'' Jak agreed. ''Remains be seen how hand takes shape. Let's go.'' He left his drink on the table and walked into a narrow hallway where he figured the washroom was. He stepped over

Sykes's unconscious body. Even without looking, he knew the three men were following him and Dean.

He walked through the door on the left, led by the stench of urine and the soured stink of sweat. The washroom was uncommonly small, decorated with pinups from skin magazines Jak had seen before. There were pictures on the walls that looked like the women in them were trying to turn themselves inside out. He'd never cared for that kind of thing, and couldn't understand how other men could. His own rutting urges were triggered by different things.

The men in the washroom gave them notice, but ignored them for the most part.

Looking at the back wall, Jak spotted the small window above the piss trough. He didn't pause, not knowing if the three men following them would figure on taking them when the chance presented itself to hem them in.

He stepped up on the trough, making a couple of the men nearest him on either side shy away. He ignored them, grabbing the window latch and unlocking it. He shoved the window open with a creak. The night air rushed in, still carrying the scent of the ville, but lots cleaner than the interior of the washroom.

Jak hoisted himself up and climbed through the window. It let out into an alley filled with grass and weeds growing up between chunks of cracked pavement. He pulled himself through, then reached back for Dean.

The younger boy slithered through all on his own, joining Jak a heartbeat later.

"Hey, they're getting away!"

Looking back into the lantern-lit room, Jak saw the three tattooed men rush to the window. They almost got into a fight with the other men. One of them unlimbered his side arm.

Jak tapped Dean's shoulder and they stepped into the darkness, out of the line of fire.

"Guess they're pretty serious about finding us," Dean said.

Jak nodded. "Probably got Kirkland's blessing. Mebbe heard left inn by ourselves, thought those coldhearts could take and question us. Then blame them we get chilled."

"Nobody would have believed that."

Jak nodded. "Yeah. But Kirkland not know that." He listened to the men yelling behind them, realizing it had to have been the others in the washroom, not the men trying to track them. "Hurry." He led Dean into the shadows. It would be better if they didn't have to kill anybody.

At least, not where the bodies would be left out in the open.

Chapter Seven

Hand lettering made the small sign look elegant. J.B. stood outside the building looking up at it after pulling the bell cord: Tinker Phillips and Sons Gun Repair and Gun Sales Straight and True Guaranteed.

Wheelgun and .45 semiautomatic images framed the announcement. Rifle images bridged the distance along the sides of the sign.

The building was compact, consisting of a single story and running back about four times in length what it was in width. White paint looked well kept, and small panes of frosted glass covered the windows and the door openings. Even in the low lantern light coming from the street, the Armorer could see the shadows of iron bars just on the other side of the glass.

The door opened softly, not drawing back much. Close-cropped blond hair hung over a pair of sky blue eyes that regarded J.B. in frank disapproval. For a moment the Armorer thought he was looking at a young man, then he saw the face had a maturity to it in spite of the fact there was no beard growth.

"Can I help you?" the girl asked. Her tone was cold, and there was no friendliness in her at all.

"Name's J. B. Dix." He tipped his fedora. Then replaced it. "I saw your sign. Noticed some light against the glass from inside. Thought mebbe you hadn't entirely shut down the business for the day." He felt an itch over his chest, like the ones he got when somebody laid gun sights over him. Riding with the Trader, traveling with Ryan, he'd learned to put great faith in such feelings. He shifted a little, taking up a stance that would make his torso less of a target.

"You're one of those people Kirkland put out the word on. The outlanders."

"Yeah." J.B. felt a little uncomfortable staring into the girl's blue eyes. He wished Mildred had come with him instead of staying at the hotel. But she'd been excited about the prospect of a hot bath. J.B. could never understand that. Cleanliness was next to godliness. Even the Trader used to say that every now and then. But the first thing the Armorer held to was being well armed. "I could come back mebbe tomorrow if this isn't a good time."

The girl shook her head. "Wouldn't want a friend of Kirkland's to run the risk of doing without something we could provide." But her eyes said she was lying. "Tell me what you want, and I'll see that you get it if we got it. I'll pass it through the drop box to you." A long box built into the side of the fortified wall pushed out partially, revealing the empty depths inside.

"Let him in," a man's gruff voice commanded from somewhere inside the building.

"Don't know that would be a good idea," the girl protested quietly, her eyes never leaving J.B.'s.

"Anna, you heard what I said."

"Yes, sir." She shifted her attention to the locks holding the door closed.

"Appreciate it." J.B. waited for her to finish unlocking all the latches and chains. He turned to the deputy standing in the shadows on the other side of the street. "You want to come in, too?"

"Naw. Be fine out here. If you go into Tinker's, there's only one way out of there. I'll be here waiting for you."

"Could be a while."

"If I get lonely, I'll talk to myself."

The door opened. The girl stood in front of J.B., wearing tight jeans and a blouse that was tucked into her waistband. The slim, curvy build left no doubts as to her sex.

"You got more of a vision problem than those glasses lead a person to expect?" the girl asked. "Or mebbe I should whistle up your dog, 'cause he sure as hell isn't doing his job."

J.B. looked into the pale blue eyes. "Sign says 'and sons.' Reckon you caught me by surprise."

"I can handle a pistol or long blaster about as good as any in these parts. And that sign's right. I'm Tinker's daughter-in-law. I help out here at the store. You got an idea of what you want? Or are you just going to wish and dream?"

"Kirkland said there'd be a line of credit," J.B. replied. "Figure on spending some of that if I can."

"There is, and you can. But you come in hungry, it'll spend right fast. Kirkland don't tap into us as much as he does some in this ville."

"I know what I need." J.B. reached into his shirt

pocket and took out one of the shotgun's fléchette rounds. "Seen anything like that?"

The girl took the shell between her fingers and turned it carefully to catch the weak light streaming down from the street lanterns. "Twelve gauge?"

"Yeah."

"Special load?"

"Fléchettes."

She nodded. "Heard of them, but I never saw a shell like this." She handed it back to the Armorer. "'Fraid we can't help you."

"Anna," the older man's voice roared, "you let that man on in here. Right now."

"Yes, sir, Daddy." When Anna stepped back from the doorway, she took a step to the side, keeping her gun hand clear. She fisted the double-action .44 Magnum Colt Anaconda in the holster on her hip. "But, Mr. Dix, remember to keep any sudden moves to yourself."

J.B. touched his hat. "I'll surely keep that in mind." He stepped into the darkened room, blinking rapidly in an effort to bring his night vision up to speed. Rather than looking directly at objects, he depended on a peripheral view, because that part of sight always adjusted first.

The forward room of the building was small and bare. Gun ports cut into the wall on the other side looked like yawning demons' mouths even in the shadows trapped inside the room. Hard metal gleamed inside.

J.B. raised his hands, making sure to keep them away from his body. "If this is going to make everybody this tense, mebbe we can do this another day."

"If I don't like what I see," the man stated, "I reckon we won't see you again tomorrow. Neither will anybody else."

"Then hurry up and make up your mind," J.B. told him, "'cause I've got to scratch my nose something fierce and I don't want to get shot for my trouble. Can't imagine anything worse than getting a belly full of double-aught buckshot and dying kind of slow while your nose is itching the whole time."

Anna stood at the side, clear of any field of fire. "You want to move away from that door? I got to lock up."

J.B. nodded slowly. "Two steps to my right, and I'm going to take them slow. Count them for you. One." He stepped, his stomach tight in anticipation. His mind was working the angles automatically, weighing the risks. It was possible he could whirl and yank the young woman into the way, then hit the door running and get away before he got shot. But he was curious, too, because this wasn't at all the kind of reception he'd expected to receive after Kirkland's invitation. "And two." He stopped.

"That's fine. Anna, get that door now."

Anna moved forward and shot the locks. "I'm going to take his guns, too, Daddy."

"No." Tinker Phillips's voice didn't hesitate. "You stay away from that man. If he's who he says he is, you'll be dead before I could tell you was in trouble."

Anna ripped her blaster free of the holster and

trained it on J.B., as well. "Well, then, I guess we're going to have to decide what to do with him. Personally I'm all for killing him and being done with it."

RYAN STOOD at the window in the hotel room, the curtains pulled so no one could see in, and the lit lantern placed so his shadow didn't skate across the rough material. The street stayed empty below, and folks who were out got on with their business. He was naked, chilled now after the hot bath. He carried the SIG-Sauer in one hand, same as he'd kept it close by during the bath.

"Anything, lover?" Krysty asked from behind him.

"No. Just looking. Ville doesn't quite fit together right." He turned to her, saw her standing there naked. He had no idea of how many times he'd seen Krysty naked since they'd known each other, but the sight never failed to make his heart beat a little faster in anticipation. Though still road weary from all the killing and the travel of the past few days, seeing her made him feel younger and stronger.

"Know what you mean." Krysty tossed back her flaming mane and ran a comb through it, her breasts heaving with the motion. For a minute, with the lantern light playing over her soft skin, she looked defenseless. The V of crimson fleece between her thighs blazed like fire. "Should be an interesting dinner with Aunt Maim in a little while."

"Either way it goes," Ryan said, "we aren't staying long. We'll get our business here done and move on.'' He moved away from the window and put his arms around Krysty. He enjoyed the smell of her, the cleanliness, and the faint scent of the musk drifting up from her arousal. She felt warm and chill all at the same time in his arms. He got an erection almost immediately.

''Something,'' Krysty said, lowering her arms and putting them around his neck, ''tells me we might be a little late to dinner.'' She rolled her hips against him, making a tunnel between her thighs that cradled his erection.

''Mebbe we can still make breakfast.''

She ran her hand down the scarred side of his face, bringing heat to the places that weren't nerve deadened. ''We've got to be there tonight. Besides being under Miss Kate's roof, I'm curious about the woman. We didn't see her at all earlier.''

Ryan kissed Krysty's neck, sucking the flesh into his mouth and biting down hard enough to almost bruise the skin. Krysty groaned into his ear, holding him tighter.

''I know it isn't so, lover,'' she whispered, ''but all of a sudden it feels like it's been a long time in between for us.''

Ryan silently agreed. He moved against her, feeling her sex opening to allow him in. He kept from penetration, though, letting the oils build up until his flesh glided against hers. ''We can take some time now.''

''Only if you promise there's going to be a later.'' Krysty's hands dug into the big muscles of his shoulders.

"Promise," he said huskily. He bent and picked her up in his arms, then carried her to the bed. She scooted back when he set her down, making room for him. Instead, Ryan knelt at the edge of the bed, shoving the 9 mm blaster between the mattress and the box springs so he could get to it easily. He parted her legs, then kissed her there. He continued kissing as her flesh melted into sugary fluid at his every lick and nibble. In moments his tongue slid freely along her parted folds, and he tasted the sweet-and-sour saltiness of the excited nubbin of flesh.

Krysty groaned and shuddered at the touch of his tongue. She locked her hands at the base of his skull and pulled his face into her harder. "Keep doing that," she whispered huskily. "Just like that, lover, just like that."

Ryan kissed and tongued her sex, feeling the tension fill his lover. After a time, she quivered like a plucked guitar string, her need the only thing at the forefront of her mind. He brought her to the brink of her climax, but didn't let her go over the edge. When she seemed to reach the edge of release, he moved to a different spot or changed the rhythm, forcing her body to adapt and long for a new sensation. She drew her legs up tight against her breasts, allowing him even further penetration of her most intimate depths. Plaintive cries ripped from her throat.

At last Ryan let her climax crest, cradling her hips against his face so he could go deeper and maintain the contact his lover desired even though her body bucked against him. He rode out the release, staying on target, feeling his own needs building even more as hers were met. After a time she went limp against him.

He drew back, smiling up at her across the flat planes of her stomach and the mounds of her breasts. "Mebbe there's something to be said for the occasional room at the inn."

"Speaking of in," Krysty said, "why don't you come up here?"

Ryan covered her body with his. He slid into her at once, going as deep as he'd ever been. She gave a slight moan again, letting him know the lovemaking wasn't completely over for her, either. He trapped her wrists in his, holding them flat against the bed as he took her. His own climax came near to bursting, only a few short movements away.

With a burst of strength, Krysty seized his wrists in hers and flipped him over on his back without losing their connection. Ryan felt her liquid desire melting down around his hardness. She held his arms down as she took him forcibly enough to make the bed creak. Ryan rode out her excitement and determination, meeting her stroke for stroke. Then it seemed like everything in him came loose and exploded.

Krysty cried out again as she hit her own peak, even harder than before. She slowed her hip undulations, bringing them down.

She leaned down and kissed him. He breathed in the scent of her, and of the soap that still clung to her skin.

"I guess there is going to be a later," she said in a throaty voice.

"Play your cards right," Ryan growled, "and there could still be a now."

"No time, lover." She kissed him again, then heaved up off him. "The best you're going to hope for right now is that the bathwater is still warm."

Ryan watched her walk back to the bathroom. He felt the grin on his face in spite of the situation they found themselves in. There was something about Krysty that had made him start seeing some of the soft sides of life again. Some days he didn't like that thought. Only a hard man survived in Deathlands.

He slipped the SIG-Sauer from under the mattress and walked into the bathroom after her.

"IT'S NOT MUCH farther now."

Doc glanced down at his small companion. Albert kept up an almost running gait to match the taller man's strides. The dwarf kept his hands on the holstered .38s.

Long shadows filled the warren of alleyways in front of Doc. He guessed that they were in the older section of the ville. Hazard had been built from some good timbers, planed and put together with skill. But here in the center of the ville where the rest of the community had evidently sprung from, most of the buildings remained cobbled-together structures made from cast-offs of other buildings.

Cobb's turned out to be one of the oldest buildings. It was a narrow, two-story structure, its eaves made up of abandoned garage doors. Whitewash covered the surfaces, but those surfaces possessed an ill fit. Plaster caulking hung in thick coats over the cracks and joints. Yellow light showed through at the top and bottom of the door, leaking through from a lantern beyond. The light also lit up a wide pane of glass with Cobb's Bookstore hand lettered across it. Masking tape held fragments of the glass together.

On the other side of the window was a group of small round tables and straight-backed chairs. A counter stood farther back, a dark rectangular shadow in front of the lantern hanging on the wall. A cigarette coal glowed orange in the darkness.

Albert walked to the door and reached up for the bell string. He pulled it vigorously three times, then waited.

Doc stood on the uneven porch beside the little man and watched as two shadows got up from the tables inside. He felt edgy and tense in spite of Albert's camaraderie.

The door creaked open, revealing a thin strip of a man's face and one piercing eye that flicked over Doc, going from up to down and back again. "Howdy, Albert. Something I can do for you?"

"I brought a friend, Cobb," the dwarf replied. "Has an interest in books and such."

"You're going armed," Cobb said. "Where's Liberty and his gang?"

"Chilled," Albert said. "By this man and his friends. Liberty's probably been turned to crow shit from the looks of things when I last left him."

The door opened a little wider, revealing both the

man's eyes now. "He chilled Liberty, and he's walking around Hazard all straight up and all. Hard to believe."

"Believe it," Albert said. "I was there." He gripped his blasters. "And now I got these."

"You should of just run on, my little friend," Cobb said.

He turned to Doc. "And you, you should have never come here, because you surely signed your death warrant." He cocked his head at Albert. "Or hasn't the little man told you that?"

"I hadn't," Albert said, clearing leather with both his blasters and pointing them at Doc. "Dammit, Cobb, I was planning on telling him at a better time than this."

Doc felt totally surprised, not believing the dwarf's allegiance had turned so quickly. He fisted his sword stick, drawing the pieces in two by a fraction of an inch. If the chance presented itself, he planned to bury the business end of the sword in the little man's throat.

"Don't do nothing stupe," Albert said. "I'd hate to shoot you, Doc, but I don't aim to die because you're overreacting to bad news. Mebbe it isn't as bad as you think."

Righteous indignation and burning anger filled Doc as he looked into the little man's eyes. "I saved your life by my own hand," he said in a hoarse voice. "And I bade my friends trust you as they trusted me. Now you betray that trust. If you know your books as you have assured me you do, you will know a passage from Plutarch that was accredited to Julius Caesar and is most appropriate for this moment—'I love treason but hate a traitor.'"

Albert gestured with his blasters. "Get on inside the building, Doc. Cobb, take that cane away from him. And relieve him of his blaster."

Doc submitted to the indignity of being left bereft of self-defense. Cobb dropped a heavy hand on his shoulder and guided him into the structure. Two other men spread out before him, weapons gleaming in their hands. Doc glanced around the small room, but his chances of escape were as dim as the lantern light.

Chapter Eight

"Can't shake them," Dean said, turning into the grade of the broken land outside of Hazard. Fear kept an edge on him like a skinning knife. "Going to have to take them." He carried the Browning Hi-Power in his fist. Glancing over his shoulder, he spotted the five tattooed men they'd picked up tailing them.

The coldhearts rode horses and carried long blasters across the pommels of their saddles. The intent and the wariness they displayed left no doubts about what they planned.

Despite the run through Hazard, Jak and Dean hadn't been able to throw their pursuers off the trail. The men had clung stubbornly, guessing where the two youngsters had headed. Finally, at the stables, they'd been cornered and driven out of the ville.

And that was the part Dean couldn't really figure. The five men hadn't tried outright to chill them, but they had left no doubts in his mind or Jak's. Still, there had been nothing to do except be driven before them.

Dean hauled up short behind a thick-boled oak, thinking about how his father and the rest of the companions had set to and chilled Liberty and his gang without warning. He wondered if these five men intended for a message to be sent to the rest of the populace of the ville.

He peered through the shadows and saw Jak only a few feet from him. The albino carefully worked a water bladder they had taken from the stables. Jak had emptied it in one of the stalls, then drained the oil from three lanterns before they'd climbed through the roof and escaped into the brush. That had been when they had first discovered that the men had at least two silenced handblasters among them.

"Not much time," the albino whispered. "This happen quick."

"What?"

"Take them," Jak said. "Chill them fast. Then find out why not try chill us fast, too."

The fact that the five men hadn't been trying to blast through the brush had bothered Dean some. The only time they had been fired upon had been back at the stable. With the silenced weapons, the coldhearts could have tried to blast them back at the gaudy house, maybe chilled them, too. But they hadn't.

"Say when," Dean agreed.

"Stay here," Jak whispered. "Wait for signal."

"What signal?" he asked hoarsely, as Jak melted into the shadows.

"Know when see it," Jak's voice drifted back.

Dean sidled up to the tree, took up a two-handed grip on the Browning Hi-Power and aimed at the riders. He braced his arm against the tree trunk.

A horse nickered tiredly, blowing fog out its nostrils in the chill air that had settled over the countryside with the coming of night. The coldhearts talked among themselves, obviously waiting for their quarries to break cover at some point.

Less than fifty yards away, Dean got a better look at the long blasters two of them carried. They weren't regular weapons, like his father's Steyr. The two blasters they had looked more like long, cylindrical tubes mounted on gun stocks. J.B. probably would have recognized the make and model, but Dean thought it was enough that he recognized they were compressed-air guns. More questions assailed his mind, but then time for thinking was well past.

A pale shadow drifted along behind the horses, cutting through the brush with an unnatural speed. A spark flared, then a flaming object slammed against the man in the center of the five, drenching him with dark liquid. The flames quickly spread across the dark liquid, though, licking eagerly at the man and the horse.

The animal panicked first, its hindquarters on fire. It broke into a sudden run, hindquarters buckling as it tried to drag its rear onto the ground. The sudden movement threw the man from the saddle. He hit the ground hard, rolling and screaming as he tried to slap out the flames wreathing him.

Revealed in the light given off by the burning man and the burning horse, Jak sprinted up behind the man on the outside, out of Dean's field of fire. The albino slapped his hands against the horse's rear and vaulted aboard. The animal whinnied in fear and reared. Jak reached around the rider and seized the reins and the pommel, holding himself and the rider on. His other hand wrapped up under the man's chin. Moonlight glinted on metal.

The rider didn't try to struggle, letting his arms go limp at his sides. The burning man's cries continued to shrill over the trail.

"Chill him, Dean!" Jak ordered.

Dean swiveled his sights over the man closest to him. The other men jockeyed to control their horses and bring their blasters to bear on Jak. One of them ripped off three shots that missed.

Curling his finger over the Hi-Power's trigger, Dean squeezed off two shots that crunched through the man's chest, blowing out his heart. The body tumbled from the saddle, and the frightened horse thundered through the forest.

Realization that they were caught between their prey gripped the remaining two riders at once. Both put spurs to their mounts. One rode for Jak, while the other crashed through the brush where Dean stood.

Dean kept his position, standing his ground. He brought up his blaster and breathed out through his mouth to relax his arms. He centered the sights over his target's chest as the man raced toward him.

The attacker fired four shots that ripped bark from the tree beside Dean and the branches above. The man yelled loudly, hoping to rattle the youth.

Instead, the youngster fired coolly, placing two shots within a heartbeat of each other. The horse chose that moment to raise its head, and both 9 mm hollowpoint rounds struck the animal's skull, exploding its head.

Dean tried to realign his sights as the dead horse fell to the ground in a tumbling heap, but the uncertainty of the shot and Jak being behind the target stayed his finger. Before he could draw another breath, the man leaped from the saddle and dived into the brush, vanishing before Dean could take aim.

In that moment he knew that their trap had suddenly turned deadly again.

J.B. KEPT HIS HANDS raised as he looked across the barrel of Anna's blaster. He didn't say anything. Words weren't his forte. But he figured Mildred would be mighty angry if he got himself killed, especially since he'd turned down the offer of a roll in the hay to get his business with the gunsmith taken care of first. If it came down to it, he'd see the young woman before him dead before he allowed himself to get killed.

"Are you really J. B. Dix?" the man asked roughly.

"Yeah."

"The one rode with the Trader in the Shens on War Wag One?"

"Can't say there was ever any other."

"Saw you once, a long time ago, but the light's bad and my eyes aren't what they was."

"Hoping your good sense is. If I have to, I reckon I'm going to find out how good your girl here is.

I'm not a man to sit for long under the barrel of a blaster. Comes time to shit or get off the pot.''

Anna rolled the blaster's hammer back with her thumb. ''You're about two pounds' pressure away from death right now, mister. I wouldn't go getting all puffed up about your situation and how bastard tough you are.''

J.B. let a smile cross his face, as cold and hard as the drawn blaster in front of him. ''You're just pushing me that much closer to taking the decision out of your hands. I got no backup in me when it comes to taking a hand in gunplay.''

''Put that blaster away,'' Tinker Phillips ordered.

''Don't know that that's a good idea,'' Anna said. She kept her eyes locked on J.B.

''Long as you live under my roof,'' Phillips said, ''you're going to be bound by my word. You don't holster that piece, I'll chill you and bury you myself.''

With practiced efficiency, the woman lowered the hammer and twirled the blaster on her finger in a flashy display. The weapon found leather and snugged in tight. ''Another time mebbe, Mr. Dix.''

''Not if I have a choice,'' J.B. replied. ''Be a shame to chill a woman who seems to know so much about firearms.''

She looked amused.

''Okay if I put my arms down?'' J.B. asked. ''I'm losing feeling in my fingers.''

''Go ahead,'' Phillips said.

J.B. lowered his arms but continued to move slowly.

At the other end of the room, a section of the wall popped forward and dropped into grooves on the floor and across the ceiling. As it slid to the side, it revealed a doorway beyond. A hunchbacked old man stood in the doorway, looking like he was carrying a pack on his back because of the deformity. But he carried an oiled MAC-11 in a gnarled fist that looked two sizes too big for the rest of his body. With his bent-over position, the man was barely five feet tall.

"Tinker Phillips?" J.B. asked.

"That's me." Phillips's face was covered by gray hair and a thick gray beard that didn't quite disguise the scarring that had eroded his features. "People tell me I'm an ugly old bastard to my face, but that don't mean I take kindly to it."

"Didn't come here to look at you," J.B. said.

Phillips seemed taken aback for a moment by the bald-faced statement, then he cackled. "Damn, but some of Trader must have rubbed off on you. That old fucker was pure mean through and through. Man couldn't handle what he had to say ought not ask him what was on his mind."

"I've got a line of credit," J.B. said. "Put up by Kirkland. Wanted to see what I could get for it." He was conscious of Anna falling into place at his back.

Phillips hung the MAC-11 in a specialty holster at his right side. He spit at his feet, then rubbed it away. "Kirkland's a smart man, but he's got the conscience of a rabid dog."

"You're the first person in Hazard I've heard speak out against him."

"That's because you haven't talked to everybody in our happy little ville." Phillips turned and walked into the room beyond. "Come on in and sit a spell."

J.B. followed the old man, noting how the hump was large enough and high enough that it almost made Phillips look like he had two heads in the darkness. He heard the movement around them and knew they weren't alone. He used his peripheral vision and noted at least three more bodies.

Phillips drew a self-light across a rough cover. Light flared to life and banished some of the shadows. He cupped the flame in his hands and moved it toward a lantern another man held out. When the wick was burning good, the man replaced the hurricane glass and adjusted the flame.

Light spread out over the room, illuminating tables and chairs and a couple sofas spread out across a generous living space. Barren walls enclosed the space, holding no windows and no decorations. Two long rectangular tables sat at one end. Four men sat around the farthest one. All of the men had hand-blasters on the table in front of them, close in beside the metal plates piled high with beans and meat, thick chunks of carrots and potatoes. A tray of yellow corn bread acted as a centerpiece for the table.

"Have you ate since you been in the ville?" Phillips asked.

"No."

"You're welcome to our table." He gestured toward the small wood stove in the corner. Two big pots sat on the surface, steam still rising up from both. "Bread's fresh, just out of the oven."

J.B. noted the design with interest. He'd seen many like it, had even helped build several when he'd been a kid back in Cripple Creek. The residual heat from the wood stove was channeled up through the flue, and a baking box was built off the main pipe. But the flue on this stove didn't run straight up as most did. Instead, it ran off to the side and disappeared through a wall.

"Got it run so it can't get blocked off?" the Armorer asked.

"Out back of the main building," Phillips said, nodding. "Tapped into a fireplace of the glassmaker. He runs his ovens most of the time because he's always making glassware. Folks use it for canning what goods they raise, and for being sociable. We don't cook unless the glassmaker is working."

"And if he gets sick or takes a day off?" J.B. asked.

"Hardtack," one of the men at the table said, "and cold biscuits. You think we don't say some prayers for that old glassmaker come sick season in winter, you got yourself another think coming." He had a full beard and a thick scar over his left eye that had blue tattooing from a gunshot fired close up.

"Nobody notices you don't have a smoke flue?" J.B. asked.

"We got one," Phillips answered. "Even run smoke through it on occasion. But tying it into our main system here and letting Kirkland and his people have us at their mercy isn't exactly what we're willing to risk."

"I'll take a plate," J.B. said.

Phillips reached up into a cupboard and took down a metal plate. He dipped a large portion of meat, beans and vegetables onto the plate, then took a big spoon from a glass near the sink area and passed it over with the plate.

J.B. walked to the table where the other men were and sat down. One of them shoved the bread over. "Got your own well, too?" the Armorer asked. He broke a corn bread square and swabbed it through the bean broth.

"Of course. Have to be self-sufficient for the necessities."

J.B. bit into the corn bread, savoring the salty grease flavor of the bean broth. The taste took him back, just as the company of rough men around him, to a time long past. He understood the siege mentality, if not the why of it. As he ate, he began to get a different picture of Hazard, and he didn't like what he was looking at.

Phillips sat across from him, getting into the chair with difficulty. "None of Kirkland's people have been this far into my gun shop since we rebuilt it."

"What have you got against Kirkland?" J.B. asked. He ate with both hands on the table, watching the company he was in. Anna stood against the wall to his left, deliberately on the wrong side for him to make a quick draw against, and in a position that gave her a full field of fire without endangering anyone else in the room.

The five men in the room besides the gunsmith were all hard and rangy. They kept their eyes on him.

"Same as most other people in the ville who kind of want to run their own lives," Phillips replied. "He keeps us here, won't let us go."

J.B. swept his gaze around the room. "Seems like you got yourself a small army here. Don't see how you could be kept from leaving if that's what you decided you wanted to do."

"Looking on the face of it, that's what you'd think. But that's just looking on the face of it. My momma, God rest her soul, popped me out of her belly after being exposed to a hot-rad area on an overland trip my daddy took when he should have been seeing to it she stayed comfortable. You look at me now, you see a man been down some hard roads. Can you imagine what I must have looked like while I was some pissant newborn? I mean, we're born into this world ugly anyway. But me?" He barked harsh laughter.

"Must have been a sight," J.B. agreed.

"Damn straight, it was." Phillips rubbed his hump as if trying to massage away the old memory. "My daddy, he was all ready to stove in my head and be done with it. Only Momma didn't let him. Said she'd buried enough dead births, and I was the first one born live. Figured she had something wrong with her insides. He left her, but she managed to keep us both alive. Turns out I was real good with my hands. By ten and twelve years old, I was helping feed us by working on things other people brought to us.''

J.B. nodded. "You going to eat, or did I take your plate?''

"We eat in shifts,'' Phillips replied. "Against getting poisoned.''

J.B. understood immediately. "You trade out for food?''

"Yeah. No room for a garden down here, and got no place to raise beef, either. Gives us a certain vulnerability.''

"So you eat far enough apart that the symptoms would show up?''

"Yeah.''

J.B. scooped up more beef and beans, chewing it thoroughly. "And if somebody gets poisoned?''

"Simple. I blow up the building and go out of business. Want some coffee sub to go with that meal?''

J.B. nodded.

Phillips looked at one of the young men, who got up and took the coffeepot from the stove. He poured a ceramic cup full, then handed it to the Armorer.

"So what's keeping you here?'' J.B. asked.

"The plague,'' the gunsmith answered. "You mean to tell me you haven't heard of it?''

Chapter Nine

Jak maintained his hold on his hostage with difficulty as the horse reared and staggered under their combined weight. He kept a steady pressure on the reins, holding the horse from bolting and running. The burning horse raced through the brush ahead of them, leaving fiery sparks in its wake. Some of those sparks fanned to life as fires all on their own.

The albino locked his right arm under his hostage's chin. Warm blood flowed down his hand from a wound the leaf-bladed knife had made on the man's throat during the brief struggle. "Move, and die," Jak promised, his lips close to his captive's ear.

"Gonna be chilled in a minute anyway," the man argued in a strained voice. "Hiram ain't gonna crawfish. And he don't give a fuck if he kills me, too." But he didn't move against the threat of the knife.

Jak watched the man bringing his horse around to face them. The man had lost control over his mount for a moment when the burning man had dropped at his horse's hooves. He pulled his long blaster to his shoulder.

The albino kicked the horse in the sides and yanked savagely on the reins. The startled animal, given its head, burst into a gallop. It vaulted over the burning man still rolling around on the grass, then it crashed against the horse carrying the man with the long blaster.

The muzzle-flash ballooned from the rifle, reaching out over a foot. Jak heard the bullet break wind beside his ear. Expertly he flipped the leaf-bladed knife at the rifleman. The blade flicked into the man's eye, burying deep into the brain tissue beyond.

Before his hostage could try to break away while the dead man fell from his staggered horse, Jak drew the .357 Magnum Colt Python and placed the barrel against the back of the man's head. He pulled on the reins, swinging the horse back in the direction where the surviving coldheart had gone to brush in front of Dean. The man was gone.

Jak raked the area with his gaze, but he didn't see Dean, either. Both of them had vanished. Then he spotted movement to the right of the tree where Dean had been. But he had no idea if the movement belonged to friend or foe.

"I THOUGHT WE HAD an understanding between us, Albert," Doc said. "I must point out your present behavior is less than exemplary, to say the least."

"This old man talks a lot, doesn't he?" Cobb asked. He stepped behind Doc and grabbed a handful of the old man's hair.

Doc managed to hold himself in check despite the pain, but he feared his scalp was going to be torn loose. He kept his hands out at his sides, but he was waiting for an opportunity.

"Cobb, I didn't want him hurt," Albert exploded. And Doc thought that was a strange thing for a man to say while holding him at gunpoint.

"You shouldn't have brought him here," Cobb said. "I don't know that I can trust him."

"Well, I do," Albert growled.

"Might I suggest," Doc said, "that you have a most peculiar way of showing it."

"It's your own bastard fault, Cobb," Albert accused. "If you hadn't started to tell him about the plague, I wouldn't have had to draw down on him. We could have taken our time about telling him proper and all."

"What do you mean about not telling him about the plague?" Cobb demanded. "Shit, everybody around here knows about Kirkland's plague."

"Doc don't," Albert said. "And neither do his friends. Doesn't that tell you something?"

Doc's mind raced, trembling at the edge of uncertainty by the bizarre turn of events. He struggled to maintain his hold on reality as voices crashed and warred in the back of his fragmented mind. He was reminded of a frigate that he'd shipped on, not knowing where, not remembering why, and certainly without knowledge due to his own patchy history of when that had occurred. The black water seemed to hover around him again, and his arms recalled the strain of holding on to the rigging.

Cobb kicked at the back of Doc's knees, causing the old man to drop to the floor. Still holding a handful of hair, Cobb bent to bring his face close to Doc's. "That right, gray hair? You don't know anything about the plague?"

"I know about several plagues, sir," Doc answered, locking eyes with his tormentor. "Name the particular one to which you're referring."

"Kirkland's plague," Cobb said. "The one he's infected everybody in Hazard with."

"I must admit, that is one with which I am not immediately familiar." Taking advantage of Cobb's proximity, Doc swung his head forward, cracking his skull into the other man's face. "However, I must object to such rough usage."

Blood spurted from Cobb's nose as he reared back and cried out in pain. He clapped a big hand over his face, dropping the cane.

Doc reared to his feet and grabbed the sword stick. Though his mind whirled dizzyingly, he twisted and jerked the cane with practiced ease, baring the hidden blade. Words came to him from Shakespeare's *Macbeth* as he turned to face Albert. "'Lay on, Macduff, and damn'd be him that first cries, "Hold enough!"'"

"Chill the crazy old fucker!" Cobb yelled, glaring up from the bloody mask his face had become. "He broke my goddamn nose!"

Doc stepped toward the dwarf, assuming a fencer's stance, the sword blade moving into position before him. "I'll not allow my life to be ripped from me so untimely, and my blade go unsullied," the old man declared. He watched the door from the periphery of his vision. Two men moved into place, blasters in their hands, as well. He could never make it through them.

"Doc," Albert said calmly, "I didn't mean any harm. I just didn't want you to go acting stupe when you heard about the plague." Slowly he holstered his blasters. He spread his arms away from his sides, then walked forward until his throat was wedged tight against the sword blade. "I wouldn't chill you. Wouldn't let anybody I know chill you. I owe you and your companions my life. God's truth on that." His Adam's apple bobbed against the sword point, starting a thin line of blood that ran down his neck. "Just wanted to get your attention. Stick me if you want to."

Doc stared into the little man's eyes, and Albert had to have seen something there that warned him. The dwarf closed his eyes. Doc drew the sword back. "I have killed many a man in my day, Albert, but I have always known the why of it. I shall know the why of it before I take your life, as well." He turned back to Cobb. "You, sir, shall not afford the same liberties."

"Damn you, Albert, for bringing this man here." Cobb wiped his bloody hands across his shirtfront. "I'll be a triple-fucked monkey if I don't chill you myself." He took a step forward.

Doc swung the sword stick to intercept the man. "I shall trouble to ask you not to do that."

Cobb pulled up short. He snorted in anger, blowing great gouts of blood from his nostrils. His lips were coated with crimson stains.

The other men in the room trained their weapons on Doc.

The old man showed them a wolf's grin. "I don't believe you gentlemen are any too willing to fire your weapons in the confines of this ville. Otherwise I would have never made it across the threshold. And that—I believe, gentlemen—is a double ace on the line."

The tension remained in the room for a handful of seconds. Doc was conscious of every tick of it. He was still confused about who was who and what was what, but that was generally the case any time he was away from the companions.

"Leave him alone," Cobb stated. He snorted again and cleared out his nostrils. He glared at Albert. "And what are you going to do if he's just somebody Kirkland sent to trip us up?"

Albert shook his head. "Kirkland figures he's got nothing to fear from us. Liberty knew I spent my free time here. And what Liberty knew about the inside of this ville was exactly what Kirkland knew. They ignored you even before I came along. You're no threat to Kirkland by yourself, but mebbe with the help of Doc and his friends..." He let the thought hang.

Doc could tell from the grimace on Cobb's face that the big man didn't like hearing that. He slid the sword blade back into its housing, snapped it closed with a click.

"Kirkland's got the plague working for him," Albert said, "and he knows that. Anybody who doesn't like what he's doing in Hazard, well, they get a berth on the last train West.''

"If you do not mind my asking," Doc interrupted, "but what exactly is this plague you persist in mentioning?"

"Nobody knows," Albert replied. "All anybody knows is that any man, woman or child who wanders out of Hazard for more than two days' travel, dies from the plague."

"How long does it take inside the ville?" Doc asked. Images filled his head of bloated bodies he'd seen in his travels over the past three centuries. Being trawled through time had the distinct disadvantage of leaving a man's thoughts addled. Some of the images in his head he knew he'd seen himself: an Indian village wiped out by smallpox, and a persecuted religious order all dead from syphilis. Others he wasn't sure of, but he thought they were from old vid, or maybe it had been new vid at the time. Names cropped up in his mind: Legionnaires' disease, ebola and AIDS, but he could put no real depth to them.

"Nobody dies inside the ville," one of the other men said.

"If it is a plague," Doc said, "then there should be an attrition within the ville, as well."

"There isn't," Cobb said. "Kirkland sees to that."

"How?" Doc's mind seized on the implications of the problem.

"Man gives out inoc—inoc—" one of the men tried to say. Then he shrugged it off. "Man gives out shots. You know, needles in the arm. That kind of shit.''

''A cure?'' Doc asked. ''Well, if he's giving out cures, any of you could get up and leave at any time you wanted to.''

''That's not the way it works, Doc,'' Albert said. ''Kirkland's inoculations buy you only a little more time. They don't cure you.''

''But that makes precious little sense,'' Doc said. ''It would be much more difficult for a medical person to design a partial cure than one that would totally counteract the affliction.''

''But that's what Kirkland did,'' Albert insisted. ''Come on downstairs and we'll talk about it.''

''Downstairs? I thought we were on the bottom floor.'' Doc glanced around, noticing how uneasy Cobb was acting. Keeping the big man in sight, he crossed the room and took up the Le Mat blaster from the table where it had been left.

''Got a basement level,'' Albert said.

He turned his attention to Cobb. ''Show him.''

''Fucked if I will. Should have never shown you.''

Albert approached the man. ''Cobb, you've been a good thinker, a good planner. But you haven't seen these people operate. I have. Mebbe they're our only chance of getting out of here.''

Cobb stared hard at Doc, then reluctantly backed down. He walked to the rear of the room and stood behind the counter. The back wall held a carved fish head. Cobb picked up a yardstick and rammed it down the fish's open mouth.

A hollow pop echoed inside the room, followed by a clattering noise. Cobb grabbed a lantern off the counter and lighted it. He glared at Doc. "Well, come on, then." He took a step forward and disappeared from view.

Doc rounded the counter and looked down at the floor. Cobb climbed through a recessed area, moving slow with the lantern. Doc looked at the inky shadows waiting below and thought about his current position again. He hadn't had the upper hand in his dealings with the other men. But in the narrow tunnel through the bottom of the floor, he would be totally at their mercy.

Cobb kept climbing. In a short while he reached the bottom of the ladder and held the lantern up. "Come on, then. You wanted to know." He twisted the wick, turning up the light.

And the yellow gold illumination spun out through the hurricane glass, opening up into a cavernous space by comparison to the narrow tunnel. Where there had been a few shelves with tattered paperbacks, hard covers and magazines littering the shelves on the first floor, the hidden floor below seemed covered with books. There had to have been thousands of books in all.

"By the Three Kennedys," Doc whispered hoarsely. All thoughts of walking into a trap left him. He stepped through the hole and followed the ladder down.

IN THE FORESTED AREA, Dean moved quietly and panther quick. He kept the Browning Hi-Power in his fist as he slunk through the brush where the man had vanished. Dean wasn't as good in the brush as Jak was, but then nobody was. It scared him some, creeping through the branches and bushes, wondering if he was as good as the man he hunted. But he knew Jak was counting on him.

He breathed through his mouth in shallow, rapid breaths that were almost soundless. The man he pursued wasn't as disciplined.

The man gasped a few feet to Dean's right, and the boy turned slowly, letting his weight shift to keep his line tight against his chosen cover. He brought up his blaster, following its lead. Once he had the weight shifted properly, making no noise at all, he completed the turn.

A footfall sounded in front of him, followed by another. The noise was almost lost in the snorting and blowing of Jak's captured horse.

Dean caught the movement in his peripheral vision. He stared at the edges of the shadow that drifted into view in front of him rather than at it. Even before his father had found him, Sharona had taught him the value of skylining.

Metal glinted in the shadow's fist.

Dean knew it was the long blaster the man carried. He sighted above it, taking another step closer to get around low-hanging branches that might have deflected his shot.

The moon moved into a clearer space of the sky between scudding clouds, and the man spotted Dean. He whirled and brought up the long blaster.

Coolly Dean moved into the clearest position he

found, his finger tightening on the Browning's trigger. The long blaster crashed thunder in front of him, the muzzle-flash looking like it might explode from the barrel and touch him. He felt the heat of a bullet sizzle past his face, then the Browning's hammer fell on the first round. He managed a tight group of three as the man levered another cartridge into the breech.

The 9 mm hollowpoint rounds drove the man back, slamming him back through the brush. He stumbled and fell to the ground, sitting with his back to a warped oak tree.

Dean moved forward, the Browning leveled at his target. The man struggled to bring up his weapon. Dean fired again, centering the round between the man's eyes. His face went bloody as his brain evacuated his skull and plastered the tree bole behind him. The corpse gave a spasmodic jerk and released the long blaster.

Staying careful and alert, Dean reached the corpse and kicked the weapon aside. The missing fragments of the man's head assured that he'd never be back in this life, but Dean had seen too many people with a strain of mutie blood in them that rewired nervous systems. Folks who should have been dead got stubborn about it, like a snake with its head chopped off.

He stripped away two handblasters, as well, tossing them to one side. The stink of blood filled the air. Mosquitoes descended in a swarm, settling over the bloody stumps of the man's skull. Night crawlers slithered through the brush and across the ground. A fat, toad-looking creature plopped from the tree overhead and dropped onto the corpse's face. Extending a prehensile tongue into the open mouth, it started feasting on the spilled blood.

"Dean?" Jak called softly.

"Yeah." Dean went through the corpse's pockets, his quick fingers identifying objects before his eyes could cut through the darkness.

"You chill him?"

"That's an ace on the line." One of the shirt pockets yielded a handful of 9 mm ammo that would fit the Browning. Dean appropriated it and shoved it into a pocket.

"You do, you tell. Get ass shot off, you no yell out." Jak sounded irritated.

"Forgot." Dean continued his search, turning up a fancy vinyl case not much bigger than his hand.

"Read nice on grave marker," Jak offered. "Ryan pretty pissed off have to write it, though."

"Okay, okay," Dean said. "I get the message. Get off my back." He popped the lock tabs on the small vinyl case. A small collection of feathered darts lay on a sponge pad, sheathed by leather straps. "Hot pipe! I found something here."

"What?"

"Darts for those compressed-air guns." Dean held one up against the full face of the moon. The liquid trapped inside the thin glass walls glowed vile amber.

"Tranks," Jak suggested. "Shoot. Make go sleep."

Dean looked at the liquid in the dart shell. "I don't think so. Mebbe we got something a little nastier here. Those men opened up on us without warning. I don't think they were intending to take us back to Hazard.''

''Got one here. Ask him.''

''Be there in a minute.'' Dean finished up his search, turning up a box of 9 mm reloads in a thigh pocket of the dead man's pants, a metal box of self-lights that looked waterproof and a packet of jolt. ''We'll ask him together.'' He put the packet of jolt into his pocket. None of the companions used the narcotic, but in a lot of places it could be used in the place of jack for trade. Of course, a man had to watch his back when trading in those places.

Dean picked up the two handblasters he'd tossed aside and discovered one of them was a compressed-air pistol. He examined it in the moonlight. The pistol was a single-action, requiring a dart to be loaded into the breech each time it was fired. When he pulled the bolt back, he saw that it was empty.

Taking the pistol and the vinyl case of darts, he went back to join Jak. He reloaded the Browning's magazine from the loose 9 mm rounds in his pocket. Firelight from the burning man on the ground played over the albino, his captured horse and his hostage.

''Anybody else?'' Dean asked.

''No.'' Jak nodded toward the man on the saddle in front of him. ''Cover.''

Dean leveled the Browning, making the man flinch. ''Sure. I got him.''

''He tries run, shoot legs, dick, not head or chest. Only need him live for little while.'' Jak shoved the hostage to the ground. The horse, relieved of its bur-

den and already spooked, reared and snorted in fear
at the new sound. It tried to run, but the albino kept
it under control.

Dean locked the Browning squarely on the man's
crotch.

The captive scrabbled at the ground, trying to find
purchase to pull himself up.

"No," Dean said. He squeezed the trigger and
put a bullet through the man's pants at the V of his
legs.

"Oh, goddamn!" the man shrilled, sitting up to
grab himself with both hands.

Jak gentled the horse again and hopped down. He
tied the reins to a tree, then returned to look at the
hostage.

The man brought his hands up with a look of
perplexion on his face. The animal mewling sounds
he made continued. There was no blood on his
hands, but clearly the 9 mm round had cored a hole
through the loose folds of his pants.

"Missed," Dean said. "Can you believe it?"

"Mebbe small," Jak suggested. He held his fore-
finger and thumb a half inch apart. "Splinter dick."
He crouched beside the man, a bloodthirsty grin
spreading across his scarred face. He held one of the
leaf-bladed throwing knives in his hand. "That
right?"

"Fuck you," the man snarled, his voice still shaking with fear.

"Already got it figured," Dean said, "that you
aren't equipped for that. Could be you piss off my
friend here, he'll use that knife of his to do a con-

version on you so you're all set to receive instead of give. If you catch my drift.''

"Piece of meat," Jak said. "Cutting change all that."

"Don't," the man begged. "Don't cut me."

"Answer questions," Jak suggested. "Lie, I cut off piece."

The man nodded, both hands protectively around his crotch. "Sure, sure."

"Tell us about the darts," Dean said.

The man swallowed hard.

Without hesitation, Jak flicked out the knife and cut across the knuckles of one of the man's hands. The man screamed out in pain, his eyes drawn to the wound across the back of his hand. But he didn't let go of his crotch.

"What did you do that for?" he demanded.

"You hesitate," Jak replied, "gives time think up lie. I want lie, I ask you question today, come back for answer tomorrow. Tell about darts."

"They got the plague in them," the man responded. "They got the plague in them, and that's all I know."

Chapter Ten

J.B. sipped coffee sub and regarded his host. "What plague are you talking about?"

Phillips massaged his hump unconsciously with one hand, grimacing a little like the action gave him some pain. "Kirkland got everything organized here in Hazard. Invited folks in. Then he kind of picked and chose who was staying and who was moving on. Took him about a year to get it all straightened away with who was what."

J.B. sopped corn bread into the soup at the bottom of his plate and chewed as he listened. He ate in spite of the churning that started at the pit of his stomach. The Trader always said that a man who didn't know for sure when or where his next meal was coming from shouldn't be shy about bellying up to a table that was offered.

"Once he had mostly everybody here that he wanted, Kirkland announced that the plague had spread. Had a few poor bastards found out in the forest that died of it."

"My husband died of the plague," Anna said.

"Sorry to hear that," J.B. stated. "How many folks died in the ville?"

"None," Tinker answered.

"You find that interesting?" J.B. asked.

Phillips grinned coldly. "Bastard right, we did. Found it more than interesting. Found it downright fucking suspicious."

"What about the bodies?" J.B. asked. "Were you allowed to claim your son's body?"

"Allowed to see it," Phillips replied. "Some of the sheriff's deputies found Eddie out in the forest."

"What was he doing there?"

Phillips scowled and looked away. "Eddie got it in his fool head that he could mebbe outrun the plague. We've been watching Kirkland and his people all this time. He's got a roving band of thugs under a man named Liberty that keeps most folks clear of the ville."

"Not anymore," J.B. said.

Phillips looked at him. "Not anymore?"

"They've all been consigned to crow meat this morning," the Armorer said. "Should be little bitty crow piles squirted out all over the ground now."

"Heard you came in with Albert," Phillips admitted. "That's what set me to suspicioning so much."

"Good thing Kirkland isn't as suspicious as you," J.B. said.

"And if he was of a mind to be?"

"Reckon we'd find out if we could feed a few more crows before we got out of the ville." J.B. held up his cup as the coffeepot made the circle of the table.

"We got more to eat," one of the young men at the table offered.

J.B. thought briefly of Mildred probably sleeping

back in their room at the hotel. He wondered if she'd eaten yet or was waiting for him to come back. Then he decided she'd probably eat before he got back. It didn't look like he was going to be leaving any time too soon. He pushed his plate forward, and it was filled again. "What made Eddie take off out of the ville?"

"Took off in the middle of the night," Phillips said. "Figured mebbe he could make it. Every now and then, you hear stories about somebody who made it out of Hazard."

"Any truth to it?"

"That's what we were going to find out. Eddie slipped off after his inoculation, figured he'd know something damn quick. Two days later they brought his body back."

"How long had he been dead?"

"Animals and insects had been at him," Phillips said. "Kind of hard to figure."

"Mebbe as much as both of those days he was gone?" J.B. asked. He helped himself to another square of corn bread. One of the young men pushed a tub of homemade butter toward him.

"Mebbe."

"Did you get to check the body over?" J.B. noticed that Anna was growing more uncomfortable with the subject of the conversation, but he had to press on with it. He and his friends were in the middle of the present situation.

"No. Kirkland always has the bodies of the reclaimed plague victims wrapped all special. Look like mummies time he's through with them."

"So what could you see?"

"Eddie's face was all blotched up. Black looking." The old man's voice roughened and broke, but he pulled it back on track soon enough.

"Rad burn will do that sometimes." J.B. spooned up more beans and meat.

"Wasn't rad burn," one of the men stated. "Damn plague is what it was."

"Kirkland come around asking any questions?"

"Oh, yeah," Phillips answered. "Wondered what Eddie was doing out in the forest. Told him I didn't know, that him and Anna had a fight. A young man during something like that forgets his good sense."

"He believe you?"

"Hell, no. That's when we started barricading ourselves in here a little tighter."

"Kirkland doesn't want you to leave." J.B. looked at the old man.

"Me and mine," Phillips announced, "we were one of the first families in Hazard. Time was we took a certain pride in that. No longer."

"Lot of work for a man who knows weapons," the Armorer said.

"Yep." Phillips gave him a wry grin. "Can't say that I see you hanging out a shingle anywhere and settling down. So don't be saying it like it's a thing to be done by just anybody."

"Too much traveling with the Trader," J.B. replied. "Fiddle-footedness gets in a man's blood after a time. Always wandering."

"Well, you and your companions surely wandered in the wrong direction this time."

"Low on ammo," J.B. explained. "We didn't have much choice."

"How come you didn't know about the plague?" Anna asked.

J.B. returned her gaze full measure. "Liberty didn't answer a whole lot of questions before he caught the last train to the coast."

"If you wander around in this area, you'll find people talk about the plague," Anna said. "Still get some folks in from time to time for trading, but it's generally those who know Kirkland's got the plague under control who show up. It doesn't set right that you wouldn't know about it."

"We've been running low to cover," J.B. said. "Before we got here, we just left a whole peck of trouble." And that was true enough.

Phillips rubbed his hump again and fixed the Armorer with a steel-hard stare. "Well, J. B. Dix, I'll promise you one thing—that trouble that you left, it isn't anything like what you got on your hands now. If Kirkland let you and your companions into this ville, it was for a reason. Whether he makes you stay here or ups and chills you people outright when the time comes remains to be seen."

"Also remains to be seen whether he can hold us." J.B. glanced back at Phillips. "Or if he can chill us."

"I like the way you talk," the old man said. "Let's freshen up that coffee sub and hear some more."

"THOSE ARE plague darts."

Jak held three of the darts in his hand. Instead of

feathers along the back of the shaft, vinyl triangles in red and yellow were designed to act as stabilizers. "What plague?"

Their captive licked his lips nervously. He was strapped to a tree in a sitting position, held in place by leather thongs Jak had found among one of the saddle kits. "Kirkland's plague."

Jak squatted on his haunches in front of the man. He flicked one of the leaf-bladed throwing knives across the fingers of his other hand with unconscious grace. He sat deliberately so the moonlight would glint off the razor-sharp edges. "He name it?"

"Yeah." The man nodded enthusiastically, but the albino noted the glance the man flicked at the cut on the back of his knuckles.

"That all he did?"

"Yeah."

Jak glanced at Dean. The boy looked impassive standing only a few feet away. Dean held one of the captured single-action long blasters in his hand, keeping watch over them. With an economy of motion, Jak stabbed the throwing knife into the man's thigh. When the prisoner opened his mouth to scream in pain, the albino yanked the knife from the man's leg and slashed his lips, cutting in a quarter inch at both corners of his mouth.

Blood gushed out with the man's garbled screams. He coughed and choked as he breathed in and sucked blood into his lungs. Terror shone in the wild whites of his rolling eyes. He struggled against the leather thongs, then broke into choking gasps and tears when he couldn't get loose.

"You bastard nuke-shitters!" he screamed, his voice echoing out over the forest.

With a flick of quick movement, Jak moved the knife again, burying the point in the end of the man's nose. The captive stopped screaming, but bloody spittle flew from his mouth as he breathed like a bellows pump. The albino ignored the blood.

"Scream again," Jak warned, "take both ears off. Understand?"

Keeping his head still, going almost cross-eyed while staring at the knife and trying to keep his tormentor in view, the man said, "Yes."

"Good." Jak withdrew the knife. "Kirkland's plague. Tell me."

The man took a long, shuddering breath, then let it out. "Kirkland made it. Come up with it somehow, from some predark book he found or mebbe just thought of it on his own. Nobody knows."

"A plague spreads," Dean said. "Man's got to be rad stupe to go fooling around with something like that."

"Not this plague. Only kills the person gets it shot into them."

"Then it's not a plague," Dean argued.

The prisoner wiped one corner of his slashed mouth on his shoulder. "Only know what I was told. Kirkland and Liberty call it a plague, they tell me to call it a plague, I fucking well call it a plague."

Jak thought about what the man was saying. He didn't have all the words or the book learning that Dean did, but he could guess at some things himself. "Why plague?"

"To keep the ville in line. There's a lot of people don't like the way Kirkland runs things. They want to leave the ville, start over again somewhere else. They figure Kirkland can have this one. But he doesn't figure Hazard is worth having without having people to control."

"The people in the ville don't know?" Dean asked.

"No. He always has Liberty schedule a group to keep watch out here. Anyone tries to get away, we take them down. Kirkland's also got people inside the ville who inform on who's thinking about slipping away."

"Kirkland controls Liberty?" Jak asked.

"Sure," the captive said. "Did, anyway. Until you hardcases came along and killed him."

"Does Kirkland know that?" Dean asked.

"Fucking right, he does. Knew that when you got to the ville. Nobody arrives in Hazard without Liberty sending someone along to say it's okay."

Jak glanced at Dean, wondering if the dwarf had deliberately set them up. "Albert know that?"

"Yeah. Him coming into the ville like that, he had to know Kirkland would know you people chilled Liberty."

"Means Kirkland has more up his sleeve than an arm," Dean commented quietly. "He figures on taking control of the group."

"Where Albert fit in?"

"Got to ask him," Dean stated flatly.

Jak turned his attention back to the prisoner. "Why you follow us?"

The man hesitated, then shook his head, throwing drops of blood off his chin. "Kirkland wanted you chilled. You turned up with the plague, your bodies would be proof they needed him. But that wasn't my idea. I was just following orders."

And that made sense to Jak. Without wasted effort, the albino teenager slashed the man's throat. He wiped the blade clean on the dying man's shirt and turned away while the man kicked out his life. "Let's ride," he said to Dean.

Chapter Eleven

"You look good, lover."

Ryan felt a little self-conscious in the clothes Aunt Maim had sent up by way of one of the maids. The pants were neatly pressed, of thinner material than he would have ever cared to wear, and the shirt had belled sleeves and a ruffled collar that looked effeminate. The short-waisted jacket revealed the fuchsia cummerbund, and the sleeves ended above the puffy sleeves of the shirt.

"Feel triple stupe," he replied. "And that's an ace on the line. These aren't a man's clothes."

Krysty slipped her arm through his as they descended the stairs down into the hotel's main room. One of the young maids led the way. "I think you look fine."

"Not me," Ryan said. "But you look beautiful."

Krysty did. The white evening gown showed off her tall, shapely figure to perfection, setting off the liquid fire of her hair. Her face was clean, made over with a light application of cosmetics that had been provided with the clothing that had been delivered to the room only moments earlier. She'd even shed her beloved cowboy boots to put on the fancy high-heeled shoes that accompanied the dress.

The hotel was lit by lanterns. Sconces along the

wall held them every few feet, beating back the shadows that threatened to fill the building from outside. The windows on two sides of the room offered two huge views of the starry sky and quiet glimpses of Hazard.

The maid led them across the wooden floor, their footsteps muted by a thick carpet. Ryan was surprised at how big the building was. From the outside, he'd known it was huge compared to existing structures he'd been in that hadn't been left over completely after the nukecaust. But obvious care had been spent in restoring the decor.

"Isn't it beautiful, lover?" Krysty asked as they entered another room. She paused to run her hand along a grandfather clock that ticked with precision. The hands showed that it was nineteen minutes past eight.

"Yeah," Ryan responded. There were some things that had been salvaged from before the nukecaust that made him really curious about how life had been lived in those times. The grandfather clock was one. He knew from experience that the people living at that time had access to comps that could be programmed to respond to voice commands and give the time out loud. Yet an object like the grandfather clock had obviously been kept even though it was obsolete. He reached out to stroke the cherrywood finish with his fingertips.

The maid waited just inside the doorway ahead of them. Lanterns hung on the wall behind her, throwing out a yellow, elongated sphere. She crossed her hands in front of her, ducking her head. Still, she regarded Ryan with what looked like thinly veiled hostility.

Ryan returned the woman's gaze. Despite the clothing that had been sent up, he wore the SIG-Sauer in its leather on his hip. The panga was sheathed on his opposite hip, ready for instant access.

"Aunt Maim, may I present Mr. Ryan Cawdor and Miss Krysty Wroth," the maid announced.

Ryan glanced at Krysty, raising his eyebrow. The titian-haired woman shook her head slightly, indicating that her mutie senses could pick up no veiled threat of danger. Ryan took the lead into the room anyway, protective of his lover.

"Relax, Mr. Cawdor," a husky voice said. "I assure you there's no reason to be afraid here. In the rest of the ville, perhaps, but not here."

The speaker sat at the end of a rectangular dinner table. Black hair was piled atop a pale oval face that looked only slightly more healthy than a corpse's. If she hadn't been sitting in a wheelchair, Ryan judged that the woman would be tall, perhaps as tall as himself. She wore a jade green dress that crisscrossed her chest. A white eye patch covered her left eye.

"I would get up to greet you," Aunt Maim said, "but I am somewhat invalided these days. Please seat yourselves."

Ryan pulled a chair out for Krysty, taking a moment to run his hand under the table's edge to make sure nothing was waiting underneath that would do them harm. He did the same at the other end of the table before seating himself.

Aunt Maim picked up a long tall wineglass in her right hand. The maid poured from a dark blue bottle. The shawl draped across her narrow shoulders hid Aunt Maim's other arm from sight. "You'll find the wine is an excellent vintage," the hosteler said.

The maid came to Ryan's end of the table and poured drinks. Ryan picked his drink up and sniffed it. It might have been wasted effort, and he knew it. The Trader had made him aware that several poisons were virtually undetectable. Krysty shook her head, letting him know she sensed nothing wrong.

Aunt Maim laughed, a full-throated bray that carried with it a hint of insanity. She caught herself after a moment, then put down her wineglass and covered her mouth. "Excuse me, but it's been a long time since I've found myself so amused."

"Mebbe you'd care to explain what you found so funny." Ryan let an edge creep into his voice. He kept his hand on his thigh next to the SIG-Sauer blaster. He'd slipped the retaining thong the instant they'd left the room upstairs.

Aunt Maim quieted with effort, but the madness lingered in the dark eye. "What I find so amusing is that you would believe you have anything to fear from me, yet you accepted Kirkland's offer to enter this ville."

"Kind of short on choices at the time," Ryan said.

"So you chose death or imprisonment over taking your chances elsewhere?"

"Mebbe you want to spit out what you're trying to say," Krysty suggested vehemently.

"I guess Kirkland hasn't told you that you're prisoners here."

"No," Ryan answered.

"And I take it you didn't know about the plague before you walked into the ville?"

Ryan shook his head. "Mebbe you should start with the plague." As he listened to the woman's story, related with a morbid fascination, he felt his stomach tighten. Sickness was something he didn't relish. A plague, unless a man found the bodies scattered ahead of him with enough distance between and the wind right, was something that couldn't be run from.

The maid came around the table as Aunt Maim spoke, unveiling the food covering the surface. Vegetables were cut in beautiful shapes, looking delicate and delicious in their dishes.

"You don't have to worry that you're receiving better fare than your friends," Aunt Maim said. "I'm having them served out of the same kitchen. Everything that is offered to you here tonight is also being offered to them."

The maid bent low to talk to her mistress.

"I'm told only one of your party remains within the hotel," Aunt Maim said.

Ryan nodded.

The woman sighed in irritation. She leaned back for the maid to place a napkin in her lap. "That's a pity," the hosteler said, "because not all of this food will maintain proper consistency for long."

"We've learned not to be picky eaters," Krysty said. "If it's edible, or even healthy enough, they'll eat."

"Still, I'll not have guests in my establishment dine on anything less than the best. Even if they insist on keeping strange hours." Aunt Maim turned to the maid. "Please inform the cooks that their services will be needed a while longer."

The maid nodded but remained where she stood.

Aunt Maim glowered at her. "Don't be difficult, you bitch. Go see to what I've asked you to do."

"Yes, ma'am, but—"

"But nothing." Aunt Maim swiveled her head back at Ryan and gave a sweet smile. "I shall be quite safe here under Mr. Cawdor's watchful eye. I think we share a singular view on the world."

The maid left reluctantly, her cheeks coloring with emotion.

The woman lifted her wineglass. "A toast, then, before we begin this charming meal. To your health—may you keep it."

Ryan stared at the woman for a moment, then lifted his own glass and sipped when she did. Krysty joined them. "Tell me about the plague," he said. "How is it spread?"

"Actually," Aunt Maim said, positioning her soup bowl in front of her with one hand, "I don't believe there is a plague. I think Kirkland occasionally chooses to infect some of the people in the ville. Usually it's only people that try to escape Hazard."

"He doesn't want them to leave?" Krysty asked.

The woman speared an asparagus chunk with her

fork and bit into it with clean white teeth. "If they did, who would he rule?"

Ryan made himself eat. Despite the talk of plague, his lovemaking with Krysty had left him famished. He sawed off a piece of steak and ate it, finding it juicy and tender, not at all like the dry, stringy stock the companions sometimes dropped for a meal.

"If you think the plague is false, why don't you leave?" Krysty asked.

Aunt Maim sipped more wine. "My handicaps are quite severe."

"And mebbe you're in this with Kirkland," Ryan said.

Color filled Aunt Maim's pale face. She sat her wineglass down forcefully. "Kirkland and I haven't seen eye to eye in a long time." The laughter came from her again, not lasting quite as long this time, but sounding more uncontrollable. She recovered. "Although it seems that eye to eye is the only way I see these days. However, just so you'll know, rest assured that in my dealings with Kirkland—" she shifted so the shawl fell away from her left side, shoving the stub of her left arm, the sleeve pinned up, through the material "—that I have found the fucker quite disarming."

DOC PROWLED through the stacks of books, carrying a lantern. He was drawn by the titles and covers. Nearly every branch of science that he'd ever heard of was represented somewhere in the collection. Albert, Cobb and two of the others sat around a small oval table in the center of the room.

"Got no time for you to be looking through the books," Cobb growled. He wiped his nose with the back of his arm, brushing away a few drops of blood that continued to seep.

Doc ignored the man. He found a section that held all of George Orwell's books. Tenderly he took down a slim hardcover edition of *1984*.

"Doc," Albert called.

Gently Doc turned the pages in the book, a passage drifting back into his mind. He remembered reading the novel, but he couldn't remember when. He shifted his attention to the dwarf and company. "'If you want a picture of the future, imagine a boot stamping on a human face—forever.'" The old man shook his head. "So true, so true. By the Three Kennedys, may you never have known how truly you spake the future."

Albert crossed the room, stepping into the aisle and into the swell of light that emanated from the lantern. "Doc, tell me how you came to Hazard."

Doc automatically put the book back on the shelf. Despite his best efforts, he felt his mind wandering, crashing through the decades, through all the information that was so mixed up in his head. "Why that's easy, dear friend. I came through the hole with Alice. No, it was Emily." Tears suddenly burned into his eyes. "No, no, that's wrong. Dear, sweet Emily couldn't come with me this time. Not this time, nor any other."

"Leave the old bastard alone," Cobb shouted. "It's evident he's fucking crazy."

Doc focused on the insult, using vestigial anger

to crystallize his thoughts. "And you, sir, are an ignoramus and a bounder."

Albert smiled. "Glad to have you back among us, Doc. Now, come on over here and let's talk."

Doc paused a moment, taking up an armload of books. He used his cane across the bottom of them to brace them while he carried them. He sat at the table, taking up one of the stools. He placed the lantern beside him, then began going through the book.

"How did you get here?" Albert asked again.

Cobb reached into one of the shelves and brought out a jug. He poured the amber liquid into five metal cups and passed them around.

Doc sniffed the cup, finding the smell of alcohol strong and burning. "My word, but do you not know the meaning of *subtlety* when it comes to home brew?"

"Don't have time to get it perfect," Cobb argued. "Answer Albert's question about how you got here."

"Why, we walked, of course."

"You and your friends?"

"My companions and I, yes." Doc sipped the brew and found it too strong for his taste. He put down the cup and began leafing through his collection of books.

"And you never heard of the plague before?" Cobb demanded.

"No."

"Somehow that doesn't sound right. You got to admit that."

Doc fixed the man with a hard gaze. "Have you ever heard of Ralph Waldo Emerson?"

Cobb looked around at the other three men in the room, disregarding Doc's frank stare. "No."

"Yet you stand in a room filled with books," Doc continued. "I even saw some of Emerson's works on your shelves. I find that it does not sound right that you have never embraced the man's writing."

"What's that got to do with—?" Cobb began.

"Exactly my point," Doc roared. "That I have not heard of the plague ere now simply means that neither I nor my companions have heard of the plague. What you actually want to know is a way out of your present problem, and with that I may be of some pedestrian help. Assuming that my companions are amenable." That, the old man knew, would depend on whether Ryan thought he could get them out of the ville without raising an army to do it. And if a way could be found around the plague.

Chapter Twelve

"Kirkland cut off your arm?" Ryan asked. He tore one of the fancy biscuits in two and spread honey butter across it.

"That isn't all." She waved to the maid, who had returned and stood in the shadows. "I'm afraid his vengeance was quite complete."

Reluctantly the maid rolled the wheelchair back. Aunt Maim pulled back the blanket across her legs and revealed that she only had one of those, as well. The other was perfect and slender, poking down from the hem of her dress, her foot encased in a jade green slipper.

"The animal took her arm, her leg, her breast, her eye, her ear," the maid said in a shaking voice.

"That's enough, Jocelyn," Aunt Maim ordered.

The maid subsided, but cried quietly into the palm of one hand. "You were so beautiful," she choked out.

"I still am," the hosteler said in a firm voice.

But Ryan heard the quaver in her words. "You still are," he agreed.

The woman covered her leg and her stump with the blanket and nodded her head in appreciation. Color touched her cheeks. "Thank you. I am not told that by enough men these days."

She glanced at Krysty. "I beg your indulgence."

"Of course," the redhead replied. "What Ryan and I have together has been through a lot. Neither of us is afraid to speak his or her mind."

"More people should be able to conduct their lives in such a fashion. Push me forward, please, Jocelyn."

The maid gently wheeled the chair under the table, then she stepped back into the shadows.

"I apologize for the inconvenience in your meal. I know discussion of such matters is not good for the palate."

"The meal's good," Ryan said. "I don't see how anything short of getting chilled is going to interfere with that."

"I'll pass your kind words on to the cooks." Aunt Maim sipped her drink.

"Cutting things down to the bone here," Ryan said, "I suppose there's a reason why you asked us here and not the rest of our people."

Aunt Maim regarded him with her one dark eye, resting her chin on her only hand. "Of course."

"Like to know what that is."

"You're a direct man, Ryan Cawdor."

"I had a friend who had a way of looking at life. Over, under or around. That was his philosophy, and it stood him in good stead."

"And where is this friend now?"

"Chilled, mebbe. Mebbe getting laid and planning his next big trade." Ryan didn't think much about how he'd left it with the Trader, but the thoughts remained with him. The Trader and Abe had perhaps given their lives to save those of the companions. "But let's cut back to the chase here."

"All right." The woman paused. "I want you to kill Kirkland."

"Couple things I see wrong with that," Ryan said. "Chief among them is the possibility of the plague chilling us right after we chill him."

A wicked smile curved Aunt Maim's perfect face. "That's only if you believe the plague is really a plague."

"Why did Kirkland do this to you?" Krysty asked.

The smile stayed in place, but all warmth seemed to drain out of the expression. "I was lucky this was all he did in a sense," the woman said. "He could have taken both of everything. He has before."

Ryan cut another piece of meat and put it on his plate.

"Kirkland worked for a baron farther east. I've even heard rumors that he spent time in Newyork. I don't know the truth of it. I first met him in a caravan headed west, through the Shens. That's how I heard about you, Ryan Cawdor. You've been gone for some years, and no one had heard of you recently."

Ryan continued eating without comment.

"Kirkland had a lot of jack," Aunt Maim went on. "I didn't. So I got close to him. Made myself available. He got interested back. I hadn't planned on a relationship with him. I don't really care for a man's sexual attentions."

And that, Ryan knew, explained the maid's interest in the hosteler.

"But I do know what a woman's face and figure can do to the right kind of wrong man. I heard about how he was going to start up a ville of his own. That ville became Hazard. Seeing an opportunity for myself, I offered my services as a hosteler. He put me into business here, for a percentage of everything I made. I thought that was fair, since it was his investment capital we were working with. I've managed a few places before, and even ran card games."

"Kirkland expected something more, though, didn't he?" Krysty asked.

Aunt Maim nodded, then sipped her drink. Her eye drifted away and became unfocused, her memories trapped in the past. "He made no bones about it. On the way over, he'd tried to be more forceful about our relationship, but the wag master didn't put up with behavior like that. And the opportunities were few."

"That changed when you hit Hazard," Krysty said.

"Yes."

"You could have kept on going," Ryan said.

"Easy for you to say, sitting there in that chair. But I see you found your way to Hazard and stopped, as well."

Ryan couldn't say anything to that.

"At the time I felt that I couldn't go on any farther. The plan was to stay here in Hazard for a time, get some jack set back, then move on."

"Only it didn't work out that way," Jocelyn

erupted in a hoarse voice rich with raw emotion. "That fucking animal came in here on her, made sure none of us was around to help defend her. By the time we got back, it was too late."

Aunt Maim's fingers circled around her glass absently. Her smile was crooked, distant and totally without mirth. "Kirkland trapped me in my office and made his intentions known."

Ryan waited, listening for what he knew would come. Rape was one thing on War Wag One that Trader and his hardcases wouldn't put up with.

"I couldn't fight him. And if I did, I knew I'd have to chill him quick if I was able. I kept a straight razor strapped to my thigh those days. Back then I was able to defend myself. So I gave in and offered oral sex. He liked the idea, said it would be a good prelude to the festivities he had planned. So I did, hoping that he was all bluff and that he wouldn't be able to get it up a second time."

Ryan waited, giving the woman time to gather her thoughts.

"Soon as he was finished with my mouth, he turned me over on my desk and started hauling my skirt up." The woman licked her lips.

Jocelyn stepped up behind her and patted her shoulders, tears flowing freely down the woman's cheeks.

The hosteler continued. "I was desperate that he not see me. I knocked the lantern from the desk, and it caught the rug on fire. The rest of the room was concrete blocks at that time. I hadn't had time to recondition and remodel in there yet, and business then wasn't what it became as Kirkland built up the population of Hazard. The kerosene burned the carpet.

"Laid flat across the desk, I was brutally sodomized. Kirkland told me he was saving the best for last. When he finished that time, he flipped me over. I tried to get to my razor, but he knocked it away. Then he saw my—my male member staring back up at him instead of what he was expecting."

Ryan had no comment for that. He glanced briefly at Krysty while Jocelyn tried to comfort "Aunt" Maim.

"You see," Aunt Maim said, wiping at her eyes, "I was stuck. Do you know what it's like to be trapped in a body, in a gender, that you know can't be your own?"

"No." Ryan's voice was tighter than he wanted it to be, but the story had caught him completely by surprise.

"I found a healer back east who had access to some predark meds. I talked him into going this far with me." She waved her hand at her chest. "But he didn't have the skill to make the final changes. I heard there was an enclave out in the west, somewhere along the Cific, that still handled operations like this. Have you ever heard of such a thing?" She looked up through her tears hopefully.

Ryan shook his head.

"No," Krysty said gently.

Aunt Maim used her napkin to wipe at her face. "It would be funny, don't you think, that I came out all this way and endured what I've endured only to find that I was chasing a lie?''

"I wouldn't think so," Krysty said sympathetically.

"We all have to chase dreams in there somewhere," Ryan told her.

"I'm going to be a lot slower these days," the hosteler replied, slapping the wheel of her chair.

"Kirkland cut her in a fit of rage," Jocelyn said. "Knocked her out and took her back to his office. He cut off her arm and her leg, then her ear and her breast, took out her eye, then—then he cut off her penis. He vowed that he'd make her half the man she'd hidden from him. He spent weeks taking care of her, making sure she was going to live, before he returned her to us."

"You see," Aunt Maim said, "I was still the best hosteler he could put into this place." She glanced around the dark room with pride. "He couldn't take that from me, and he would only have been hurting himself by trying to put someone else in here. But I have to wonder how many days I've got left now that Kirkland's tightened his control over Hazard. Not many people come to the hotel these days."

"Well," Ryan said, "I'm here to tell you that you still set a fine table."

"Thank you." Aunt Maim fixed her single eye on Krysty. "Your lover is a man, Miss Wroth, so he's probably already got his mind made up as to how he's going to handle the situation with Kirkland. But I'd like you to persuade him, if you can, to kill this monster before you quit this place."

"Ryan usually can't be talked into anything," Krysty said.

"Please try. Strangely one of the things that hurts me the most is the fact that Kirkland denies everything that happened that night. When I tried to tell the original settlers in this ville all those years ago what happened to me, he stated that his vengeance was only an example to let them know what would happen to anyone who tried to steal from him. That if they weren't willing to give him his half, he'd take his half out of them." Her voice cracked, but she made herself go on. "He denied that he'd ever desired me or taken advantage of me."

"He's a bastard monster," Jocelyn said, putting her hand on Aunt Maim's shoulder. The one-eyed woman shoved Jocelyn's hand away.

Krysty shot Ryan a look. He kept silent, knowing there was nothing either of them could say.

"I apologize for interrupting such a good meal with my tale of woe," the woman announced after a short, uncomfortable silence. "And now I find myself feeling inadequate for any other conversation." She waved at Jocelyn, who pulled her chair out from under the table. "If you'll excuse me, I think I'll turn in for the evening."

"Of course," Krysty said.

Jocelyn turned the wheelchair and pushed Aunt Maim away.

"Do think about what I said, Mr. Cawdor," the hosteler called back. "I hadn't cheated Kirkland out of any of his proceeds before the night that he ruined me, but I've cheated him out of plenty since. I've got a lot of jack put back for a rainy day. A large chunk of that is yours—if you chill Kirkland.''

Ryan picked up a knife and cut a thick slab of cherry pie sitting in the middle of the table. The berries and the cooked sauce ran out, thick and dark as spilled blood across the small plate he put it on. ''Like a piece?'' he asked Krysty.

''I'm afraid I've lost my appetite, lover.''

Ryan placed the pie in front of her. ''If you've got the space, eat. We're not staying in this ville one chron tick longer than we have to. Don't know when we'll have it so good again.''

Krysty picked up a fresh fork and started in. ''So where do we go?''

Ryan cut another piece of pie and put it on a plate in front of him. ''Back to the redoubt. Shortest distance to the safest point. Liberty and his gang weren't the only guns Kirkland has access to.''

''There's always the sheriff and his men.''

''Yeah.'' Ryan sectioned off a bite of pie with his fork. ''Once we get back to the redoubt and get inside, nobody'll be able to follow us.''

''Hopefully we'll end up somewhere better than this,'' Krysty said.

''Can't see how it would be much worse.''

J.B. OPERATED the reloader with skill. Lantern light filled the room, kept tight underground so no one outside would know what was going on. His chron showed it was almost eleven o'clock. He knew Mildred would be pushing past the irritated stage into the worrying stage, but there wasn't anything to be done about it at the moment. His work had to be completed if the companions were to be properly outfitted.

Phillips, Anna and the weaponsmith's sons and daughters-in-law helped with the making of the fléchette rounds for the M-4000. Ammunition in 9 mm, .38 and .357 was plentiful. Most of the work Tinker Phillips did was in those calibers. The special loads for Doc's Le Mat blaster had to be hand tooled, as well, but after the Armorer had explained and shown Phillips and his clan what had been needed, the shells were assembled quickly.

J.B. readied another line of shotgun shells for packing. Anna brought over a plastic box of fléchettes, deadly little triangles cut from thin sheets of metal with a die press. Together, they worked the fléchettes into the plastic shotgun casings. Phillips also kept a number of shotgun casings on hand, which made the job faster and easier. They were already primered and powdered, needing only the loads to be set into place. Usually the gunsmith filled them with double-aught buckshot.

"Are you really going to help us?" Anna asked as she helped J.B. pour the fléchettes into the plastic casings.

"By helping ourselves," the Armorer answered truthfully. "From what you tell me, Kirkland let us into Hazard for a purpose. I don't see that he's going to just let us walk back out of here. Over, under or around. That's what Trader used to say. And that was only if you couldn't go through something. If Kirkland tries to stop us, which he's going to have to do, I've got a feeling Ryan will go out of this ville roughshod right through the bastard.''

"If people here see you ride out of the ville, they'll follow,'' Anna said. "It'll be enough to break Kirkland's hold over them. They'll leave, too.''

J.B. tapped the end of one of the shotgun shells into place and sealed it. "Might not have to leave. Best thing might be to mebbe just have a necktie party at a local gallows with Kirkland as the guest of honor. The ville's set up in a good place. Folks can make a living trading off travelers coming through the Shens.''

"Mebbe you're right.''

"Something to think about,'' the Armorer said.

Anna poured more fléchettes into the casings. "But you're not going to stay?''

"No.''

"Why?''

"My friends and I,'' J.B. said, "we're looking for something.''

"What?''

J.B. shook his head. "Won't rightly know until we find it.''

"Could be you'll spend an awful lot of time just looking,'' Anna said.

"Could be,'' J.B. agreed. "Can't help but get about the doing of it, though.'' And he turned his attention back to the shotgun shells.

Anna went away, her face a mask of blank emotions.

After a few minutes Phillips joined J.B. The old man rubbed his hump and waited until the Armorer glanced over at him. "You do good work," Phillips said. "The things I heard about you, I guess they were all true."

"Mebbe not all," J.B. replied, "but enough. When it comes to gunsmithing, I know my way around. A man learns to be careful around something he's working with that can blow his fool head off if he thinks he knows his business before he does."

"One of the two most dangerous fields in the world," Phillips agreed.

J.B. took off his glasses and cleaned them, waiting. Phillips had something to say, so he let the man choose how and when to say it.

"Well, fuck me," the old man growled. "You're a hardcase, J. B. Dix."

"Been said a time or two already."

"Can't believe I'm seeing it, but I think Anna likes you. There's ways you got that remind me, and probably her, of Eddie. Set your mind to it, you probably couldn't do much better."

"Kind of quick to even be thinking such things, isn't it?" J.B. asked.

"Most folks get a short shake at life in the Deathlands," Phillips said. "Hell, I know. I may be racking up some years myself, but I've buried a wife and three children. Things like this, you know what you want. Anna, she knows what she wants."

"Couple hours ago," J.B. said, "she was all set to ventilate me."

"Mebbe she would have, too. Something to think over, J.B."

"Can't." The Armorer tapped another shotgun shell together. "I've already got somebody."

"She hold a candle to Anna?"

J.B. looked at the old man. "Best tread lightly when you go there."

The old man's gaze met J.B.'s squarely. "No harm meant, for fuck's sake. Just asking. Conversation, that's all."

J.B. let the silence between them hang for a moment. "Yeah. The woman I know holds a candle to Anna."

"Well, I guess that's that."

The Armorer nodded. He turned his attention back to his work. From the way things were going, he figured they'd be done by three or four o'clock. He felt tired, but he forced himself to go on.

And he thought about Mildred, wishing there was some way to get a message to her.

Chapter Thirteen

Mildred Wyeth came awake with a hand over her mouth in the darkness of the hotel room. She reached under her pillow for the Czech ZKR 551 but barely had her fingers curled around its butt before a fist rammed into her stomach.

Pain bounced around crazily inside her head, warring with the fatigue that had put her to bed in spite of her anger and worry over J.B.'s absence. She'd expected the Armorer to be gone for a while. Outfitting the group was a primary concern, and J.B.'s fascination with firearms was prodigious.

Stubbornly she tried to cling to the target pistol. The fist crashed into her stomach again, making her retch.

"Look here, bitch," a man's rough voice whispered in her ear. "You want to live to see morning come, you mebbe want to just do what we want."

The hand over Mildred's mouth crept higher, cutting off her breath through her nostrils, as well. Panic shrieked loose inside her. She flailed, curving her fingertips into talons. A set of fingernails found flesh, carved deeply.

For a moment she thought she might get free. Then something hard and unforgiving crashed into the side of her head, and she drifted away suddenly in a fog of cottony darkness.

"SHOULD WE WAKE Mildred?"

Ryan glanced at the door down the hall. "Let her sleep. Until the others get back, we can't plan on much." He used the key and let them into their hotel room. He stood just to one side of the door and peered in, his hand resting on the SIG-Sauer.

None of the shadows inside moved wrong.

He let out a tense breath and entered the room, taking the time to check the windows and the bathroom, as well. A careful man, the Trader had always said, always spent time looking things over, even after he'd looked them over a couple times already.

"Aunt Maim's story wasn't exactly made to set a mind at ease," Krysty commented. She straightened the mess of bedclothes, smoothing them.

"No." Ryan stood at the window and gazed out. He saw a few men moving about, but none of them appeared headed in the direction of the hotel.

"What do we do now?" Krysty asked.

"Wait," Ryan said. "Jak, Dean, J.B. and Doc are still out there. Give them some time, see if they come back." He took the chair against the wall and rammed it under the doorknob. It stood to reason that the key they'd been given hadn't been the only key Aunt Maim had for the room. Then he sat out of sight beside the window and waited.

"You should get some sleep, lover," Krysty suggested.

"I will in a couple hours," Ryan said. "Or when J.B. makes it back."

"He should have already been back. Are you thinking about going looking for him?"

"No. If anything wrong had gone down with J.B., we'd have heard about it by now. You get some sleep. If nothing happens in the next couple hours, I'll wake you, get some sleep myself."

"Good night, lover." Krysty rolled over on the bed.

Ryan listened to her breathing gradually deepen. He waited with the patience of a great cat stalking its prey. Some of the cards of the hand they'd drawn blind had been turned faceup on the table. But Kirkland hadn't known everything they knew, either. It remained to be seen who got stuck with the joker in the deck.

DOC LEFT Cobb's at just after midnight by his old chron. Albert went with him. Cobb and his cronies hadn't been happy about seeing them leave, but there hadn't been much choice. Doc carried with him a slim volume of Robert Frost's poetry. Cobb had somehow managed to come up with three paperback editions and two hardcovers.

Raucous piano music came from farther down the street, and Doc spied yellow lantern light pouring out onto the wooden sidewalk.

"Now, there's a happy tune," Doc commented.

"Yes," Albert agreed, "but it only disguises a den of inequity."

Doc glanced at the dwarf. "A den of inequity, dear Albert?"

The little man blushed strong enough to show even in the darkness.

"I must say, your command of the language seems to ebb and flow," Doc said. "At times you seem to speak most eloquently, and at others you can be very inelegant."

"Self-taught in a lot of matters," the dwarf replied. "I don't get the chance to actually hear a lot of what I read. I'm most comfortable talking the way I was brought up."

"There is nothing wrong with it," Doc said. "I meant no offense."

"None taken. But I know my shortcomings." Albert grinned. "Been there most of my life."

"Cobb, despite all the books he has access to, does not seem as erudite as you."

"Thank you."

"Oh, dear Albert, that was not intended as a compliment—though you may certainly take it as such—but as an observation." Doc tapped the silver lion's head of his cane against his temple. "I am merely exercising my brain." And enjoying the clarity he seemed to possess at the moment.

"I don't know that Cobb likes books," Albert said, "as much as he likes to think books are going to give him the edge on everybody else. He thinks he's going to glean all this knowledge and set himself up somewhere as a baron in his own right."

"And you?"

Albert shrugged. "I just love the stories and the

poetry, Doc. Most of them kind of turn out to be the things that bind us all, you know?''

"I know very well indeed." A fragment came to Doc's mind, drifting in from somewhere. He nailed it down with effort. "I am reminded of a passage presented by John F. Kennedy regarding both power and poetry."

"One of the three you're always swearing by?" Albert asked.

The question threw Doc off his stride. He reached back into his mind, but he didn't know. "I am afraid that I could not tell you." He heard the quaver in his voice as the uncertainty inside his mind seemed to beckon to him.

Albert reached up and patted him on the arm. "It's okay, Doc. Doesn't matter if this John F. was one of those three or not. What did this Kennedy say?"

Remarkably the passage remained in Doc's brain. He felt calmer as he put it to tongue. "It was in an address before a college, unless I misremember, and I do not think that I do. It went something like this.

'When power leads man toward arrogance, poetry reminds him of his limitations. When power narrows the areas of man's concern, poetry reminds him of the richness and diversity of his existence. When power corrupts, poetry cleanses, for art establishes the basic human truths which must serve as the touchstone of our judgment.'''

"That's beautiful."

"When I read it, I liked it well enough." Doc

kept walking, listening to the comfortable thump of his boots across the wooden boardwalk. His attention was drawn to the gaudy house, pricked by the loud strains of the piano. "Mayhap we could just peek in."

"Bad place to be, Doc." Albert scowled.

Ignoring the little man, Doc strode up to the batwing doors and peered in. The smoky haze robbed the scene of its color, but he saw enough. The girl on the stage had a live snake and was totally obscene in her actions. "Upon my soul."

"Warned you," Albert said.

"So you did." Doc drew back from the doors and avoided the drunken men sprawled on the boardwalk. "Then let us return to the hotel and perhaps see if there is any grape to be had. I shall endeavor to tell the others about the plague on the morrow. There is nothing to be done about it yet."

Albert led the way across the dirt street. Before they gained the other side, a horse-drawn wagon clattered out of an alley. The driver whipped the horses unmercifully, making them go faster. Their hooves pounded into the dry ground as the wheels cut across the ruts. Three other men sat in the flat-board back, hanging on. A fourth person lay prone between the three men.

Doc got only a glimpse of her face, but he recognized her immediately as Mildred. A cold fist of fear closed around his heart.

"Hey," Albert said, "wasn't that—?"

"I fear so," Doc said. He pushed himself into

motion at once, following the horse-drawn wag through the shadows. "Go warn the others, friend Albert, whilst I endeavor to track these louts." He left the dwarf behind in a handful of strides, barely holding his own with the disappearing wag. He hoped they didn't have far to go.

RYAN SAT QUIETLY near the window, his chin resting against his chest. He kept his eye closed, but he didn't truly sleep.

A light tapping sounded at the door.

Ryan uncoiled, slipping the SIG-Sauer from leather and walking to the door. The tapping repeated, one of the codes he and the companions had designed to recognize each other in the event they were separated. "Who is it?" he demanded.

"Me, Dad," Dean answered. "And Jak. We need to talk."

Ryan moved the chair from the door, glancing at the bed. Krysty had roused herself and had her pistol to hand, covering the door. Unfastening the latches, he stepped back and let the two boys into the room.

Dean started to talk first, sitting on the floor so he couldn't be seen through the window from the street level. Ryan didn't interrupt, learning about the plague darts and Kirkland's own intentions of killing the two boys and blaming the plague.

Before Ryan had the chance to progress with his questioning, another knock came on the door. This one didn't have any of the patterns the companions agreed on.

"Who is it?" Ryan asked.

"Albert," the dwarf said in a loud whisper.

"Where's Doc?"

"Doc sent me on." Albert sounded slightly out of breath or nervous.

Ryan didn't know which it was. He rolled back the SIG-Sauer's hammer with a thumb, lessening the pull tension on the trigger to something over two pounds. "Why?"

"Kirkland's people have got Mildred," the dwarf said.

"How do you know?"

"Me and Doc saw her ourselves."

Ryan gestured at Jak. The albino stood, filling his hands with the leaf-bladed throwing knives. Ryan signaled Jak to take the dwarf.

The teenager nodded.

Pulling the door open, Ryan leveled the 9 mm blaster between the dwarf's eyes. To his credit, Albert already had his hands up. Nobody stood in the hallway behind the dwarf.

"Get in," Ryan ordered, keeping the SIG-Sauer still.

Dean took the .38 pistols out of the little man's holsters while Jak pinned him in place with a blade on either side of his throat.

"You don't have to worry—" Albert began.

"Shut up," Ryan commanded. He walked into the hallway with the 9 mm blaster beside his leg. His senses were on triple red, reading every shadow before him. He tried the door to J.B. and Mildred's room and found it open. That discovery created a bad feeling in him that only got worse when he found the blood spots on the white sheets of the bed.

He returned to his room. "Fireblast!" he swore.

"Mildred?" Krysty asked.

"Somebody took her," Ryan answered.

"Was she still alive?" Krysty asked Albert.

"I couldn't tell," the dwarf said.

"Where's Doc?" Ryan repeated.

"Went after the wag they were carrying her in."

"Who?" Ryan asked.

"Only person I can figure," the dwarf answered, "is Kirkland's people."

"The sheriff?"

"He wasn't one of the men I saw."

Ryan went to their gear and picked up the Steyr. He glanced back at Krysty. "I'm going after J.B., let him know what's going on. Everybody just sit tight here until I get back."

"Be careful, lover," Krysty cautioned.

Ryan nodded. He put the Steyr over his shoulder, barrel pointing down, so he could swing it up into position.

"Him?" Jak pointed to the dwarf, not removing his knives.

Ryan stared hard into the little man's eyes. "Cut him loose, but watch him. Right now the only people we trust is ourselves." He left the room by way of the window.

"Dad," Dean called back, "I can come with you, cover your back."

"You'll cover my back better here," Ryan said. "Man doesn't have a place to come back to, he's a dead man running. Could be we'll have to fort up in here. You and Jak have a look around—without alerting any of the staff here—and see if there's anything we can use."

Dean nodded, accepting his father's decision.

Ryan glanced at Krysty. "Back as soon as I can." Then he made his way along the eaves overhanging the boardwalk below. The clouds remained generous, masking his movements. He moved slowly and carefully enough that there was no sound.

At the end of the eaves, he dropped into the alley and headed for the gunsmith's shop.

COLD WATER DOUSED Mildred and brought her back to wakefulness. "Goddamn," she shouted. "Do that again and I'm going to find you some day and choke you to death with your own entrails." She blinked the moisture out of her eyes, trying to clear her blurry vision.

"Not quite the sentiments I'd expected to hear from an educated woman."

Mildred focused on the voice, making out Kirkland seated in a chair across the small room. Two men, one of them carrying a small metal bucket, gathered to his left.

"Go fuck yourself," Mildred said.

Kirkland only laughed. "I assure you, I am not quite the refined and eloquent man that you perhaps thought I was earlier in the day."

"I never made that mistake," Mildred replied.

Mildred shifted on the straight-backed chair she sat in. Leather straps held her in place. Her hands were tied behind her, and her ankles were tied to the chair legs. "Maybe you want to explain this." She let her peripheral vision skate around the room.

Simple and plain, with only a few shelves against the walls, it looked like a concrete bunker that Mildred remembered from her days before being cryogenically preserved. The jars on the shelves held canned foods, vegetables and fruits. The concrete walls had been poured rather than mortared of blocks. Two lanterns hung on the walls, creating a pall of smoke that clung to the low, untextured ceiling.

"You," Kirkland said, "have had the misfortune of becoming a bargaining chit in the game I intend to play with your leader. You see, there have been stories of a plague that haunts this ville. Yet none of the seven of you seemed to be aware of it. And you came into the ville in the company of Albert, whom I personally know Liberty only keeps around as a token of amusement. Albert must be setting might high store on himself these days if he thinks I believe Liberty would let him come into Hazard alone with strangers."

"Or maybe he wasn't crediting you with being too intelligent," Mildred replied.

A cold smile twisted Kirkland's face. "At any rate, all of you made mistakes regarding me."

"That remains to be seen," Mildred replied. "I guess you figure on using me against Ryan?"

Kirkland spread his hands. "That, I would think, would be fundamentally clear at this point."

"Maybe so." Mildred smiled coldly back at the

man. Inside, she was afraid. She didn't like the idea of being trapped and helpless. However, one might be true, but the other wasn't necessarily so. She already felt some slack in the leather around her left wrist. "But you made a mistake, too."

"Would you care to explain?"

"Sure. You made a mistake in thinking a man like Ryan would give a rat's ass about me."

Kirkland's brows knitted. He leaned forward in his chair. "I find your idioms, madam, most interesting. When I take in the fact that you seem to be somewhat skilled in the field of medicine, you become even more interesting."

"Maybe you could cut me loose from this chair," Mildred suggested, "and we can find out just how interesting I can be."

"I don't think so." Kirkland stood and walked to one of the lanterns nearest him. "Though that suggestion may further inspire my curiosity at a later date."

"I'll be waiting," Mildred promised.

Kirkland blew out the lantern's flame, dimming the light in the room. "I assure you," he said, "that you will have no choice in the matter." He took the second lantern from the wall and headed up a set of rickety wooden steps that further led Mildred to believe she was somewhere underground. "I do hope you're not afraid of the dark."

Mildred forced herself to keep still as she watched Kirkland and his two men crawl out of the room through a trapdoor at the top of the stairs. Thrown bolts spilled heavy echoes into the room. The acrid stink of smoke made Mildred sneeze.

She waited a few beats in the complete darkness, struggling with a fear that threatened to consume her. When she heard no other noises, she began to work on the leather binding her left wrist. The rough material chafed her skin, settling into a fierce burn that forced her to give up. Loose as it was, the leather thong still maintained enough friction to restrain her.

Then she thought about the jars of foodstuffs sitting on the shelves. They'd contain juices. Gingerly she leaned forward in the chair, struggling to clear it off the ground. Her ankles ground in pain as her feet rose heel up, her weight resting on the ball of her foot. Cautiously, knowing if she tipped over she'd never have another chance to save herself, she scooted over toward the shelves she remembered being nearest.

Her efforts yielded her less than an inch at a time, and the pain involved was great. The increased effort also caused the knot of swelling on her right temple to throb even more painfully, and her bruised stomach muscles rebelled at the demands being made on them.

After six attempts, she was forced to rest. The sound of her gulping air was the only sound in the room. She sat, trying to quieten her quivering stomach muscles so they would be ready for the next round of agony.

She took solace in the fact that she was six inches

closer to her goal. Then she pushed the chair up again and continued to move forward. She wasn't going to just sit there and be used against her friends.

Chapter Fourteen

Ryan spotted the deputy across the street from the gun shop long before the man knew the one-eyed warrior was there. He knew from the man's stance that he was watching the gun shop, and that he'd gotten bored with it. He also saw moonlight kiss the deputy's star on his chest.

Ryan stayed in the shadows as he turned the corner. He walked casually, as if he were a man with another place to get to and in no real hurry to get there. It fit in with the handful of other men he'd seen on the streets.

The deputy gave him a quick scan, then turned his attention back to the front of the gun shop. He kept his hands folded across his chest.

While doing a recce around the building, Ryan found the second man working backup. The second deputy sat high on a balcony over the general store, surveying the street from a folding canvas chair. The station was a good one for watching over the man at street level, but it left the man on the balcony vulnerable.

Ryan circled the building and found a plastic drainpipe bolted to the wall beside the balcony, leading down into a rain barrel that was half-full. Though the pipe wouldn't hold his weight, the rain barrel did put him within reaching distance of the balcony.

He shed the Steyr, knowing it would be too hard to move while carrying the big weapon, then thumbed the restraining strap over the SIG-Sauer. He stepped onto the porch quietly, then moved up onto the rain barrel. Straightening himself and maintaining his balance, he caught the support struts of the balcony.

Gently Ryan eased his weight from the rain barrel to the balcony struts. He knew the deputy was facing away from him, so all he had to do was remain silent. Holding all his weight on one arm while he moved the other higher was a strain, but he managed it.

He drew his head up slowly, maintaining the illusion of the shadows. He peered between the bars and saw the deputy still facing away from him. Chilling the man was optional; keeping him from yelling a warning wasn't.

He pulled himself up over the edge of the railing and onto the balcony. The deputy never heard him coming. Ryan reached for the man's head, gripped it firmly, then twisted hard before the man could cry out or start to struggle.

The harsh crack signaled the separation of the man's skull from his spine. Flatulence ripped through the man's pants as his bowels released.

Ryan left the corpse where it lay in the chair and climbed back to the ground. In a matter of less than a handful of minutes, he'd recovered the Steyr and crept up on the other deputy.

With the man out in the open the way he was, Ryan had no choice but to take him quick. The one-eyed warrior bolted around the corner and came at the deputy at a good stride.

The deputy came around to face Ryan, uncertainty in his movements. He was young, used to handling an area that didn't have much rebellion in it. Too much power took the edge off a man. "Can I help you?" he asked.

Ryan said, "Sure," then kicked the younger man in the crotch. The deputy doubled over, grabbing for his groin. Ryan swept the Steyr around to buttstroke the deputy, breaking the back of the man's head. He died in a single breath.

Crossing the street, Ryan knocked on the door to the darkened gun shop.

"What do you want?" a young man's voice asked, so quiet it didn't drift more than a few feet.

"To see J. B. Dix," Ryan replied. "And make it bastard quick. I've already chilled two men coming this far. One of them gets discovered, we're going to be up to our ears in Kirkland's sec teams."

"I'll be back."

Ryan waited, staying in the shadows. He didn't know how long it would be before someone came along to change the guards.

"Ryan," J.B. called less than two minutes later.

"Here." Ryan stepped in through the open door, noting the woman and the two men that flanked the Armorer, their hands on their weapons. "There's a lot of things we've got to talk over."

DOC SAT on his haunches and watched the barn. The wag carrying Mildred had disappeared inside almost a half hour before. Cloaked in the shadows of a nearby residence, crouched behind some bushes, he kept his Le Mat blaster across his knees. He held the slim volume of Robert Frost poetry in his free hand, forcing himself to be patient by trying to recall all he could of the poet's work.

He was torn between going back to Ryan and the others to let them know where Mildred had been taken, and not wanting to desert the woman.

His mind conjured up torture scene after torture scene, refusing to give him any rest. Too many of the vulgar violences that traveled through his brain were too clear, too much a part of what he had lived through.

Doc had witnessed the evil that lurked in the hearts of men. He stifled a burst of laughter that threatened to tear free inside him, not knowing what had sparked it.

Voices warned him that men were coming back out of the barn.

Doc drew back into the shadowy embrace of the hedges beside the house and curled his finger around the Le Mat's trigger. He had it set for the massive .63-caliber shotgun load. If all hell was going to break loose when he had to use it, he figured on clearing the decks as much as possible beforehand.

Kirkland walked out of the barn in the company of two other men, all of them illuminated by the lantern the healer carried. One of them Doc recognized as being one of the men aboard the wag that had taken Mildred. Kirkland led the way into the back of a large manor house that showed evidence of skilled carpenters who had built it.

When the men disappeared into the house, Doc waited a little while longer, then eased out of hiding and took long steps toward the barn. The door was left unlocked, so he crept inside.

The stink of hay and the animals filled his nostrils as he passed inside. He used his cane much as a person without sight would, feeling for uneven surfaces ahead of him.

With a dull thunk he found an object before him that turned out to be one of the wag wheels. He pocketed the Frost book and whispered hoarsely, "Mildred! Mildred! Dear lady, it is I, Doc. If you can hear me, please let me know." He searched frantically, feeling across the buckboard, sorely afraid that Mildred's corpse would be the only thing left lying there.

Thankfully, in a sense, the buckboard was empty. That still left finding Mildred almost an impossibility. Doc prayed as he searched, hoping that the woman was still alive.

A sliver of moonlight above him caught his attention as it threw a narrow shaft onto the stalls in front of him. It vanished a moment later, obviously having been reflected from some other surface outside. Still, it presented possibilities.

Working from the brief glimpse he'd gotten, Doc found the ladder leading up to the hayloft and climbed it. When he gained the top, he used the sword stick again to search the area before him, making his way to the small doors fronting the barn. The moonlight rimmed them, drawing them into squares almost three feet across.

When he reached the doors, he pulled the bolt back and opened them. Moonlight invaded the barn, falling down over the horses below. Most of the stalls contained animals. With the unaccustomed light invading the barn, some of the horses started nickering restlessly. Still, the natural light flooding the barn would be much less obvious than lighting a lantern.

Doc climbed back down the ladder and rounded the buckboard. A quick check let him know that Mildred wasn't in any of the stalls. His mind flew, racing with possibilities. He glanced upward, seeing nothing but the hayloft above.

He then moved to one side of the stall near the barn door and started stamping his foot. All he encountered for a long time was the dull splat of his boot striking nothing but hard ground.

He was beginning to think that if there was an underground room, it was buried so deep that he wouldn't be able to hear the difference. Fearful disappointment filled him, and the madness seeped into every chink such negative thinking created.

Then the sound changed when he stamped. Instead of a dulled thud, he heard a hollow *thomp*.

Marking the area with the sword stick, Doc sprang for the pitchfork hanging on the wall near the tack and harness. Determined effort and some work allowed him to track the underground room to the rearmost stall on the right. The stall was empty, and straw covered the floor. Doc scraped the straw away and found the square-cut door beneath, collared by two-by-fours. He grasped the steel ring set in the door and yanked it open to reveal a yawning black abyss below.

He felt inside and found a ladder built onto one of the walls. Voices outside startled him, coming closer.

Quiet as he could be, Doc climbed inside the doorway and pulled it closed behind him. He waited for a moment, hardly daring to breathe.

And the voices came closer. "I don't care what Kirkland says about that bitch," a man said. "Damaged goods isn't gonna keep her from being worth just as much to the bastard outlanders. I see Kirkland took a woman from the gaudy house tonight, so I know he isn't needing relief the way I do."

"I don't know about that, Harold," another man said. "You go messing with that woman, Kirkland's liable to chill you over it."

"Fuck him. I'll just tell him she's lying. I don't think he's going to be handing her back to those outlanders alive anyway. Never saw him be overly generous about such things, and they got something he wants or he would have killed them outright anyhow."

Doc explored the floor below him. The sword stick quickly touched walls on all sides of him, letting him know he was in a very small room. Kneeling, he dragged his free hand across the floor, spreading out his fingers so he could cover more ground. He found another steel ring and pulled it up.

The footsteps coming from above continued their approach, growing louder.

Doc took the second ladder down, sensing movement too late above him. And below him was the sound of breaking glass.

AGAINST THE SHELVES now, Mildred shoved hard. Her shoulder met a gallon jar with considerable force. The jar rocked across the shelf and collided with another from the sound of the breaking glass. Liquid ran down her arm.

Twisting in her chair, Mildred let the liquid run onto her other arm, drenching her wrist where the leather thong had grown more loose. She knew leather also stretched when it got wet. The water that had been dumped on her earlier had probably loosened the thong as much as it had.

The liquid—brine, from the smell of it—thoroughly soaked the thongs holding both wrists as bits and pieces of vegetables slid across her fingers. She pulled against her restraints, finally able to get her hands free.

Then she felt along the floor for a chunk of glass to use on the thongs binding her ankles. She found a piece only a few inches long that had razor-sharp edges. While she was picking it up, she accidentally sliced her thumb. The brine burned the cut, but she ignored the pain while she cut herself free.

A muted banging noise sounded above her where she judged the trapdoor to be. In the darkness it was hard to tell, hard to remember. Using both hands now, she gently searched through the glass fragments until she found a bigger one that she could use as a weapon.

She dragged her knuckles across it, keeping the softer parts of her hands protected from the edges. The piece she held was nearly eight inches long.

The banging from above repeated, louder this time. Men's voices also drifted into the room.

Mildred ripped a shirtsleeve free, then wrapped it around the bottom four inches or so of the glass shard she'd picked up. The cloth wrapped around enough times that the glass didn't immediately slash through. She fisted it, feeling somewhat better for having it.

The glass shard wasn't much of a weapon, but she could make do.

The trapdoor opened. More darkness greeted her, this slightly more gray than the shadows filling the underground room. She didn't know why the man entering the room wasn't carrying a lantern.

Reaching out, she touched the ladder, making sure of the distance. Then she tightened her grip on the glass shard and waited.

The footsteps continued coming down the ladder for another few rungs, then halted. "Mildred?" whispered a voice she recognized.

Positioned behind the old man, Mildred halted her blow just in time. She'd intended to slash across whoever was hanging from the ladder. Legs or back, the wounds would have given her an edge.

"Doc?" Mildred whispered back.

"It is I, dear lady, come to your rescue I had

thought. But I fear we are not going to be alone for much longer."

Without warning, light appeared around the edges of a second door above Doc. The weak yellow illumination flared down through the sides of a second trapdoor above the one Doc was halfway through.

"Somebody's been here, Harold," a man said in a quiet voice that barely got through the muffling effects of the trapdoor. "All the straw's been moved."

"I can see that, Miner. Get that lantern over here and let's take a look before we get anybody else."

"Betwixt a hard place and a rock," Doc whispered, "that's surely where we find ourselves in this quandary."

"Haul your bony butt down off that ladder," Mildred ordered. "All you're doing up there is making a fine target."

Doc clambered down.

The shadows drew back as the light from the lantern above filtered into the room. Dust particles raced like wild comets through the haze drifting through the trapdoor above.

"Your blaster, Doc," Mildred prompted. "That scattergun of yours is good in close quarters. And those bastards aren't going to have many places to run." She hung on to her anger, using it to force her fear away.

Doc's Le Mat clicked as he made the adjustments necessary to swivel the shotgun barrel into the active role. "Stand back, dear Dr. Wyeth, because those concrete walls are going to be just as hard on us as they are on them.''

Then the trapdoor above opened.

Pulled back against the wall, Mildred suddenly went deaf and blind as the Le Mat discharged. Shotgun pellets bounced wildly, and men started to scream.

Chapter Fifteen

"Jak and Dean have got horses rounded up and waiting for us just outside of Hazard," Ryan said to J.B. He sat at the table in the back of the gun shop. "If we make it that far, we can get out of here with a whole skin."

"Sounds to me like your skin is the only one you're worried about."

Ryan looked at the woman, remembering her name with effort. "Anna, my skin and those of my friends are the only ones I ever worry about."

From the looks on the faces of Tinker Phillips and his sons, Ryan's views didn't sit well.

"If it hadn't been for us," Anna protested, "you bastards wouldn't have been outfitted as well as you're going to be."

Ryan knew that was true. J.B. had already shown him the ammo that Phillips had contributed to the cause. He fixed the woman with his hard stare. "Just because I'm making plans to take care of my people doesn't mean I'm leaving you out in the open with a busted wheel. You expect somebody to come riding into this town like some kind of vid hero and chill Kirkland?"

"Been nights I dreamed of nothing else, mister," one of the men commented.

Ryan shook his head. "You people have been cooped up in this retreat too long. I just chilled two men to get in here and talk to J.B. Kirkland's going to know about it, and he's going to know pretty much who did it. I don't see him letting us walk away after that."

"And he has Mildred," J.B. put in. "Kind of makes everything personal." He cleaned his glasses and put them back on, the steel rims hard and shiny. "We aren't going to leave without her."

"We're going to take Kirkland on," Ryan said, "because we don't have a choice. If we chill him, that's fine, but it's going to be because it happened, not because we planned on it."

Anna sat back from the table. Her right hand was below the table, out of sight.

Ryan didn't doubt for a moment that the woman had a blaster on him, just as he knew J.B. had her covered while he sat beside her. "If you people want your freedom—or this ville as your own—that's up to you. Fireblast! You're still going to have to go through Kirkland's sec team to do it."

"Man's right," Phillips said. "It isn't his fight. Never was. Never will be." He massaged his hump. "How do you plan on getting the woman back?"

Ryan swiveled his gaze to the old gunsmith. "I'm going to have to take a hand in Kirkland's game. If we try to run, I don't see that we're going to get past his sec team without getting run to ground. Even with horses."

"So what do you have in mind?"

"Make him bring his sec force back into the ville

to contain an insurrection," Ryan answered. "Provided you can persuade a few people to join up."

Phillips shook his head. "Don't see how that's possible. There's the plague to consider."

"The plague's a damn lie," Ryan growled.

"I got your word on that," Phillips said, "and I'm mostly willing to believe you. But those people out there, they've seen plague victims come in for a few years. They believe. Give me a week or so, mebbe I could make believers out of them. But not in one night. And we've only got half of that left."

Ryan pushed up from the table. "I don't aim to wait, Tinker. Kirkland's going to shove it right up to the line in the morning, and I'm not going to back down from him. You want to make a difference, you'll be ready to take a stand, too."

Phillips shook his head. "Got to think about that."

"You do that," Ryan said. "I've got to get back to my people. J.B.?"

"I'll be along in a bit. Another hour or two, and I'll have enough shotgun loads for the M-4000 to last for a while." He looked up at Ryan. "If you hear anything about Mildred—"

"I'll come myself," Ryan promised.

"You going looking?"

"If Doc comes up with something we can work on."

"You'll let me know?"

"Any way it goes, you'll be the next man I tell," Ryan answered. He took his leave from the gun shop, feeling the heat of the woman's angered gaze.

In a way she was right. He was thinking only of his own skin. And knowing that didn't feel comfortable.

He walked out onto the boardwalk, making certain the dead deputy across the street hadn't been replaced. There was a time when he rode with the Trader on War Wag One he might have taken a firmer stance in Hazard. The Trader wouldn't have put up with what was going on in the ville.

Any way it went down in the morning—if things saw fit to wait that long—there would be more than a few people catching the last train to the coast.

DOC MANAGED the recoil from the Le Mat with a little trouble. He'd squeezed off the shot before he was truly ready, and there had been the matter of footing. Still he readied another blast as the echoes of the first slammed against his eardrums in the tight confines of the room.

One of the two men broke away from the second trapdoor above, screaming hoarsely that he was hit and bleeding badly. The second man shoved the snout of a revolver into the hole and squeezed off rounds as fast as he could.

Doc dodged back, feeling one of the bullets yank at his coattails, creating another mending job for a time when things were decidedly calmer.

The pistol bullets bounced and whined from the walls a few times before expending the energy that propelled them. Glass containers broke, spilling smells and foodstuffs to the floor. The light trickling down from above was barely enough to let Doc see Mildred taking cover across the room.

Knowing they didn't have time to spend exchanging shots with the men up above, Doc glanced upward and saw the man above shoving his arm into the trapdoor area again. The old man brought up the Le Mat and pushed it into the mouth of the bottom trapdoor. He dropped the hammer on the round, aiming for the wall, unable to fire at the gunner without exposing himself.

The double-aught shot bounced off the wall and smashed into the gunner's arm. He wailed in pain.

Doc readied another load into the Le Mat. "Are you ready, Dr. Wyeth?" He had to shout to even hear himself.

"Yes," Mildred roared back.

"Then follow me, and pray that the Almighty continues to look after fools." Doc grabbed the ladder and bounded up the rungs. He kept the Le Mat in one fist, managing the climb with the other.

Up above, the second trapdoor remained open and free of gunmen.

At the top of the ladder, Doc made his way to the second trapdoor and climbed onward. He stayed low when he climbed out at the barn floor level again.

One of Kirkland's men lay to one side, sightless eyes staring at the ceiling. His chest was a bloody ruin where the initial double-aught charge had caught him.

Doc paused, hunkered down and cut his eyes around the barn. His hearing was still hampered from all the crash and din that had been released in the underground room. Then he spotted the fleet-footed shadow speeding toward the barn doors. He lifted the Le Mat and fired again.

The shotgun charge caught the man in the back and hurtled him forward, sprawling him out almost within reaching distance of the doors.

Doc turned and offered his hand to Mildred as she climbed out of the trapdoor. "My hand, dear lady, while I have the strength in me to help."

Mildred grabbed his hand and scrambled out of the hole. "Now what?"

Doc raised his eyebrows. "You propose that I had an actual plan in all of this?"

"Would have been a great help, Doc." Mildred stripped the blaster from the corpse and started moving toward the tack and equipment area.

"I had thought of taking the horses," Doc admitted, "but I was uncertain what shape you might be in."

"I'm all for getting the hell out of here." Mildred took a pair of bridles from the wall and tossed one to Doc. "Everybody else Kirkland has at this place is going to be all over us like flies on shit."

"Those," Doc assured Mildred as he crossed the stable area to one of the horses, "are my sentiments exactly." He thrust the Le Mat into his belt, then grabbed the mane of the horse in the stall beside him.

The animal tossed its head a few times, but came into the bridle easily enough. Despite the ringing in his ears, Doc thought he could hear men yelling outside. He forced the bit between the horse's teeth, then fit the bridle strap behind the horse's ears.

Mildred led her chosen mount from the stall it was in, and swung up onto its bare back. The horse bucked for a moment, but she fought it into submission, holding the reins tight.

Doc clambered onto his horse's back, feeling the ridge of its backbone shove insistently into his crotch. The ride definitely wasn't going to be one of comfort.

"Ready?" Mildred asked.

"As much as I dislike these animals, I feel I have little choice."

"Then ride!" Mildred flicked the reins against the horse's neck, causing it to break into a gallop. She headed toward the barn doors, left slightly ajar by the men who had entered the structure after Doc.

Struggling to lock his legs around the creature he rode, Doc followed the woman. He didn't think she knew the way back into Hazard where the hotel was.

They burst through the barn doors almost neck and neck. Mildred and her mount slammed into the door and knocked it open still farther. Shots greeted them when they emerged from the barn, drumming a rapid tattoo across the doors.

Doc thrust the Le Mat at two men running from the back door of the manor house, then pulled the trigger. The shotgun blast drove them backward.

Mildred's borrowed blaster cracked harshly, dropping another man shooting from a second-story window toward the back of the house.

Doc managed the manipulations that moved the barrel holding the cylinder of .44 rounds into play.

He fired at targets, not really hoping to hit any of them, but wanting them thinking he was armed.

"Which way?" Mildred asked.

Doc kicked his horse into greater speed. Kirkland's hostile blasters faded quickly behind him. "This way." He led her back through the rutted roads of Hazard.

"Got company," Mildred yelled up.

Twisting, Doc glanced back behind them, spotting five riders traveling along in their wake. A bullet ripped through the air above his head. "Then we have no choice but to make haste."

POUNDING HOOVES caught Ryan's attention. He came to a halt beside the hotel, getting ready to clamber up to his room, then turned and glanced back down the street.

Two riders rode hard for the hotel, followed by a handful of others. Moonlight glinted from Doc's silvery mane and from some of the lighter beads worked into Mildred's hair.

"Krysty!" Ryan called, raising his voice.

"I see them, lover."

Ryan pulled the Steyr to his shoulder, putting himself against the hotel. He centered the sights over the lead rider of the five pursuers, putting the crosshairs on the man's face. He guessed that Doc and Mildred were still seventy yards out, and the men following them were about another twenty after that.

Detonations cracked, and Ryan saw Doc's horse stagger slightly before recovering itself. Changing his mind, Ryan put the crosshairs on the lead rider's horse. He let out half a breath and squeezed the trigger.

The bullet sped true, crashing through the animal's forehead and spewing the contents of its brainpan over the rider. Reflexes gone, the horse tumbled in the street, throwing the rider in one direction while it fell in another. The falling horse took out another rider and mount, and became a hazard for the rest.

Then a barrage of fire chopped into the riders chasing Doc and Mildred. Ryan recognized Krysty's and Jak's blasters, then the high-pitched report of Dean's 9 mm Browning joined in.

The line of riders wilted at once. But more gunmen joined them from the gaudy house down the street.

Fifteen yards out, Doc's horse was shot out from under him. The old man and the dead animal went down together, tumbling across the rutted street.

Ryan lifted the Steyr and blasted two men who tried to urge their mounts over the downed riders. Two horses with empty saddles ducked into the nearest side street.

Amazingly Doc scrambled to his feet and ran toward Ryan, looking none the worse for wear. "By the Three Kennedys!" the old man yelled. "I thought the next thing these old ears would be hearing was sweet refrains from Saint Gabriel's horn."

"Get to the hotel, Doc," Ryan ordered. He kept covering fire going, but the return blasterfire was building, as well. Bullets thudded into the wall nearby.

Mildred rode her horse onto the wooden boardwalk, then abandoned it in front of the doors. She tried the doorknob, but it didn't open. Before she could move, though, Jak was there, opening the door and letting her in. Doc thumped across the boardwalk, as well, keeping his head low.

"Ryan," Jak called.

Wheeling, Ryan sprinted to the door and pushed through. The albino teenager fired past him at Kirkland's sec team.

Inside the foyer, Ryan spotted one of the dead deputies sprawled across a sofa in the waiting room. His throat had been slit from ear to ear, and the blood patterns across the cream-colored antimacassar suggested that he'd been held in place while he died.

"Mildred," Dean called from the second-floor landing.

The woman glanced up in time to catch the big blaster Dean tossed down, then she caught the box of shells that followed. With grim efficiency, she broke the pistol open and checked the loads. Then she snapped the ZKR 551's cylinder. "Thanks, Dean. Where did you find it?"

"Your room," Dean replied. "Reckon the guys who took you overlooked it."

Ryan reloaded the Steyr from loose rounds inside his shirt. The blasterfire coming from outside continued unabated, letting him know the attackers weren't going to give up easily. The thick walls of the hotel kept the bullets from coming through, but several of them punched through the windows, ravaging the decor.

"What the hell is going on?" Aunt Maim rolled into view, propelled by Jocelyn. Both of them only wore sleeping robes.

"Looks like mebbe you're going to get your wish after all," Ryan said. He fell into line beside the window and peered out.

More bullets crashed through the windows. Spinning shards of glass whipped through the air and rained over the furniture.

Jocelyn yanked Aunt Maim back, keeping her behind the heavy counter. The maid pulled a heavy double-barreled shotgun from behind the desk.

"The bastards are shooting up my hotel," the woman shrilled. "That wasn't supposed to happen!"

Ryan lifted the Steyr and put the crosshairs over a man taking cover at the corner of a building. He squeezed the trigger and watched the man's head go to pieces. More men rode up on horses, muzzle-flashes flaming from their weapons.

"Where's John?" Mildred asked as she reloaded. Her accuracy with the target pistol was telling, as with all of the companions. The sec force might have gathered dozens out in the street, but none of them appeared anxious to charge toward the hotel.

"At the gunsmith's," Ryan answered. "Getting the ammo we need. I figure the noise from this is going to draw him soon enough." He sighted on one of the riders, then punched a heavy-caliber bullet through the man's chest.

The corpse tumbled free of the saddle, and the horse bolted for cover.

Hooves crashed heavily against the boardwalk outside. Ryan looked frantically, knowing a rider had to have come up on the boardwalk from his blind side. Then he heard Doc's Le Mat blaster cut loose in a full-throated roar. A heartbeat later a riderless horse galloped by his window within reaching distance. A dead man trailed along behind it, his foot caught in one of the stirrups.

"Hold up, everybody!" a man roared out in the street. "Just hold up and wait! Get that building surrounded and let's hold them there until Kirkland gets here!"

The blasterfire ceased outside as the newly arrived riders spread out and took control of the sec men's guns.

Ryan watched as the men moved with grim efficiency, cutting off their every chance of a bloodless escape. "Fireblast!" he snarled.

"I must apologize, my dear Ryan," Doc said from across the hotel room. "I appear to have brought the proverbial hornet's nest descending upon us like a judgment from a dark and dire god."

"Not your fault, Doc." Ryan reloaded the Steyr again, weighing the chances of moving during night as opposed to moving after daybreak. "At least you got Mildred back safe and sound." He watched the street, seeing lanterns being spread among the men. They hustled in twos and threes, running like wolf packs.

Ryan sighted on one of the lanterns, led his target

a little, then let out half a breath and held it. His finger tightened on the trigger until he felt the rifle recoil against his shoulder.

Across the street, the lantern exploded into pieces. Oil splashed over the man carrying it, then ignited as the flames caught. He screamed in pain as the fire burned deep, wreathing him.

Mildred's pistol cracked, adding two more burning men to the pyre. Lanterns started going out all around the ville.

"Keep this floor covered," Ryan told Jak, Mildred and Doc. "Jak, you take the rear of the hotel. Mildred, you and Doc spread out here. I'll be back."

Jak faded into the shadows, his pale body lighted for only a moment as he passed. Doc and Mildred took up windows on opposite sides of the hotel wall facing the street.

Ryan sprinted up the stairs. It was going to be harder than a blue freezie's ass in January to hold the hotel. But it was also going to cost the sec men dearly if they tried to invade.

He found Krysty upstairs putting ammo for her blaster in small heaps beneath the windows of three rooms facing the street.

"Guess we stepped into it this time, lover," she said.

"Been there before," Ryan replied. "We'll see our way clear of this one, too." But at the moment he wasn't quite sure how. "I'm going up on the roof. Get a clearer vantage point from there."

"Do you want company?"

Ryan shook his head. ''The rooftop's probably going to be the first position we have to fall back on.'' He gave her a brief kiss, then headed out of the room.

Ryan shook his head. "The rooftop's probably going to be the first position we have to fall back on ..." He gave her a final smile, then headed out of the room.

Chapter Sixteen

"You got a back way out of this place?" J.B. asked. He stood near one of the barred windows overlooking the main street. The hotel was only a few blocks down, ringed by gunmen who had overturned buckboards and brought out crates from the general store to build a barricade.

"Your friends are dead," Phillips replied. "They got no way out of that hotel. Whether Kirkland's men get them this hour or the next, it's going to happen."

J.B. turned a harsh glare on the gunsmith, making the other man drop his gaze. "Mebbe so. But I'm not going to sit down here all high and dry and pretend it doesn't matter to me. My place is with them, and that's bastard sure where I'm going to be."

Phillips stared hard at him. "Mebbe you think me and mine should throw our hand in with yours."

The Armorer spoke quietly. "Appears that's what you were asking Ryan to do earlier."

"It's different. That man is facing a certain chilling in the position he's in now."

"I don't see it much removed from what you were asking," J.B. argued. "Except that you aren't standing in there with him like you talked like you would.''

"You trying to shame me?" The old man's voice grew harsh and cold.

J.B. shook his head. "You asked me a question, I answered it. You don't like the answers I give, don't be asking questions.''

"If the plague isn't real," Phillips said, "then mebbe we got a chance of getting shut of this place. Start over somewhere new. Always a place in a ville for a man knows blasters.''

"Can't argue with that," J.B. said. "And I wouldn't want to. But I got to get to my own work.''

"You're throwing your life away, J. B. Dix," Anna told him.

"They aren't dead yet, and neither am I. We've come out of tough spots before. Probably going to see a few more before any of us catch the last train to the coast." He flicked his gaze back to Phillips. "Come on. You've got to have a white rabbit's bolt-hole around this place somewhere.''

Reluctantly the old man nodded. "We got a tunnel that will get you out of here.''

"Where does it come up?''

"At the blacksmith's shop next door. Got a corral there, and sells green-broke horses. Times got hard, we always figured a man a-foot wasn't going to make it. Needed him a horse if he was going anywhere.''

"Show me," J.B. said. He readied his weapons as he walked.

"You're a fool, J.B." Anna grated.

"I guess we'll see about that after the smoke clears," the Armorer told her in a cool voice.

THE TRAPDOOR at the other end of the tunnel was heavy with packed earth. It took real work to get it up, and the whole time J.B. had to wonder if one of Kirkland's sec men was going to be standing at the other side of the room waiting for him.

Nobody was there, though.

He climbed out of the tunnel and brought up the duffel containing the ammo he'd gotten from Phillips and put together himself, but stopped when Anna grabbed his pants leg. She surged up out of the ground to join him, fisting his shirt.

"You don't have any idea what you're walking away from," Anna told him, pulling her body close.

J.B. felt the heavy pressure of her firm breasts against his chest. "I got an idea."

"And you're still going to walk? Even walk into your own death?"

"Made a promise," J.B. said, "that I'd be there. I'm not the kind of man to walk out on people."

"If things had been different, then?" She looked into his eyes wistfully, not bothering to disguise the desire burning there.

J.B. looked at her, admitting to himself the desire he felt for the young woman. But it was only passing fancy, and he knew himself well enough to know that. What he had with Mildred, there had never been anything like it in his life. She understood him in ways that no woman ever had, while at the same time remaining one of the most vexing creatures he'd ever encountered.

"Mebbe," he said, just to give her that.

Anna pulled him close. "There hasn't been a man for me since Eddie died. Mebbe there never will be. But if you get back this way, or you hear of Tinker Phillips's Gun Shop, you come on around for a visit."

"Sure," J.B. said, and the lie tripped from his lips with no effort at all.

She pulled his face into hers and gave him a burning kiss that he felt clear down to his toes. Then she broke the kiss and walked back to the trapdoor. Her walk suggested the curves and the passions that burned under her clothing.

"You put up a hell of an argument," J.B. said in a thick voice.

"But you're still going."

"Yeah."

Anna stepped back into the tunnel and climbed down. "I wish you well, then." She pulled the trapdoor closed.

J.B. went over to the horses, his Uzi canted at his hip and gripped in one hand. Anybody that came through the door while he was bridling a mount was fair game. Moonlight and lantern light drifted in through the patchwork glass windows.

He took down a bridle and fitted it over the head of a bay gelding that seemed gentle enough. He didn't bother with a saddle because he felt he was already working on borrowed time. Then he led the gelding to the rear doors of the blacksmith's shop.

Pulling himself onto the animal's back, he put the duffel across his lap, then thumped the horse in the sides with his heels and headed through the alley. Two men stood at its mouth, peering down the street at the hotel. Both turned to look at J.B., but neither of them recognized him.

He rode past them.

"Man, get your fool self chilled out there bastard quick," one of the men said.

J.B. ignored the warning and rode straight for the hotel, knowing there was every chance he'd get chilled in a cross fire between his friends and Kirkland's people.

The sec men stared after him as he rode out into the center of the street. They froze, not knowing what to do. A ragged cheer burst out from some of them as they thought one of their own had gotten courageous enough or stupid enough to try another attack on the hotel.

"Go get them outie bastards!" someone yelled.

And that, J.B. knew, might very well be the kiss of death because Mildred and Ryan were good enough to empty the horse's saddle even now. He raised his voice. "Rider coming in! It's J.B.!"

It took only a moment for what was truly happening to crystallize in the sec men's minds. Then they opened fire.

J.B. stayed low, aiming the horse at the front doors of the hotel. He kept his stomach pressed tight against the duffel bag so he wouldn't lose it. Twisting, he brought the Uzi to bear, raking a line of 9 mm bullets across the sec men behind him.

The bullets chewed through kegs, an overturned buckboard, and tables that had been brought out of various establishments. A handful of sec men went down under the blasterfire.

J.B. didn't let up until the Uzi was empty. He turned his attention back to the hotel, holding on to the horse's mane as it vaulted up onto the boardwalk. He knew it had taken some hits during the firefight; he'd felt them shiver through the animal's flesh. Two bullets had grazed the Armorer's left side, tearing through skin and glancing off the bone beneath.

The doors opened ahead of him just before he thought the horse was going to smash into them. The animal struggled to keep taking steps, blood flecking from its nostrils and blowing back into J.B.'s face in warm, wet drops.

The Armorer tried to pull the animal up short, but it was nearly dead, ignoring the pain in its mouth from the rough handling of the bit. The horse's front legs went out from under it as it fell forward.

J.B. leaped off his dead mount, pulling the duffel clear. New pain flared through his bruised side when he hit the floor. He skidded across the wooden floor and smashed into a big chair. Bullets ripped through the fabric over his head. The strange thing was, the bullets came from inside the hotel.

"Hold your goddamn fire!" Mildred yelled. "He's one of us!"

J.B. glanced across the room and saw the two women huddled behind the counter. One of them sat in a wheelchair, brandishing a huge blaster.

Muffling a groan as he pushed himself to his feet, J.B. reached for his fedora and clamped it onto his head. He gathered the straps of the duffel and pulled it over his shoulder. His side felt as if it were on fire.

Doc shoved the doors back together, then put the lock bar back into place. "John Barrymore," the old man said, "I was not sure if we would see you again in this life."

"I'm harder to get rid of than that," J.B. declared. He stepped across the mess the dying horse left when its bowels evacuated across the wooden floor. "You get Mildred back?"

"The gods permitted me to perform that small task." Doc took up a position at the window and blasted a charge of buckshot that elicited a scream of pain from outside. "But I fear I have escorted your dear lady from the frying pan into the fire."

"You know my views on that," J.B. said, joining the old man at the window. "Get a bigger frying pan." He recharged the Uzi and hammered out a series of bursts that drove the advancing sec men back to cover. "Where's Ryan?"

Then he heard the distinctive boom of his friend's Steyr.

"Up top," Mildred said.

J.B. crossed to the woman and gave her a brief kiss. "Keep yourself safe until we get out of this."

"You do the same," Mildred said.

The Armorer went up the stairs, talked briefly to Krysty and found out Ryan was on the roof. He located the inside ladder and went up. "Ryan."

"Come ahead," Ryan called.

Straining, J.B. barely made out the big man in the shadows. He heaved himself onto the roof with the duffel in tow. "Got good news and bad. Which do you want first?"

"The good," Ryan answered. "Mebbe it'll make the bad go down easier."

"The good news," J.B. said, moving painfully into a sitting position, "is Tinker was willing to part with some plas ex. Got a mighty big store of it for one man. Said he's been saving it for a special occasion."

Ryan nodded, scratching at the rough leather of his eyepatch. "Figure on boobying the building for when they decide to rush us?"

J.B. grinned. "Like that song Gimball used to play back on War Wag One. 'Hotel California.' Everybody's gonna check in when they come for us, but nobody's gonna check out. If they give us enough time, I'll have the plas ex set so it'll take out the bottom three floors and leave the structure standing. If we get godawful lucky, we can get away in the confusion."

"Draw it up and let me know when you need me," Ryan said. "I'll get Dean up here with the Steyr. He's good enough to snipe anybody who gets to feeling too lucky."

"Give me a half hour." J.B. felt the warmth sticking to his side, but knew the wound was already starting to coagulate. His eyelids felt grainy from lack of sleep and overexertion.

"What's the bad news?" Ryan asked.

"If you're expecting people in this ville to rise up with us and take a stand against Kirkland, it isn't going to happen."

"Tinker Phillips and his family?"

"Dealing themselves out of it."

Ryan didn't look surprised. "Can't say that I blame them on the face of things. We'll do what we can."

J.B. nodded, reaching out to clap Ryan on the shoulder. "Over, under or around. One of them will get it done."

"Always has," Ryan said.

Chapter Seventeen

"Outlanders!"

Ryan roused himself from the semisleeping state he'd allowed himself to drift into during the past hour. He and J.B. had spent two and a half hours setting the plas ex around the hotel, tying all the remote-control detonators into the broadcast unit J.B. had. All of them would detonate at prearranged times, only seconds apart.

Ryan trusted the Armorer's skills in the demolitions area. J.B. had brought down several structures when they'd been back with the Trader on War Wag One.

"Outlanders!"

Peering over the rooftop's edge, Ryan picked up the Steyr.

Kirkland was out in the middle of the street, standing there in what looked like a glass box that sat in the back of a horse-drawn wag. A dozen gunners stood around the wag, protecting it.

Ryan couldn't believe it. He shouldered the rifle, keeping the barrel back far enough that none of the sec team could see it. He put the crosshairs over Kirkland's broad face. Taking up trigger slack, he breathed out, then squeezed through.

The bullet slammed into the glass box, sending

fracture lines running across one of the flat surfaces. But it didn't penetrate. Ryan studied the bullet hanging in midair above Kirkland at an angle that would have taken the man through the face if it had gone through.

Inside the glass box, Kirkland had flinched, but stopped short of throwing himself flat. The sec men surrounding him weren't as cool about getting shot at. They went to ground and started to fire back at the hotel.

"Stop firing, you stupe bastards!" Kirkland roared. It took a couple minutes for the blasterfire to subside.

"Okay," Ryan called back, "you got my attention."

Scrambling noises sounded beside him, then Krysty joined him. "He's built himself a bulletproof box of armaglass, lover."

"Putting on his own private show," Ryan agreed.

"You people are in a coffin," Kirkland yelled.

"And still got plenty of room for company," Ryan called back. "How many of you want to be chilled trying to nail the lid on?"

"There's another way we could work this," Kirkland said.

"Tell me."

Ryan turned to Krysty and spoke in a lower voice. "Get the others. We're going to get out of here."

"I know you chilled Liberty and his people," Kirkland said. "Proves you're harder to deal with than he was. The position of outer-perimeter sec chief is open."

"Don't see how we could trust each other," Ryan responded.

"We've got to start somewhere."

"Sure. I trust you and I end up with a back full of bullets. You trust me, how are you going to know I won't take up that outer-perimeter position and just keep on riding?"

"Have you heard about the plague?" Kirkland asked.

"Yeah," Ryan replied. "I also heard it's a fake."

Kirkland glanced around the street. Shopkeepers hadn't opened their buildings that morning, but they were around.

"You tried to kill two of our people last night," Ryan went on. "Only they killed your men instead. They found those air rifles and the darts you use to administer the bacterial injection you refer to as the plague."

"You're lying!"

"Got no reason to at this point," Ryan said. "Jak!"

Below, the albino teenager threw the captured air rifle and darts into the street.

"We didn't have those when we rode into Hazard yesterday," Ryan called out. "People that saw us know that. Word's going to spread, Kirkland, that your plague is just a big fake. Then you're going to be flat out of power in this ville, if they don't string you up."

"You're lying," Kirkland said. "You're just trying to get these people to throw their lives away in an attempt to save your own ass."

Ryan watched the storefronts. People of the ville had gathered within the shops, not wanting to be caught out on the streets. But they were drawn to the approaching storm of violence all the same.

And they were hearing his words.

"You chose how it was going to be when you made an attempt on my people last night," Ryan said. "And when you kidnapped one of them to use against us. Today all bets are off, and devil scrog the hindmost."

"You're signing your own death warrant," Kirkland warned.

"Hell of a lot of signatures before you decided to add your Hancock to it," Ryan answered. He glanced back as the rest of the companions and Albert joined him on the rooftop.

Ryan felt restless energy fill him. Time to shit or get off the pot, and he knew it. Kirkland was going to know it soon, too. The one-eyed warrior watched as Kirkland glanced around at his troops, getting ready to make the call.

Incredibly a high keening noise cut through the air.

"Upon my soul," Doc exclaimed, "do these old ears deceive me, or is that the sound of calliope I hear playing?"

"That is a calliope," Mildred agreed.

The music echoed over the ville, sounding cheerful and happy, totally out of sync with the events unfolding in Hazard.

"'Bring in the Clowns,'" Mildred said.

"Not see clowns," Jak said. "See wag. Look."

He pointed out of the ville, down the route the companions had followed.

"'Bring in the Clowns' is the name of a song," Mildred said. "A lot of carnivals used it for their theme music. What the hell is that?" She shaded her eyes.

Ryan took out his field glasses and studied the approaching wag.

In another life it had to have been a recreational vehicle. Ryan recognized it from vids he'd gotten a chance to look at. But now it was weathered, new metal spliced over on top of old, probably replacing rusted areas. Almost thirty feet long, it sailed along over the broken terrain on drastically altered suspension that raised it nearly four feet from the ground. The vehicle was painted a rainbow of colors. Big clown faces in white greasepaint adorned the sides. The eyes were made up of the windows in the rear section. Dozens of balloons were tied to the upper deck of the RV. Crates festooned the vehicle, some held in cargo netting and others strapped to the metal sides.

A sign on the side read Uncle Joe's Traveling Wild, Weird West Show. Two mutie pig skulls were mounted on top of the engine cowling, and plastic eyeballs on springs dangled from the empty eye sockets.

Ryan scanned three men inside the RV's cab. One of them was behind the wheel, and the other two sat to the right. All of them were dressed up in outlandish clothing.

"A traveling circus?" Doc asked. "Did I read that aright, my dear Ryan?"

"Appears so," Ryan replied.

The calliope music continued its happy tunes over the countryside, growing ever louder. It had more noise than rolling thunder.

Inside his bulletproof cage, Kirkland began to yell out orders. The loud circus music kept Ryan from hearing what was being said, but he watched the sec team fan out to meet the approaching wag.

Dust spanned out behind the RV as it glided into Hazard. But other telltale dust spumes trailed it.

"Big wag's not alone," J.B. commented. His face looked gray and haggard.

Ryan knew they all needed some rest. Maybe back at the redoubt it would be possible. But first they had to get out of the ville in one piece. He trained the field glasses over the terrain, spotting at least five other dust trails.

"We're on triple red," he told the others, "and who knows what's about to come leaping out of the bag."

The circus wag braked to a halt, the gaily playing music louder than ever. Suddenly a voice blared through a PA system mounted in the vehicle.

"Citizens of Hazard, Uncle Joe's Traveling Wild, Weird West Show is pleased to make your acquaintance!"

The man's voice sounded vaguely familiar to Ryan, but it went back a lot of years. He picked over his memories, searching for it. But he kept his eye on the dust trails circling the front of the ville, as well.

"We're here for your amazement and edification," the announcer continued, "and for the amusement of children of all ages! Come see some of the strangest mutie creatures ever taken into captivity. She-She, the two-headed woman. Drynk, a scabbie so twisted by rad-corrupted genetics that he has no bones in his body and sleeps in a five-gallon pail. And more. For the next little bit, sit right back and let us entertain you. All just for a little jack everybody can spare."

"I know that voice," J.B. said.

Ryan nodded. "I do, too."

"Remember Handsome Wyatt?" the Armorer asked.

Below, clowns with green-and-red wigs hopped out of the circus wag and began to open crates on the sides of the vehicle. Inside the crates were metal cages containing live muties. The side Ryan could see held five of the creatures. One of them was She-She, the two-headed woman. The second head lay behind the first, not really a head at all, but some kind of spongy growth that possessed eyes and a mouth, and the same blond hair the mutie woman had on her real head. She was old and nearly naked, with running sores all over her body. She sat placid and docile, spittle running down both sides of her mouth as she ignored all the activity going on around her.

"Yeah, I remember Handsome Wyatt." Ryan stopped looking at the muties. They were there to draw attention away from the circus wag. He already spotted movement through the thick armaglass. "I cut off his left thumb for stealing gas from War Wag One."

Handsome Wyatt had ridden with the Trader for a while before Ryan and J.B. had signed on. The man hadn't lasted long after Ryan came aboard and discovered the man had been siphoning gas from the Trader's wags for personal profit. The Trader had been lenient the day Wyatt had been caught, and Ryan had only taken a thumb from the man instead of his life.

"Well," the Armorer said, "this looks like something Handsome Wyatt would come up with."

Stories had traveled with and to War Wag One in those days. The Trader was known to pay for stories that he considered investments. Some of those stories had always been about members who had drifted onto the crew of War Wag One, then drifted out. Trader's family had spread out, and people were always eager for news.

"You figure he brought his act back closer to home?" Ryan asked.

"That's his voice," J.B. said, "and that's an ace on the line."

"If he finds out you and I are here," Ryan said, "he'll chill us as soon as he can put a gun sight on us."

"Yeah." J.B. turned to Ryan and cleaned his glasses on his shirt. He smiled coldly. "Could be this party is going to be even bigger than we thought."

"He's got at least five other wags waiting out in the brush," Ryan observed.

"Play our cards right," J.B. said. "We wait, see what happens, and mebbe he won't miss one during the confusion. He doesn't know how this hotel is about to come apart."

"Or mebbe you aren't interested in what ol' Uncle Joe has for you because you've got your own act going on," the voice thundered from the PA system. "I see a man in a glass cage out in the middle of the street in this ville, and that's something you don't see every day, either."

The clowns continued unveiling cages, stripping canvas from some that held hideously malformed animals. The sec force working Hazard started to spread out, getting into position.

"If either one of those sides get overly ready, it's going to make things more difficult for us," Ryan said.

J.B. nodded.

Ryan lifted the Steyr. "So let's open the ball for them. I've got the clowns."

"Leaves me the Hazard sec teams." J.B. took up the Uzi and leaned out over the rooftop.

"Now!" Ryan said. He squeezed the trigger.

The bullet caught a clown full in his greasepaint-coated face, turning it from white to red in a heartbeat. As the body arced backward, thrown by the force of the round, Ryan settled the crosshairs on another target. He fired again, catching the second man in the shoulder as he turned.

The rest of the clowns pulled blasters and took

cover around the circus wag. The top of the wag popped up, and a man flipped an M-60 machine gun out on a tripod.

"They come carrying heavy," J.B. commented.

Ryan nodded. He glanced at the line of sec men the Armorer had blasted. Four of them were down in the streets, and only one of those was still alive.

In heartbeats the main street cutting through Hazard was a bloodbath in the making.

Ryan swiveled his attention back toward the ville's perimeter. Dust trails from traveling wags flared up again as they roared into the streets like great mechanical cats. They were small passenger wags, two of them pickups that rode on high suspension like the circus wag. But these were painted camo military colors and stripped down to necessary armor to lighten the weight.

The small wags flared out at once, letting Ryan know they were following preplanned routes. The highway jackers had a sizable amount of firepower, and evidently the ammo to spare to properly show it off.

Bullets popped paint from the circus wag, but didn't look to be penetrating either the metal or the windshield. Kirkland's sec forces gave ground before the predators.

"Kirkland's targeted us," Mildred said, pointing to a team of sec men charging the hotel.

"We knew it wouldn't go easy," Ryan said. He studied the circus wag as it moved toward the line of men Kirkland had posted in the street. The wag carrying Kirkland's armaglass cage backed away in front of the circus wag. Bullets struck the cage repeatedly, smashing dozens of fractures across the clear walls. It was a miracle the glass held, but it did.

Kirkland's wag pulled into an alley, and the man stepped out, yelling orders to his sec men.

Ryan drew a bead on the doctor, intending to shut him down once and for all. Then he heard J.B. yell, "Incoming!" and automatically went to ground.

An explosive round smashed into the corner of the hotel roof, debris raining over the friends. The tar-and-rock surface of the roof cut into Ryan's cheek and chin. He coughed as his lungs rebelled against the dust he was sucking in, and his eye teared up in an effort to clear his vision. He maintained his grip on the Steyr. "What the hell was that?"

"Rocket launcher," the Armorer said. "One of the small wags was packing one. Looked like an RPG-7."

"Reloads?" Jak asked, brushing splinters from his snow white hair.

"Yeah, they can be reloaded," Ryan growled, "if they got them." He crawled back to the edge of the roof after making sure all of the companions were moving around. Down in the street, the circus wag was plowing through the barricade that had been erected in front of the hotel.

Handsome Wyatt hung on to the outside of the circus wag. Ryan recognized the man even with the white greasepaint staining the other man's face.

And Handsome Wyatt recognized him right back.

"Cawdor!" The name ripped like an oath from Wyatt's throat.

Ryan brought up the Steyr and leveled it. Before he could get the man in the open sights, the M-60 gunner opened up, unleashing pure, hot lead hell on the rooftop. The one-eyed man went to ground.

The bullets chopped into the roofline and sprayed wood fragments into the air. Before they stopped, another rocket-launched round slammed into the hotel. The building shivered like a palsied dog during a cold bath.

"They come," Jak said. "More sec men, more clowns in building."

Ryan avoided the front of the building, which was still taking a barrage of fire. He peered into the alley, spotting one of the pickups pulling to a stop to disgorge more of the jackers. They blew the door below with plas ex and forced their way inside. The rooftop was fast becoming a no-man's-land that was going to be filled with chilling.

"Cawdor!" Wyatt screamed from below. "Why don't you come out and play, you one-eyed bastard!"

The big circus wag ground gears out in the street, bullets pinging from its metallic skin.

Ryan looked at Jak. "Get that rope ready. We're going to need it."

The albino nodded, then strapped his gear around him. He coiled the end of the hundred-foot rope they'd scavenged from the hotel's stockrooms around his waist, then took a running start at the side of the building.

Blessed with uncanny acrobatic skills and a sense of balance, the albino sailed across the intervening gap to the next building nearly twenty feet away. With the hotel being the tallest structure in Hazard, the building next to it was only two stories tall.

Ryan watched Jak drop onto the opposite rooftop, landing lithely and rolling to keep from injuring himself. The albino was up in seconds, pulling the slack out of the rope as Dean fed it through to keep it clear.

"The wag in the alley?" J.B. asked.

Ryan nodded. "We make a run for the horses Dean and Jak stashed, they're going to hand us our heads."

Blasterfire sounded from inside the hotel, letting Ryan know the two groups had found another battleground.

"Go!" Jak called, twanging the rope to show that he had it taut.

Even with him tying it to the other side of the building below, the descent grade was steep.

"Cawdor!" Wyatt shouted again. "We got an account to settle up."

"Over here!" someone yelled from below. "They're trying to get off the building!"

"Mildred," Ryan growled.

The woman nodded and ran over to the side of the building facing the alley. She took careful aim with the ZKR 551 target pistol and began to bang off shots.

Ryan went to the front of the building, scouting for the wag with the rocket launcher. He spotted it with difficulty, but watched Wyatt waving it forward.

Settling in behind the sights of the Steyr, Ryan shot through the wag's front tires. The vehicle went out of control and slammed into the front of the general store, coasting through the main window. The men aboard scattered at once, bailing out with their equipment. Ryan sighted on the man carrying the rocket launcher and put him down with a bullet between his shoulder blades that ripped through the front of his chest.

His next rounds were directed at the RPG-7. At least one of the rifle bullets ricocheted off the rocket launcher before another jacker grabbed it and hauled it to safety.

"Fireblast!" Ryan cursed. He turned the Steyr on the circus wag and banged off two rounds that kicked the open door against Wyatt. The man was completely hidden by the armored door—except for the hand on the door.

Ryan grinned coldly, then sighted through the scope. A moment after he squeezed the trigger, he saw blood spray from the jacker leader's hand.

Wyatt withdrew into the cab of the circus wag, screaming in pain and rage.

"Handsome!" Ryan yelled over the rooftop. "You might want to think about coming up against me again. You're running out of fingers, you stupe bastard!" He pushed up from the roof and ran to the alley side. "Get across the rope, Dean. You can help some of the others on the other side."

His son nodded, then wrapped a leather thong

around the rope and jumped over the side. The rope bowed with his weight, but the thong slid freely.

"Doc goes next," Ryan said as Dean hit the rooftop, cradled partially by Jak. "Then Mildred, Albert, Krysty, J.B. I'll bring up the rear."

"My dear Ryan," Doc started, gazing across the expanse between the two buildings, "truly I wish you thought of another—"

"Get on with it, Doc. You're going to get someone chilled by hesitating."

The old man wrapped his leather thong around the rope, then leaped over the side with a harsh yell of "Geronimo!"

"A little more quiet would have helped," J.B. said.

The other companions and the dwarf quickly slid along the rope, as well.

Just as Krysty swung out over the alley, the first of the jackers reached the rooftop. The man opened up with his blaster, slamming bullets into the rain barrels atop the roof. Ryan threw himself to one side, then swept up the SIG-Sauer from his hip. He drilled the man three times, dropping him to his back.

"Blow the building," Ryan told J.B.

The Armorer nodded and jerked the radio-controlled device from his jacket pocket. He flicked off the plastic protective cover, then depressed the plunger.

The roar of the erupting plas-ex charges was deafening in spite of the calliope music still sounding in the street below, and the wild bursts of blasterfire.

The hotel trembled, swaying far more than Ryan had figured probable with the amount they had used for the demolition work.

For a moment he was certain they had managed to blow themselves up when a huge section of the rooftop collapsed in the center of the hotel. Then the rumbling died away.

J.B. took the rope and leaped across the alley, with Ryan following almost right on his heels. They hit the other rooftop almost at the same time, letting go to drop the final distance.

Ryan pushed himself to his feet, ignoring the painful scrapes he'd gotten on the side of his face and along one arm. He fisted the Steyr and ran for the side of the building facing the hotel. Broken glass and debris from the structure littered the rooftop they stood on. Fires raged inside the building, licking at the gaily patterned curtains.

At the side of the building, he looked down and found the small wag still sitting below. One of the men was down, covered by a section of the building that had popped his skull like an overripe tomato blistered by the sun. The driver struggled to get out from under the debris.

Ryan brought the Steyr to his shoulder and shot the man through the head. J.B. burned down a couple of stragglers trying to recover from the blasts. Shouldering the Steyr, Ryan slipped his panga free. "Get Jak to pull the rope to the other side of the building. I'll get the wag, bring it around over there and we can board."

"I'll give what cover I can."

Ryan slashed the panga through the rope, watching the free end jump away as he held on to the other end. He leaped upward and grabbed a fresh hold. The twenty-foot span across the alley would put him closer to the ground as the rope dropped.

He leaped over the edge of the building and swung toward the hotel. Lifting his feet, he caught himself parallel to the side of the hotel, then dropped to the ground.

Fisting the SIG-Sauer, he sprinted to the wag and yanked the dead driver from behind the wheel. Seating himself, he pressed the starter button patched onto the console in front of him.

The engine turned sluggishly at first, then caught. It gave a throaty roar, then he let out the clutch. Debris fell away from the wag. Men poured out of the hotel behind him, dust covered and injured. From the looks of things, the jackers were winning over Kirkland's sec forces.

Ryan roared around the building, handling the wag with brute strength across the ruts. A wag came at him from the left, catching him from his blind side. It rammed into the pickup, carrying enough weight and speed to lift Ryan's wag from the ground for a moment.

The driver of the other vehicle fed more power to his machine, a reconditioned jeep that had seen hard times.

Ryan drew the SIG-Sauer and blasted the man from almost point-blank range. The bullet blew the back of the jacker's head out in a gush of brains. Metal shrieked as Ryan swerved around the corner and found his friends taking up positions in the alley.

J.B. and Jak climbed onto the wag's running boards and shoved the rest of the debris out the back. The Armorer took the shotgun seat while the others piled in back.

Krysty sat behind Ryan, one hand touching his neck.

Ryan took the shortest course out of the ville, putting the accelerator to the floor. The wag's engine sent them surging forward.

"My dear Ryan," Doc called from the back, "I am afraid we have not quite escaped the ville without notice."

Ryan had to glance over his shoulder, as the wag had no mirrors. He spotted the wag pulling into their dust trail. Jak and Krysty had already opened up on the vehicle, with Dean joining in a heartbeat later. But it was Mildred with her steady hands and keen eye that put a bullet through the driver's chest.

The trailing wag slewed sideways, giving up the chase.

Ryan kept his attention on the narrow, twisting road. With luck they would be back at the redoubt in under an hour. He glanced back at the ville one last time, seeing how the streamers of black smoke were gathering above it.

"That ville," Doc announced, "was aptly named."

"No," Dean stated. "Needs a new name. Longer than the original. Mebbe call it Hazardous."

Doc laughed delightedly. "Ah, young Master

Cawdor, your education has not been for naught, has it?''

Ryan ignored the merriment in the back. The redoubt was tucked away so that most people couldn't find it. But Handsome Wyatt had been with War Wag One and the Trader when they had looked for nothing else.

And he had to wonder if Hazard had been the only thing to bring the man to the area.

Chapter Eighteen

For a time Ryan didn't think the wag would have enough gas in it to take them to the redoubt. The needle, if it was accurate, hovered just above the quarter-tank mark and stayed there. But it was the road that finally gave out, getting passable only on foot or by horseback.

Four miles out from the redoubt by estimation, he pulled the wag over to the side. The steep grade allowed them to easily tip the wag into the gully below. They spent a few minutes gathering brush to cover it up, hacking it free with their knives.

"Dust line headed this way," J.B. called. He squatted farther up the hill, binoculars to his glasses.

"Didn't figure it would take them long to catch up," Ryan said. "How far out?"

"Four miles, mebbe five. The wind's blowing this way, so it might actually be a little ahead of them."

"Are you sure it's them?" Ryan checked his gear. The ammo J.B. had scavenged from Tinker Phillips's gun shop had been split up on the way over.

"Still got balloons tied to the bastard circus wag," J.B. said laconically.

"Thought all be bust in firefight," Jak said.

"Such are the vagaries and whims of the gods," Doc stated.

"Got no time to waste," Ryan said, feeling the miles evaporate between them and the wolves chasing at their heels. "Jak, Dean, take point. Figure we're operating on condition green and nothing's going to be ahead of us."

Both boys hurried ahead, already knowing where the redoubt was because they were in familiar territory.

"Doc, you and the short man go next. Albert, if you can't keep up, you can't go. And Doc, if I see you trying to carry him this time, I'm going to shoot you myself."

The old man fired off a snappy salute. Albert set himself to match Doc's pace.

"Mildred, you and Krysty go next. Walk a secondary drag. J.B. and I will bring up the rear a couple hundred yards behind. If we have to, mebbe we can buy some time."

THE FOUR MILES WENT quickly as they followed the sun to the west. Even Albert was able to stay the course.

Ryan watched the dust cloud trailing them draw closer, pausing now and again to study Handsome Wyatt's collection of jackers as they milled around where the road ended.

"More like jackals than jackers," J.B. commented as they crouched in the brush farther up the rough terrain than the wags were. "Running around in packs."

"Dangerous enough, though," Ryan said. "There's some who would say we were cut of the same cloth as those people back there. And like Kirkland."

"Mebbe. But we know where the difference is. You've seen the difference between a pack of jackals and a pack of wolves, Ryan," the Armorer said. "Jackals, hell, they'll kill just for sport. But a wolf pack, they hunt for food, shelter and some form of security. That's the way of the wolf. And that's the way Trader taught us. Lot of difference between a wolf and a jackal."

Ryan nodded, knowing it was true. "Hooray for the difference, but let's put some more distance in there, too." He turned and faded back into the brush.

LESS THAN FIVE MINUTES later, Ryan watched a band of jackers peel away from the wags. He counted twenty-three men in all, counting Wyatt, who had one hand bundled up in bandages.

"No way that bastard stupe finished raiding Hazard before he came after us," J.B. said.

"Kirkland's people could have managed to dig the jackers back out of the ville," Ryan replied.

"You really think that happened?"

"No."

J.B. shook his head. "So that means he's burning up our backtrail looking for a quick dose of get-even."

"Mebbe. And mebbe he talked to somebody about that anesthetic we brought in," Ryan said. "Could be he figures we found a major stockpile."

"Man's making a big mistake leaving those wags with so few guards."

"Yeah. Well, let's just make sure we don't make any right along with him. The sooner we get back to that mat-trans unit, the sooner we're out of here."

RYAN HAD TO SLOW a little to give his friends the room they needed to reach the redoubt ahead of him and J.B. If the Armorer noticed that he was hanging back, he didn't say anything.

But the decrease in speed allowed the jackers to draw closer.

"Going to be a near thing," J.B. said.

"Yeah, but we're on the downhill side of it now." Ryan kept moving, and kept his attention spread out across the forest. The grade was gradual now, sliding into the valley where the redoubt was housed. More than anything, he needed sleep. Fatigue ate into his bones and joints like acid rain.

KRYSTY STEPPED into the small stream and followed it against the current to the base of the towering silver-leafed maple the companions had chosen as a marker to remember the trail. She carried her .38 in her fist. Liberty and his gang might no longer be a threat in the area, but they had spotted mutated beasts in the forest.

Jak and Dean were far ahead of her. She glanced back in Ryan's direction, but didn't see him or J.B.

"They're okay," Mildred said quietly. "Would have been shooting if they hadn't been."

Krysty nodded. Her sentient hair coiled tight

against her scalp. Perhaps it was from the cold, and maybe even from the dread of the coming jump. A trip through a mat-trans chamber was never any of the companions' idea of a good time.

She stepped out of the stream under the maple and walked along the bank. Her wet socks reminded her of the holes she had meant to have mended while in Hazard. Then she remembered that there were a few extra socks from that mall in the Carolinas where they'd picked up some necessities.

A little farther on, she found Doc and Albert waiting beside the stream. Frogs croaked in the wide spillway beneath moss-encrusted boulders towering thirty feet above the ground.

The dwarf wheezed hard, coughing a little as he tried to regain his breath. He excused himself in a squeaky voice as the two women approached.

"You did good, little man," Mildred complimented. "This is rough country."

"Been a rough life," Albert wheezed. "Had to get hard or die." He glanced around. "How much farther?"

"We're here," Krysty answered.

Albert appeared puzzled. "You've got to be joking." He waved at the rock and trees surrounding them. "This is a box canyon. Those jackers following us will leave our corpses out here for the animals."

"We won't be here by the time they get here," Dean said. He stood on a shelf of rock twenty feet up the rock face. His Browning Hi-Power blaster was in his hand.

Krysty noted with satisfaction that the hammer on the blaster wasn't rolled back into the ready position.

Five minutes later J.B. and Ryan joined the group. "They're still behind us," the one-eyed man said. "Be here in a couple minutes."

Even now, with her mutie sensitive hearing, Krysty could pick up the sounds of men talking and breaking through the brush. They were careful men and didn't make as much noise as most, but if a listener knew what to listen for, the sounds were evident.

"Jak," Ryan said, "take us in. Condition yellow. Light up a torch. Krysty, you take up a torch, too. Make sure we can see where we're headed."

Krysty followed Mildred, climbing up onto the rock to a narrow shelf just below where Jak and Dean stood. Both the boys had already disappeared into the crack that sundered the wall of rock from top to bottom.

There had been a tunnel at one time, Krysty knew, but it had most likely caved in after the nukecaust. However, even as warped nature had taken away, it had also provided in the form of the crack that ran deep into the heart of the hill.

Krysty turned sideways and eased into the crack. The dim sunlight, already blunted by the leafy canopy overhead, darkened quickly to full black. She felt her way along cautiously, using her mutie senses, as well as her hands and feet.

"When those jackers get here," Albert said, "all they're going to have to do is cover us over."

"My dear, diminutive friend," Doc said confidently, "trust in us and fear not. For this path truly is our salvation from this grievous situation we currently find ourselves embroiled in."

"Still feel bad not knowing where we're headed," the dwarf replied.

Krysty felt along the wall, glancing back in time to catch sight of Ryan filing into the crack behind her. A cool wind breezed from the depths below.

Another dozen steps and the constricting crack opened up. Light flared in front of her as Jak cracked a self-light and ignited the oil-based torch they had set up after their arrival. The redoubt hadn't been stocked much in the supply department. Everywhere they had looked, there had been signs of looting and scavengers who had known their business. They had, however, managed to find several useful items. A collection of skeletons remained below, three of them with their skulls bashed in.

"Krysty," Jak called, holding out another torch. The light from the one he carried lent a yellow parchment color to his features.

Krysty took the torch and slipped a self-light from her pocket. She cracked it to life with her thumbnail, and the sulfurous fumes flooded her nostrils. She applied it to the oil-soaked material of the torch, and the warm flame crawled all over the sheet remnant they had used.

The trail wound down again, going through a natural archway so low all had to duck except Albert. Thirty yards farther on, the crack led into a concrete arm of the redoubt. The first glimpse of the metal housing occurred when the lantern's light gleamed from the opening ahead.

Jak made the short drop into the access tunnel. He lifted his torch high to illuminate the interior.

Krysty scanned the access tunnel, matching what she saw with what the companions had left behind only a few days earlier. Debris lay scattered across the concrete floor, covering the metal tracks laid in grooves in some places. Nearly twenty feet across and almost that in height, the tunnel had to have been part of the supply zones back before the nukecaust.

Krysty clambered into the tunnel and stood by the opening to light the way for J.B. and Ryan while Jak went on ahead. They wound through the long tunnel, following a sharper grade as it continued to go underground. At the end of it, they found the large freight elevator they had used to ascend.

Energized by nuclear power, the redoubt had survived the nukecaust and the hundred-odd years that had followed skydark, with every indication that it would continue functioning for hundreds more.

If they had found the redoubt before it had been gutted, Krysty knew it would have been a great find, the kind of find that had first set the Trader in business all those years ago.

The companions assembled in the elevator. J.B. manned the controls.

"Everybody's on condition red," Ryan said. "Wyatt and his jackers might find their way into the redoubt, as well, and we don't know that this place is still empty. Keep your blasters out, but be sure you know what you're aiming at before you squeeze the trigger.'' He glanced at Krysty.

She shook her head, letting him know her mutie senses hadn't detected anything. The redoubt felt as lifeless as a crypt.

"All right, J.B., let's go."

The Armorer hit the control panel, choosing the level indicator for the lowest section of the redoubt. The doors closed, taking their time and squealing in protest. Despite having nuclear power that would last for centuries, regular maintenance had been missing for a long time.

After the long series of earsplitting screeches, the doors closed. Enclosed within the elevator cage, the smoke from the two torches quickly pooled against the ceiling, forming a black cloud.

The elevator dropped through the bowels of the earth.

Albert moaned and dropped to his knees.

"What's wrong, friend Albert?" Doc asked, bending to put a hand to the little man's shoulders.

"Sick," the dwarf gasped. Then he threw up. "Feels like I'm falling, but I see the floor right here."

"This is your first time with an elevator, then," Doc said.

Albert's shoulders heaved again as he threw up once more.

Krysty took a step away. Luckily the freight elevator was large enough none of them were too close together.

"Read about elevators before," Albert groaned.

"Never saw one until today. Never want to see one again."

Jak laughed, a short, harsh bark of sound. "Think elevator bad? Wait till mat-trans."

The elevator cage shrilled to a jerky stop, metal grinding against metal. Without some kind of overhaul, Krysty doubted that it would last more than a few more trips to the surface and back.

"Everybody alert," Ryan ordered.

The companions tramped through the dust, Doc reaching down to hold the back of the dwarf's jacket to keep him upright. At least Albert's nausea seemed to be gone for the moment even if he hadn't gotten his land legs back.

Krysty probed the darkness with her mutie senses. Between her and Jak, she knew most of anything that might be waiting for them in the darkness would be caught.

The albino teen hugged the walls, following the blue line that marked the floor under the layers of dust. Every now and again he had to scuff his foot across the floor to make certain the line was still there. He correlated those with the marks put on the wall by the companions when they had come through the first time.

"What is this place, Doc?" Albert asked in a voice not much above a whisper.

"A long time ago," Doc said, "well before sky-dark even, there was a government entity that operated under the aggrandized nomenclature of the Totality Concept. They constructed these redoubts, and stocked them with myriad things. The mat-trans unit that we are seeking here was developed by a further division of secrets called Overproject Whisper under the code name Cerberus.''

"Heard of Cerberus before,'' the little man said. "Some kind of three-headed mutie dog supposedly watching over hell. Called it Hades. The Greeks made up all the stories.''

"That is correct. And as it turns out, the name was most aptly placed, because this Cerberus does open unto the very jaws of hell.''

"There's one thing I always found curious about the Greeks' stories,'' Albert said.

"What's that, dear fellow?''

"They wrote about this hell like it was some kind of bad place.''

"Yes.''

"But, Doc, none of it really seemed as bad as what Deathlands turned out to be.''

There was silence for a time. "My friend,'' Doc said gravely, "I believe that is because a healthy mind could not really envision how badly things could go for the human race once something like this happened.''

Then Jak's torch lit up the door ahead of them. The albino keyed in the code, and the vanadium door slid open with near silent shushes. The friends cast aside their torches, as the redoubt was awash with cool fluorescent light.

Jak led the way inside, and they followed a twisting corridor, avoiding the other empty rooms they had found their first time through. From the way most of the rooms had been systematically stripped,

Ryan and J.B. had speculated that the military personnel who had survived the nukecaust had evacuated the structure at some point. But what had become of them remained a mystery, like so many other things after the world had died.

The end of the corridor opened into a large room that contained the mat-trans unit. The chamber was hexagonally shaped, and metal disks set in the floor and ceiling glowed with a pulsating light. Thick armaglass walls the color of fresh-cut jade shut them off from the mat-trans unit.

"What is that?" Albert asked.

"That," Doc said dryly, "is the very maw of perdition like none of you have ever seen, my little friend."

"Oh."

Krysty watched the dwarf and felt sorry for him. Doc could have gone on and elaborated more about what was going to happen to him once the transfer sequence was activated, but it would only have been cruel. When staying wasn't an option, a person had to go. Krysty had gotten that from her Mother Sonja.

"Everybody in," Ryan ordered after hurrying forward to open the door.

The companions filed into the gateway and stripped off their gear, making themselves as comfortable as they could across the glowing metal disks set into the floor.

"Is this another elevator, Doc?" Albert's voice held worry now, but he stripped off his blasters and the pack he carried.

"No," the old man said, stretching himself out

prone. "I assure you, this grim piece of business is in nowise nearly as comforting as an elevator ride. Settle down as best you can, friend, because life as you know it—for a time—shall be over."

Albert glanced back through the jade armaglass walls. "Mebbe we should try to find another way, then."

"There is no other way," Mildred snapped.

Krysty knew the woman wasn't angry with Albert, just nervous about the upcoming jump.

"We came in the only way out," Krysty said, leaning in close to Ryan. Sometimes it helped if she touched her lover before they went under the mattrans effects. Even then, she hardly ever woke up next to him.

Albert sat, stretching his legs before him as he put his back to the armaglass wall.

Ryan shut the door to begin the jump, then hurried to Krysty's side. The metal disks in the floor and ceiling glowed more brightly, and a fine mist descended from the ceiling.

Krysty twined her fingers in Ryan's. "Hope you have pleasant dreams, lover."

"Or at least," Ryan said, "ones that aren't too bad."

Nightmares and nausea seemed to be the two most prevalent byproducts brought about by the jumps. Rarely had the companions avoided them.

As she breathed in her first full, deep breath of the mist-laden air, Krysty's brains seemed to turn into oatmeal, dulling her mutie senses with a sensation of being suffocated.

Doc's voice singsonged from the corner, filled with a strength and vigor that was surprising. ''Here we go, my friends. Can you envision some future when we can look back, and see our alternate possibilities—if we chose this or that option? Could we ever say 'two roads diverged in a wood, and I—I took the one less traveled by.' I think Robert Frost summed up our present state quite well. Don't you?''

''Don't you?''

''Don't you?''

And as Doc's words seemed to hang in the air, growing more and more indistinct with each echo, Krysty knew the jump had begun. There was no saving them from the nightmares now.

Chapter Nineteen

"A man lives long enough and slows down his life," the Trader was saying, "he's going to have a lot of regrets."

In the jump dream, Ryan walked with the older man. The Trader carried his Armalite and hacked and coughed just the way Ryan remembered. Only the one-eyed man knew almost for a fact that the Trader was nowhere around Hazard, and probably nowhere near around where they were jumping to.

He scanned the hostile terrain they were in, all rad-blasted and shooting up twisted trees from a ground that looked like burned glass. He couldn't say that he'd ever been to such a place, but it didn't seem too far from reality for Deathlands.

The next couple steps, though, brought them to the edge of a thickly wooded area that looked like something out of a painting Doc had once shown them. The trees stood straight and tall, reaching up into the white fleecy clouds that had taken the place of the rad-dust-filled clouds that had hovered overhead earlier. Those had been purple and cancerous, greenish around the edges.

"I don't have any regrets," Ryan said.

The Trader shrugged and came to a stop, looking

out over the forest. "I know you don't think you do now, but you're getting long in the tooth."

A boy's face peered through the branches. Innocence gleamed in his bright, impossibly blue eyes, followed by a shy smile that promised mischief. Ryan figured the boy hadn't seen ten years yet, and probably hadn't been past the forest's edge.

"You're older than I am, Trader," Ryan said. "Mebbe you got regrets."

The man shook his head. "No regrets for me. Did everything in my life that I set out to do. Ain't the same with you."

Ryan's vision misted red as his anger took him. "How do you figure that?"

The boy across the glade stepped into the open. And the full impossibility of him stepped into Ryan's view. From the waist up, the boy looked totally norm, but from the waist down he was all horse. His upper body swayed sinuously as his lower four legs moved him forward. He darted forward in a quick thumping of unshod hooves, like he was going to come right up to Ryan and the Trader. Then he stopped, still a dozen feet away, and galloped back to the tree line.

"Play?" he asked in a melodious voice.

"Got no time to play," Trader growled. "Go away, boy, you're bothering me."

Two other centaurs came from the woods, one male and one female, her pendulous breasts swinging freely. The male carried a bow with an arrow already set to string. The female carried a spear with a long blade set on the other end.

"You didn't answer my question, Trader."

The man swung around on Ryan and caught him with a backhanded slap that sent the one-eyed man crashing to the ground. Black comets swirled in Ryan's vision, bouncing crazily off each other.

"Don't you be getting uppity with me," Trader snarled. "I made you who you are. I can damn sure unmake you—make you a follower, or a lone wolf."

Ryan forced himself not to draw the SIG-Sauer. After he'd located the Trader, they'd had some harsh words between them, but nothing like this. "Okay, Trader. Sorry. Mebbe I was out of line."

"You were out of line," Trader agreed, "and you're never going to be in line again. You want to know why?"

"Sure." Ryan went along with the dream, hoping it would end soon.

He walked with the Trader again, threading through the forest. Then the terrain shifted, and the Trader walked without concern across the ocean that stretched beneath him.

Ryan followed, not as able to walk on the water as his companion. His boots sunk ankle deep into the emerald ocean.

"It's because of your son," Trader said. "Because of Dean that you'll never be without regrets. Having children does something to a man. Takes his edge off, takes away his zest for life and the unexpected that makes him the adventurer he's supposed to be. And having children replaces those things with fear. Lock, stock and barrel, and you better bastard believe it."

"Dean's making me stronger in some ways," Ryan argued.

Trader shot him a murderous glance. "You daring disrespect my view, you worthless baron-get whelp?"

Ryan forced out a no. But he noticed that his disagreement with the Trader caused him to sink in the ocean up past his shins. The going got tougher as he fought the water. Whatever surface he walked on beneath the water also felt more spongy.

"Good, because I don't want to see you drown out here, Ryan. Truly I don't. I looked after your ass for a number of years, and I don't like to see all that time go to waste."

Ryan struggled to keep up with the older man, losing nearly half a step. And there was no end of the ocean in sight.

"Dean's going to pull you down," Trader went on. "You're going to want more for the boy than you'd want for yourself. A man knows his own limitations, knows the hardships he can handle. Always makes the wrong call when he tries raising children. That's woman's work."

Ryan knew the real Trader didn't feel like that. Not exactly. But the voice carried a timbre of truth with it.

"You'd been better off if the boy had been stillborn," Trader said. "You're always going to be risking what you have to make a better shake for Dean. And for what? Paying penance for a quick roll in the hay with that slut Sharona? Man should put a higher price on his future than that."

The Trader was out of reach now, and the ocean sucked at Ryan's boots.

"That's not true," Ryan yelled. The ocean drank him down, swallowing him up to his hips. "Dean can carry his own weight." Suddenly he couldn't move forward anymore.

The Trader turned and put his hands on his hips. "Look at you now, Ryan. You're about to be in over your bastard head, and you can't even admit it. You used to be more pragmatic than that."

"Fuck you!" Ryan exploded, trying to pull himself through the chest-high water. "You aren't Trader! Trader wouldn't say anything like that!" He struggled now, trying to keep his head above water.

"Dean's just Sharona's way of dragging you down even after she's caught the last train to the coast herself," Trader said.

The water closed over Ryan's head. He fought clear of it with difficulty, smashing his arms against the ocean. But he knew the sustained effort would exhaust him in short order.

Then something closed around his crotch and yanked him down. Underwater now, he glanced down to see what had hold of him, surprised he didn't feel claws or teeth. Some of the mutie fishes living in the rad-blasted oceans were spun right out of nightmare.

Only it wasn't a mutie fish or a water monster that held him. It was Sharona Carson, the dead mother of Dean.

She was as Ryan remembered in her better days, golden haired and looking as beautiful as any woman could want to be. She wore a purple diaphanous gown that hugged her curves and clung to her breasts.

Before Ryan knew it, he was naked. Sharona had hold of his erection, continuing to pull him down into the waiting darkness. Ryan's lungs ballooned up inside his chest, threatening to explode. He reached for her wrist, trying to find a pressure point.

Only this Sharona's wrist was as hard and as slick as any sec droid's. She held him effortlessly in one hand.

"Coming to stay with me this time, Ryan. We'll talk about Dean. You'll like that, won't you?"

Weak now and barely able to move, Ryan felt his senses swirling. But he saw Sharona's mouth open, saw her starting to take his hardness in. Her teeth glinted like diamonds, edged like razors.

Ryan screamed a denial, and the word took form in the shape of an explosion of bubbles around him. His last breath left his body as he grabbed Sharona by the hair and tried in vain to keep her razored mouth back.

She bit down.

ALBERT LOOKED AROUND, surprised to find himself in a cave. "Doc?"

There was no answer.

The cave in front of him seemed to stretch on like some dark, ugly throat. Wind blew its fetid breath over him from somewhere ahead, carrying with it the stench of sulfurous farts.

He turned and tried to go back, but all he found

was solid rock blocking his way. He didn't understand that at all. It was funny that he couldn't remember waking up, walking out of the mat-trans unit. But it wasn't humorous.

The fetid wind continued to blow over him, feeling like it was drying him out. He guessed that after a couple hours of standing around in it, a man might begin to resemble a hunk of jerked beef.

He drew his .38s and called out for Doc again. All he heard was the distant rolling thunder of his own voice. Having no other choice, he went forward through the cave.

Light gleamed all around. At first he thought the walls were rad-blasted and he was walking into certain death, but then he saw that lichens gathered on the rough stone surfaces. It was their internal glow that lighted the way.

The tunnel continued down, and the wind grew hotter. Albert sweated profusely. His clothes were soaking wet before he figured he'd gone half a mile.

Then the path he followed leveled out and widened, opening onto a big cave that he couldn't see across. A small dock jutted for a short distance into the calm black water, hewed of logs that had to have been carried a long way because Albert saw no trees nearby.

Beside the dock was a long, narrow boat, whose ends rose up in five-foot-tall spires that turned into carved goat's horns.

Because of the distance, Albert wasn't sure if he really saw movement in the boat. But it looked like one shadow shifted slightly.

Then a self-light flared to life, held in a bony, spectral claw. It burned, creating a nimbus of light that hurt the dwarf's eyes even at the distance. The man holding the self-light wore a long purple robe that seemed mottled with black mushrooms that grew out of it.

"Are you coming, Albert?" The voice sounded like something from the last gasp of a grave.

The robed figure put the self-light to a lantern hanging from the boat spire behind it. The wick caught, flaring up like it had been dry for days, before the heat pulled the oil through the strands. Then the robed figure threw the self-light onto the dark water of the underground river.

Albert could see that it was a river now, could see bits of flotsam along the left. With the lantern light going now, he also saw they were bits and pieces of corpses. An arm floated by, missing three fingers and whose stubs showed they had been gnawed off by some kind of animal.

"No, I'm not coming," Albert replied.

"Stay there and you'll die," the robed figure whispered.

"And if I go with you?" Albert demanded.

"Oh, you'll still die." The robed figure chuckled, and it was the sound of dry bones rubbing together. "But it'll be later."

"Fuck you," Albert said, pointing his blasters at the boatman. "You can't make me go."

"No." The boatman settled the hurricane glass over the lantern. It was tinted a light blue, the color of a vein beneath a light covering of flesh. And it was in the shape of a fat-bodied spider, with ruby-colored mandibles protruding from its fierce mouth. With the wick burning and shifting inside it, the legs looked as if they were moving. "But I can make you stay here." He picked up a long pole made up of what looked like shin bones. "Mebbe it's worse than what you think might be up ahead."

Albert turned as the earth shivered behind him. Without warning, the smooth slope of the short beach leading to the river ruptured in dozens of places. Things that might have once been human surged up from the ground.

Lifting a blaster, Albert fired at the nearest one, expecting to see the .38 load knock the thing on its butt. Instead, a puff of dust rose from the thing's chest, and it kept coming.

"Your choice," the boatman declared. "Mebbe you should think about the boat less traveled by." The dry bones laughter echoed mockingly throughout the huge cave.

Greenish saliva dripping with maggots crusted the undead creatures' mouths as they came for Albert. Their chests were alive with eel things that looked every bit as hungry as their hosts.

Albert fired both .38s empty, but the flying lead didn't slow the undead things at all.

"Time grows short, Albert. You have to go to the lady in the lake if you want to survive."

Abandoning his position, Albert raced for the boat, his boots thudding against the hewed logs. The boatman had already pushed it out into the current, so he had to leap to get there.

"Who are you and what the hell is this place?" Albert demanded breathlessly. His hands shook as he struggled to reload his weapons. He scanned the beach anxiously, watching the undead things walk into the water. He shivered uncontrollably, thinking how the creatures might walk out under the water and gain on the slowly drifting boat.

"My name is Bob," the boatman said, "and hell is precisely what this is."

"Where are the others?" Albert demanded as he snapped the cylinders closed on the .38s.

"There are no others," Bob answered. "You are the only one." He turned his tattered face toward the center of the river.

"What are you doing here?"

"Me? Why I was scheduled to pick you up. I assure you, I had much better things to do. Napoleon was all set to conquer Europe again, but he didn't know Joan of Arc had risen once more to lead William's troops into battle. Or that General Custer had crossed the Atlantic after winning at the Battle of Little Bighorn to help the Germans."

Listening to the boatman speak made Albert's head hurt. Some of what the robed man said made sense, but it was all jumbled up in there, as well. He pointed his blasters at the boatman. "You say you're taking me to see the lady in the lake."

"Yes." Bob regarded him calmly. "That is your destiny. It has always been your destiny."

"I don't know a lady in the lake."

"Albert, please, you must calm down."

"I am calm." But Albert knew he was lying because his hands shook as he held the .38s.

Abruptly the spider-shaped hurricane glass pulled free of the lantern, somehow keeping the burning wick trapped inside it. The glass spider with its belly full of fire climbed down the spire and started along the edge of the boat for Albert.

"Now see," Bob said irritably, "you've gotten Morris upset again. Put those bastard guns away or he might bite you."

Instead, Albert turned the blasters on the glass spider and ripped off two shots. Both of them hit the spider but ricocheted off.

"You can't harm it," the boatman said. "Remember? Or mebbe you don't remember anything at all."

Albert shook his head in disbelief.

"Every time it gets harder for you," the boatman stated. "I worry about you when you're gone." He raised his voice, but it was only a stronger, sibilant whisper. "Morris, leave him be."

The glass spider froze, glinting cobalt blue crystalline. It stood up on its back four legs and raised the front four as if scenting the sulfurous air. Reluctantly it began the journey back to the lantern base.

"I want to go back with the others," Albert said. "And if you can't arrange that, I want to go back to Hazard. At least there I understand things."

"Everything here will be made clear soon," Bob said in a gentle tone. He continued poling, pushing them out into the center of the river.

"Who is the lady in the lake?" Albert asked.

Even though he knew his blasters were pretty much useless, he found he couldn't holster them. The idea of going through this with empty hands turned his stomach. Sweat dripped from his face, and he realized that some of the heat he was feeling came from the river water.

More body parts drifted by, some of them bumping briefly against the boat with soft thuds before floating on. There were, he saw, a great number of internal pieces now, as well as body parts. Gobby masses of intestines floated past, looking like obscene jellyfish. Chitin-covered insects clung to them like they were life rafts.

"To know her is to love her," Bob said with a sigh. "I know I do."

"What does she want with me?"

Bob turned his rad-blasted face to Albert. "I don't know. Honestly. The whole concept of her needing you is beyond me. I never thought she did. And I don't think you've fooled her into thinking you care for her." He poled once more, waited a moment, then put his pole in front of them. "Well, here we are."

The boat stopped, cresting the gentle current of the slow-moving river.

"Here we are where?" Albert asked. He looked all around the boat, seeing only the black water. But the thought of the undead corpses walking along the bottom unnerved him.

"Where she is," Bob answered. "The lady in the lake."

"How deep is the water here?"

Bob took a moment to think about the question, then glanced at the glass spider. "Morris, do you know?"

The glass spider did some quick arithmetic on its four front glass legs, then twisted toward the boatman. The legs flew in quick answer.

"About ninety feet, give or take two or three," Bob replied.

"Your pole isn't that long," Albert argued.

"A gentleman doesn't talk about the length of another gentleman's pole." Bob the boatman drew himself up to his full, tall, thin height and wrapped his robes more tightly around him as if incensed.

"You can't have been touching bottom all the way to pole us out here."

Bob drew the pole up, displaying the cracked but polished collection of shinbones that made it up. "Albert, haven't you ever noticed that no matter how tall or short a man is, his legs always touch the ground? The pole, just because it is a pole, has not lost that ability."

To Albert that made no sense. Without warning, nausea seized him again, feeling like it had back in the elevator in the redoubt. He dropped his .38s and fell to his knees, retching as he clung to the side of the boat.

The water roiled in front of him, tossing the gobby chunks he'd just spit up back into the boat and over him. When they landed, they started running around, forming tails and legs.

"She's coming!" Bob cried in his thin, dry voice. "The lady of the lake is coming!"

"This is a river," Albert argued, "not a lake." Somehow it seemed important to point that out. "Shouldn't she be called the lady of the river?"

Before Bob could answer, a typhoon suddenly took shape beside the boat, erupting from the water. Gory parts of corpses and whole bodies twisted up in a column of water that shot over twenty feet into the air. A woman formed of the water, as black as ebony and smooth as marble. Her eyes were green rot scraped from a mildewed coffin, and her teeth as hard and thick as tombstones.

Still, she was beautiful when she smiled.

She reached for Albert, lifting him gently from the boat. At first her watery grip felt soothing and warm, like a bed in the middle of winter.

Then the flesh began to melt from his bones as the acid ate into him.

Chapter Twenty

"You've gone far from your roots, Krysty. Far, far away. You may never become at home again. Just a rolling stone, and rolling stones gather no moss. No more gathering ye rosebuds as ye may."

Krysty Wroth walked through the garden and felt sick to her stomach. Everywhere she walked, all the green and growing things died. She halted and looked back along the path of destruction she had made through the garden.

"Who are you?" she demanded.

The voice belonged to a female, but that was all she was certain about. And the words were hauntingly familiar.

Ryan and the others walked ahead of her, easily within hailing distance, but Krysty chose not to call out to them. They walked in formation, the way Ryan would have ordered them to, but no way would she have been walking drag at his request. Not unless Ryan or J.B. was severely wounded. They all appeared healthy. Where they walked, the grass didn't die beneath their feet.

A wild rose vine brushed against the back of her hand. Immediately, as if in fright, the vine recoiled like a child shrinking from a nighttime monster.

"Gaia," Krysty said, turning her face up to the rad-blasted orange sky, "help me to understand."

"Gaia no longer hears you," the voice continued in a childish taunt. "You are only fallow ground as far as the Earth Mother is concerned. You have no future, Krysty, and now you have no past. You have only today, and that is but fleeting hours."

Krysty cried, feeling the tears course down her face. She called out to Ryan, but evidently he didn't hear her. She was torn, unwilling to continue across the beautiful garden and leave only blighted ruin in her wake.

The companions drew even farther away from her, not even bothering to turn to look in her direction to make sure that she was there. Ryan always made sure when they were on patrol that two others watched over one, and the one was responsible for looking over two others. It was a network that had saved their small party a number of times in the past.

"Ryan!"

Even Krysty didn't hear her own voice this time, though she knew for a fact that she had screamed her lover's name. Frightened now, she ran across the garden, taking huge bounding leaps so she wouldn't trample as much of the greenery. But when she looked back, she saw that a wide strip of the garden was dead anyway. All she had to do was pass over it, not simply touch it.

"Your time is past, Krysty," the voice taunted. "All that you've been taught to revere, you've walked away from. Mother Sonja wanted you to build, but you haven't built. You've had a hand in more destruction than anything else. You and your precious Ryan Cawdor.''

''Not true,'' Krysty denied. ''Sometimes we couldn't fix the horrors, or we would have been killed ourselves. But at times…we made a difference.''

''Lies,'' the voice contradicted her. ''You're misremembering events and things as badly as that old cretin, Doc Tanner. Do you know why he forgets? Because it's bastard convenient, that's why. But Gaia doesn't forget, Krysty, and you've broken covenant with her. Time and again you've asked her to help you, asked her to help you help your precious companions. And what have you done for her?''

Krysty ran on, feeling her lungs burn in her chest. She shouted to herself, trying to drive the maddening voice from her head. It was no use; she continued to hear it plainly.

''Nothing,'' the voice shrilled, ''you've done nothing for Gaia, but you've expected everything in return. Now Gaia will have her own back.''

A summer storm gathered in the orange sky above in a heartbeat. The wind picked up speed, becoming a raging vortex that sucked cankerous clouds into the area overhead that looked like a collection of bruised boils.

Ryan turned then and came running back to her. His face was a mask of concern, given darkness by his black eye patch.

Tears streamed down Krysty's face as she reached for her lover. But a white-hot lightning bolt sizzled down to touch her with its caress. The world exploded in a bright flash of incandescence. She dropped, seemingly lifeless, to the ground, unable to control her body anymore. She felt the grass curl away beneath her, pulling back into the ground.

"Somebody help me!" Ryan shouted, kneeling beside Krysty. "Mildred!"

Mildred rushed over and grabbed Krysty's wrist.

Krysty's eyes remained opened. She saw everything that was going on, but she couldn't move. And she couldn't feel. That was the worst thing of all. She knew Ryan was holding her head in his lap, but she couldn't feel him at all.

"She's dead," Mildred replied. "I'm sorry, Ryan, but she's dead and there's not a thing I can do about it." Tears welled up in the woman's eyes, then spilled down her cheeks.

"No," Ryan said hoarsely. "She can't be dead. I won't let her be dead."

"You don't have a choice," the Trader said, stepping up somewhere from behind the companions.

Krysty thought it was strange that she hadn't seen the old man earlier, but she'd seen stranger things in the past few minutes.

"You take her any farther from this spot, you'd just be carrying a corpse on your back. But you aren't going to leave here without burying her," the Trader said. "None of those people who traveled with me are ever going to be left behind without a proper hole to be covered up in. Won't allow it."

Krysty watched, unable even to blink, as Ryan and the others dug a hole for her. She wanted to cry, but even that was kept from her. She prayed to Gaia to have mercy on her, but only silence greeted her prayers.

The hole was finished in short time, only things didn't go exactly as Krysty thought they would. They put her in the grave, but they put her in it standing up, like they had dug a well instead of a gravesite.

She lay back against the side of the strange grave, looking up at the man she loved and the best friends she had ever made, listening to Doc say words over her as if she really were gone.

"I am reminded at this time," Doc said, his white hair whipping around his face, "how we humans have a span of time between two eternities, and into that last eternity we now send reluctantly one of ours, she who was like a flame that could warm and burn and heal. May your emerald eyes light the ways of angels. Gaia keep you in her graces, dear sweet Krysty."

Krysty tried to move, but her limbs lay leaden. She tried to shout, but her voice stayed removed from her. Then a wild burning began in her toes. They moved. At first she thought her paralysis was draining away. But that was before she felt her toes elongating and stabbing deep into the rich, dark earth. Her arms rose at her sides, reaching toward the sky above. Somehow the rain clouds had all blown away, leaving only the dreadful orange sky above.

Her skin sloughed away, revealing hard bark beneath. Ryan and the others stepped back, their faces dropping in shock at what was happening.

And Krysty continued to grow. Her arms split out and became branches that changed the course of the mild breezes blowing over the garden. Her hair became foliage festooned with bright blossoms. Mixed in with her branches, though, were whiplike, barbed appendages that coiled restlessly.

Ryan came forward, calling out to her.

Krysty felt the hunger building in her, an appetite like none other she had ever known. The barbed appendages slithered through her branches, tracking their prey.

She still had a face; she felt the rough bark skin that overlaid it. But she had no voice. She wasn't able to shout a warning to Ryan.

The barbs leaped from her, swift as striking cobras. They penetrated Ryan's body, shooting completely through his chest, killing him instantly.

"As this man took you from Gaia," the feminine voice spoke, "so shall you now take what you need to replenish yourself for the Earth Mother."

Krysty felt Ryan's blood coursing through the appendages to fill her and whet her appetite. She drank hungrily, tasting the salt of his blood, hating every drop, watching Ryan's body turn white in her deadly embrace.

RYAN OPENED his eye.

His mouth felt like desert sand, and his head throbbed like someone had slammed it with a thirty-pound sledge. He ached all over.

Cautiously, afraid his head might drop from his shoulders if he moved too quickly, he turned to search the mat-trans unit for his companions. Krysty lay beside him, tears running down her temples and blood dripping from the corner of her mouth where she had bitten herself during the jump. She mewled in pain, but he felt it was more from whatever she was imagining than from any real physical discomfort.

Ryan sat up with care, feeling his head go spinning around him. He glanced up at the armaglass walls, finding them as white as mother-of-pearl, almost angelic. The room on the other side of the walls was dark, so he couldn't discern any details yet.

"You know," J.B. said from somewhere over to the left, "at first when I saw these white walls, I thought maybe this was one jump we didn't make it through. Still kind of crosses my mind as I sit here. Be interesting if we open up that sec door and step out onto a cloud."

In spite of the pain crashing through his head, Ryan laughed. Then he regretted it almost at once as renewed pain proved to him that he hadn't been feeling as bad as he could have. The pain got a lot worse.

"Heaven?" Ryan asked. "Somebody who's been through Deathlands the way we have? We won't even get visitation privileges."

"That's probably true," J.B. agreed. "But you know what?"

"What?" Ryan growled, irritated at the way even the Armorer's voice seemed to inflict more pain.

"Chances are, nobody we know is going to be there."

"I guess that means we won't miss anything."

Both men laughed, and Ryan knew that was because they felt all jumbled up inside, and because they were relieved to have lived through yet another mat-trans jump. He ran his hands along his weapons as he glanced around for the others.

Mildred lay curled up next to J.B., almost in a fetal position. Jak lay by himself, bleeding from his nose, his eyelids flickering.

"You awake, Jak?" Ryan called.

"Yeah. Talk too loud."

Ryan moved his blurry gaze on, finding Dean sprawled on the other side of Krysty. His son looked like he was breathing okay, but his tan color was paler than normal. He held his Browning Hi-Power in his fist. "Dean?"

"Yeah, Dad. Just don't make me move yet." Dean's voice sounded like a dry croak.

Doc had thrown up, and a pool of bile sat on the floor beside him and smeared one sleeve of his frock coat. The old man's eyes were open, but only the whites showed, threaded through with red veins.

Albert rolled over like a fish flopping on a bank, then threw up a bilious mess.

"What a stench," J.B. complained. "We're going to have to get out of here just to get some clean air."

The thing that struck Ryan the most was the cold, however. It seeped into his bones, coating the exposed skin. He ran a hand up to his head, hoping that massaging the back of his neck would relieve some of his headache. Then his fingers touched the ice crystals in his hair.

He pulled his hand down in wonder and stared at them. He couldn't stare long, because they didn't last long. Hardly had he time to draw a breath than they were gone, leaving only wet traces against his palm and fingers.

"J.B., how long have you been awake?"

"Didn't check the chron."

Ryan ran his fingers through his hair again, finding more ice crystals. He glanced around the metal disks of the mat-trans unit's floor. Little patches of ice gleamed against the vanadium. "Give me a guess."

"Ten, fifteen minutes mebbe."

"You notice how cold it is in here?" Ryan asked.

"Sure. Hard to miss."

Fear put a surge of adrenaline through the one-eyed man, giving him the strength to haul himself to his feet. "You think it's getting any colder?"

J.B. glanced at him, then noticed the frost on his glasses. "Mebbe, now that you mention it. Just figured it was my blood feeling thin after the jump. Don't always know how bad you really feel until after you start moving around. Kind of wanted to put that off for a bit."

Swaying slightly, his sense of balance still affected by the jump, Ryan put his hand against the armaglass. Burning cold pressed against his palm, cold enough to make his teeth ache in sympathy. He breathed out deliberately, watching as a plume of fog spilled out against the armaglass in front of him.

"That's not white paint," he told the Armorer. "That's ice caked on the armaglass outside. We're frozen in."

Chapter Twenty-One

Ryan crossed to the door, slipping once on an ice patch in the center of the mat-trans floor. He wasn't worried about being trapped because there was always the LD button that could whisk them back to the redoubt near Hazard. Going back might entail a few days of running from Kirkland or Handsome Wyatt if the jacker leader had stayed in the area, but it beat being stuck underground in a block of ice.

"Is it just me," J.B. asked, "or does it seem to you that the lights in here aren't as bright as they usually are after a jump?"

Ryan glanced at the glowing disks on the floor and ceiling. Usually they carried a residual glow after usage, and emergency lights flared on until the unit was cleared. Now they were dim, rendering only a twilight inside the gateway.

"Power's not what it should be," Ryan agreed.

"Could be failing as we stand here talking," the Armorer warned.

"Then let's see what's what." Ryan lifted the lever that was supposed to open the door.

Nothing happened.

"Fireblast!" Ryan snarled. "Bastard door's stuck."

"Try this." J.B. handed over a camp ax from his gear.

Ryan slammed the blunt end of the head against the lever. Reluctantly, the door opened to about two-and-one-half feet before its progress was impeded.

Only ice appeared to be on the other side of the door.

"What is it, lover?" Krysty asked, sitting up and holding her head.

"Looks like we've jumped into a block of ice," Ryan said. He put his hand against the ice and tried to push. It didn't budge. "Bastard thick."

"We stuck in here, Dad?" Dean asked.

Ryan looked at his son, sitting up now and wrapping his arms around his legs. Like all of them, Dean wasn't really dressed for the sudden winter weather. And Ryan could tell the interior temperature of the mat-trans unit was continuing to plunge.

None of them would last long if they remained inside the gateway.

"Only stuck as long as we want to be," Ryan replied. "Over, under or around. There's always a way. Just need to find it."

"Best way might be to go back," Mildred said. "If this jump is going to start out this bad, give us this kind of crap to deal with from the git-go, I'm ready to take a hint. If you know what I mean."

"Another jump?" Doc groaned. "So soon? By the Three Kennedys, I fear it would be the death of us all."

"Another jump won't kill us," J.B. said. "We'll just wish it did."

"Beats slow death," Jak added. "Freezing not good way die."

"None of them are. That's why we're not going to do that." Ryan shut the door. "Everybody get set."

"Damn," Albert moaned. "Don't know that I can do that again."

"Find out in a minute, little man." Ryan pushed the LD button.

The metal disks tried to glow more brightly, but they were slow about it. Ryan sat beside Krysty, feeling the cold eating into him more now. He counted down, waiting for the mist to fill the chamber.

It didn't.

"Not going work," Jak said.

And that, Ryan knew, was the size of it. They were trapped.

SWEAT COVERED Ryan inside his long coat. His breath gusted out of him in gray plumes as he worked with the camp ax. His arm felt leaden, but he didn't want to give in to fatigue. More ice chips and chunks flew when the ax bit into the solid mass on the other side of the mat-trans unit's door.

He'd excavated a hole some two feet wide that went back almost eighteen inches. The hole got narrower as it went, too, because he couldn't work the ax very well.

"Ryan," J.B. said gently. "Take a breather. Can't do this all on your own."

"Fireblast, I know it." Reluctantly Ryan yielded the ax.

The Armorer stepped up to the ice hole and began methodically to hammer away.

Ryan crossed the floor and dropped into a seated position beside Krysty. The metal floor was so cold now it nearly froze his rear end to sit on it. Krysty took his left hand in hers. He was surprised to find that her hands felt even colder than his.

"Hungry, lover?" she asked.

"Yeah. Big meal we had at Aunt Maim's seemed to have worked itself through me."

Krysty popped the tab on a self-heat and passed it over.

Ryan relished the heat of the container when she passed it over. The aroma was thick and not terribly appealing, but he breathed it in anyway because it was warm. Anything to get warmth back into his chilled body. He drank the broth from the container, and chewed the long noodles that were packed into it. He thought it might have been Oriental seasonings, but it could have been anything else, as well.

"We still have some plas ex," Dean said. "I've never known a time when J.B. got rid of every bit he had. He's always keeping some stashed somewhere."

"What are you thinking?" Ryan asked, looking at his son. "We might blow our way out of here? Have you given any thought to how much damage we might do to this unit if we did that? Or what could be waiting on the other side of that ice wall?"

Dean grimaced. "I thought about it some. I

thought mebbe it was better to take the chance than to sit here waiting." The boy looked crestfallen.

"And I thought I taught you better than that. When you're forced to make a move, especially when you're in a tight spot, you've got to shave the odds."

Dean nodded, not meeting his father's eyes.

"That ice wall could be keeping things out, as well as us in," Ryan went on. "Suppose we're underwater? Blow that ice wall out, mebbe we all drown before we can get that bastard door shut quick enough. Keep the hole small and manageable, we can get it plugged before the mat-trans unit fills up."

"You think that's it, then?" Albert asked. The dwarf's eyes showed white with fear. "You think we're underwater?" He glanced at the hole where J.B. worked with steadfast determination, and at the growing pile of ice chips.

Disposing of the ice they were bringing into the mat-trans unit was a real problem. Depending on how much they had to store, Ryan knew they might not have enough room to take it all in.

"Don't know," Ryan answered. "Be just as likely that we're sitting at the top of a brand-new mountain range along the western coast that would drop us as part of an avalanche if we set off any plas ex."

"My dear Ryan, is it necessary to worry Albert so?" Doc admonished. "He's new to the worries and whims of capricious fate when dealing out the ill hands in regards to these demonic devices."

"A man who doesn't want to know the answers, Doc," Ryan said with some irritation, "shouldn't be asking the questions."

"The reason I asked about the plas ex," Dean said quietly, "is because we may need to use it soon."

"What the hell for?" Ryan snapped. "Still got plenty of room to haul in more ice. We can keep working that hole for hours."

Dean nodded. "Mebbe. But mebbe we aren't—"

"Don't," Krysty chided.

"But mebbe we don't have hours," Dean repeated. "You notice how stale the air is getting in here? Breathing up all the oxygen, we're going to have to start worrying about getting some fresh air before long."

Ryan paused with his spoon midway to his mouth. He glanced up at J.B. "You think about that?"

The Armorer flushed, then went back to swinging the ax. "Not me. I've been contemplating mostly on how thick this ice is and what's going to be on the other side of it. Boy's right, though."

Ryan felt a surge of pride go through him, erasing some of the anger that he felt at himself for not realizing the potential danger. "You did good to think of that, son."

Dean smiled. "Wasn't really my thinking. Just something I remembered from the survival classes taught at school. We had a history lesson about miners, way back before skydark, and how they used to cut coal out of the earth. Sometimes they'd get so far down in the mine shafts that no fresh air would

come in, and some of them died. That's why they
started taking parakeets in cages down in the shafts
with them. Bad air would chill the bird before it
chilled a man. Miners kept watch over the birds.
Bird turned up dead, miners caught the next elevator
to the top of the shaft, ace on the line.''

"No parakeets here," Jak said with an evil grin.
He hooked a thumb at Albert. "Got little man. He
dies, time to blast.''

Ryan turned his attention back to the self-heat.
"Good thing you brought that up, Dean. Now I'm
going to make it your responsibility to keep an eye
on things. We start acting too stupe for our own
good, it's up to you to get us to blast.''

Dean nodded.

Ryan ate, listening to the steady attack J.B. made
on the ice wall. The hot food and the sound of the
ax falling seemed reassuring, until he heard the hollow booming echo of the thuds in the mat-trans unit.

ALMOST AN HOUR later, while Jak was taking his
turn with the ax, they broke through the ice. Ryan
was just about to call it wasted effort and use the
plas ex J.B. had because all he wanted to do was go
to sleep. He knew it was more than simple tiredness
and had a lot to do with the stale air trapped inside
the gateway.

Jak paused, then pulled the ax back and peered
through. "Through. Inside redoubt," he announced.
"Ice everywhere.''

Ryan forced himself up and went for a look. His
joints seemed stiffer than ever, and his teeth had

started to chatter. He stared into the hole Jak had made through nearly three feet of ice. It was scarcely more than three inches across, but it provided enough of a view even in the dim light on the other side of the wall for him to know they were unmistakably in a redoubt.

But this one looked like it had barely survived an ice age. Ice coated all the walls and comp banks.

"What do you see?" Mildred asked. She and J.B. sat together, arms wrapped around each other, sharing the warmth. Dean had joined Krysty and Ryan, all of them huddled together. Even Doc and Albert sat close together.

"Redoubt," Ryan said. "But it doesn't look like it's in any better shape than this mat-trans unit."

THE BITTER COLD really set in after they had broken through the ice wall over the door to the gateway. Muted light somehow survived from the nuclear reactors buried somewhere below, glowing from behind inches of ice that covered every surface.

The companions broke out all the extra clothes they carried in their gear, but it wasn't much. Ryan wore his long coat, but even it didn't cut the chill by much. Wind breezed into the big room where the gateway was, carrying a cold that he felt he'd never experienced before.

"If we don't find some way soon to warm up, lover," Krysty said, "we're going to be dead in a few hours."

Ryan nodded, knowing it was true.

"The ice evidently has been a long time in building up," Doc stated. "Witness the fact that there appear to be no broken pipes, no sources of water. It has to be carried in by the wind from somewhere as tiny crystals. Then they cling to other like crystals to form the icy exoskeleton you see overlaying this room."

"All of which gets us what?" Ryan asked irritably.

"Why, my dear Ryan, it lets us know this redoubt is obviously open to the outside world. Else where would the wind and the airborne moisture come from?"

Ryan saw the sense in that. "Best way to find our way out is to follow the wind, then."

Doc smiled. "Precisely, my dear fellow."

"Something else to consider that Doc must have overlooked," Mildred said, coming up to join them. She took a handkerchief from her pocket and tied it over her nose and mouth. "If there is much moisture in the air, and I think there is, breathing all of it in could cause pneumonia. Get a build-up of moisture in the lungs, you're definitely going to come down with a hellacious case of it. And then we're talking serious trouble."

"Masks?" Ryan said.

"Or stop breathing," Mildred answered.

"TAKE SOME WORK," J.B. told Ryan an hour later, "but I think mebbe we can chip away enough ice to shut the emergency doors. Get this room to seal off." He pointed to a section of wall he'd been working on earlier. "I checked the relays over there, and found that power seems to be getting through the systems okay.''

The emergency doors were caked in ice, held fast in the walls that shielded them. The housing over them was frozen solid.

"How much time?" Ryan asked.

"Working with the knives, ax and what tools we brought?" J.B. shrugged. "Mebbe an hour. But if we block off some of this wind, could be the room will warm up some.'' He cleaned his glasses and peered up at the roof panels. "If I get the chance, I'm going to take a look up there and see if I can trace out the environmental controls for this room. They should be on a separate relay, as well.''

Ryan nodded. "Don't like splitting up the team when we're in a hard spot like this.''

"But you like the idea of sitting around waiting to see if anybody comes calling even less," J.B. agreed. "I know. Been having some of the same thoughts myself. Leave me with Doc and Albert. You take Jak, Dean, Mildred and Krysty on up ahead and see what you can see. We'll be here, watching your back and keeping a light on for you until you get back.''

"Sounds as good as it's going to get.''

J.B. grinned. "One thing about it. I don't think any predators would hang around here waiting for a meal. Too bastard cold and unfriendly.''

"Yeah.'' Before Ryan could turn and address the others, letting them know what the plan was, a horrendous crack sounded somewhere off in the distance, rolling like a peal of thunder. Then the redoubt shivered like a dying wag-hit hound.

"Was that an earthquake, lover?" Krysty asked. Her face was mostly covered by the handkerchief she wore to protect her lungs. Ice crystals had already formed on the blue material, just as they had formed on everyone else's masks.

"Mebbe," Ryan said. "But it didn't feel like any earthquake I've ever been through before." He'd been with the Trader out along the Western Islands when he'd first experienced earthquakes. They had made him sick with fear back then, because they made every physical law he'd clung to for security seem worthless. He had seen the Cific Ocean drink down islands, seen new mountain ranges born fresh from the womb of the earth and watched trees fall like kindling for miles.

"Do you know what it reminded me of?" Doc mused. Nobody asked what, but the old man continued on anyway. "Like a big ship foundering in deep water, battling an unexpected turbulence or righting itself after a gale has torn her sails to shreds and near to capsized her. That is definitely what it reminded me of. Is that not the oddest thing?"

Nobody commented.

AFTER AN HOUR of fruitless searching through three tunnels with doors that were frozen shut, Ryan followed the main access corridor, trailing the wind that came from somewhere outside.

The access corridor was twenty feet across, covered with a thick sheet of ice that kept them inches off the actual ground. It was thick enough that Ryan almost missed the first corpse.

Chapter Twenty-Two

It was the body of a man, a pathetic and twisted caricature of what he had to have been in life. The light from the fluorescent strips overhead barely revealed him through the ice coating.

"Mildred," Ryan called out, squatting to rub the loose ice from the years-old accumulation.

"Son of a bitch," Mildred said as she approached. She pressed her hands against the ice and got almost nose to nose with the corpse.

"I didn't see a gunshot wound," Ryan stated. "No stab wound. Not even any blood. Know what killed him?"

"Not without digging him up," Mildred replied. "But whatever it was must have come for him bastard quick."

Ryan nodded. "Thought so myself. Still got his military uniform on. After nukecaust, he'd have gone on."

Krysty knelt and put a hand over the dead man's face. Her touch had to have reached past the inches of ice, though, because Ryan saw the redhead's face knot up with distaste and pain. "He died burning," she said.

Mildred peered closer. "Can't be. I don't see any

tissue damage that looks anything like burns. And there aren't any signs of it on the wall, either.''

Krysty shook her head, clearly not understanding everything she was picking up through her mutie ability. "Not from the outside. From the inside. Something that affected his lungs. His chest got tight.''

"You can feel all that?" Dean asked.

She nodded and took her hand away. "Can't do it with old dead every time, but sometimes, if I put my mind to it, I can get a feeling about their passing. I don't like doing it, but this time, I thought mebbe we should know.''

"Let's move," Ryan said, curiosity eating at him. They were clearly in a military installation. Where they could read them, signs were in military jargon that the one-eyed man found only partially decipherable.

More dead followed, all encased in ice, and all in uniform.

"Died after nukecaust," Jak ventured as they found a group of corpses lying on top of one another farther down the hallway. "Or wouldn't be many so close. Wouldn't all be uniformed.''

"Something else about the condition they're in," Mildred said as she studied the latest accumulation of corpses. "The cold had to have hit them soon. Otherwise we'd be finding skeletons here and there instead of whole bodies. Either the elements would have stripped them down, or predators would have.''

"The redoubt's integrity was compromised suddenly," Ryan said, "allowing in the cold. As thick as this ice is, as strong as it is now, there must have been a lot of water here at one time."

"Mebbe close to the sea?" Mildred suggested.

Ryan nodded. "That's what I'm thinking. That could account for the thickness of the ice."

"A flood would have washed these bodies out of the corridor."

"Could have," Ryan agreed, "and this is where they ended up." He got the companions up and moving again, following the tunnel. Another thing that totally confused him was the direction they were traveling in. According to the signs posted on the tunnel walls, they were in the south wing, supposedly heading south. Instead, according to the compass he had, Ryan charted them as going west.

Another quake shook the redoubt.

Ryan pressed up against the wall, holding on to Krysty as the sound of the intermittent, booming cracks filled the corridor. This time Ryan got some of the feeling Doc had talked about. It felt like the redoubt did bobble slowly a bit. After he was sure all the ices chunks that were going to drop from the ceiling had fallen, he pulled back.

When he checked his compass again during a breather, he found they were now progressing down the tunnel in a northwesterly direction instead of mostly west. The tunnel hadn't changed direction, just continued straight

And he had no explanation for that at all.

"NERVE GAS," Mildred said, pointing to a metal canister held in the frozen grip of the ice. "I recognize the toxin classifications."

Ryan took a closer look at the metal canister. It was pressure sealed, like a lot of other storage containers they had found in other redoubts, and marked with a skull and crossbones. "Somebody set it off inside and chilled everybody here?"

Mildred shook her head. "I don't think so. Look at the tear in the side of that canister. See how jagged it is? Leads me to think it was hit from something outside the canister, but maybe still inside the redoubt. Could have been sabotage."

"Sabotage?" Dean echoed.

"Boobied it from the inside," Ryan explained. "By somebody who was acting like he was one of them."

"Or she," Mildred said. "Don't forget which is the deadlier of the sexes."

Ryan knew she was only halfway joking. "These were Americans by the looks of their uniforms. Mebbe the Russians brought them down."

"That would be my guess," Mildred agreed. "With this much ice around, we've got to be somewhere up north. Mebbe even as far as Russia. If we are, that was a long jump."

Ryan nodded. And it would be an even longer walk back to familiar territory if they couldn't get the mat-trans unit operational again.

Farther on, they found the room where the bomb had to have gone off.

Ryan stood on the lip of the room, gazing down into what appeared to be a research lab of some kind. A lot of comps, frozen over now, sat against the wall along a ring that encircled the hub of the large room. Mechanical claws hung from the ceiling, black power cords as thick as pythons leading down from them.

He made his way gingerly to the edge of the railing and peered down. The light fixtures below weren't operational at all. All he saw was a thick pool of frozen water, interrupted occasionally by bulky equipment that thrust up from the level surface.

"How far down, Jak?" Ryan asked.

"Fifteen feet, mebbe twenty. Light not good. Hard judge distance."

"Yeah."

"You can figure there's probably thirty feet of ice before you reach the concrete bottom of that room," Mildred said. "This must be where they were storing the nerve gas."

Ryan silently agreed. His eye scoured the walls, seeing signs where explosions had ripped into the metal. Huge gouges lay under the sheets of ice, disfigured by the depth.

"I get bad feelings about this place," Krysty said in a soft voice. "A lot of people died right here."

"Took a lot of water to fill this room, Dad," Dean said. "Kind of curious about where it came from."

"Me, too," Ryan said, but he felt a gnawing certainty that he knew where it had come from. He'd had to knock ice from the handkerchief around his lower face three times since they had begun to walk. Every time he had tasted the ice through the material, and every time it had carried with it the distinct taste of salt.

Salt water could only mean a sea or an ocean. But there were a lot of those in the world. It also meant that wherever they were, it was cold by a damn sight because salt water took longer and colder to freeze than fresh water.

Another rumble shook the ground. Metal creaked this time, and huge sheets of ice ripped free of the walls in the room. Some areas had already been bared by the earlier quakes, but not all of them had torn free.

A sheet almost twice the size of a man crashed onto the railing in front of Ryan. The impact reduced it to fist-sized pieces that pelted them with bruising force and smashed into the walls around them.

Then the quake finished with a final spasmodic quiver that sent ice chunks skittering across the frozen surface.

"Getting worse," Jak commented as they pushed themselves up.

"Didn't feel any worse than the last one," Ryan said. He held a finger to the side of his nose, stemming blood flow where ice had hit him.

"Mebbe," Jak said. "But was." He pointed at the floor.

Fractures ran through the inches-thick accumulation beneath their feet. Ryan guessed that a few had been there from earlier, but in no way were they as bad as what he was looking at now. "Let's get a move on," he growled, "before this whole fire-blasted place comes tumbling down around our ears.''

"THE EXPLOSION MUST have taken place around the time of the nukecaust,'' Mildred commented. She ran her hands through the pockets of the dead man they found in the corridor. More of the ice lining the floor had buckled, making footing even more treacherous. ''Got paperwork here with a January 18, 2001, date on it.''

"What paperwork?'' Ryan asked. He moved forward, squinting in the dim light to look at the paper she offered. She gave him three sheets, all covered with feminine handwriting.

"Personal letter,'' Mildred said, shivering from the cold. She ran her hands along her arms, her gaze still captured by the young corpse on the ground before them.

The man looked to be in his early twenties. His hair was crew-cut blond, and his staring, dead eyes were hazel. A dimple centered in his chin gave him a look of arrogance, but the ice pieces clinging to his frozen flesh stripped him of that full effect. Sergeant chevrons marked his short-sleeved shirt. Some decay had set in before the freezing temperatures, and the ice had preserved what was left of his corpse. His body showed a watermark where blood had settled into his exposed limbs and the back of his neck.

The letter was just that, a message from home, written by a young wife who hoped to see her husband in two weeks for the first time in nearly eight months. Sections of the letter were covered over by black marker. From reading the text, Ryan knew the references had to do with where the young soldier had been stationed.

"Evidently this place stored a lot of war chems, lover," Krysty said. They had turned up more of the canisters. Some of them, however, hadn't been broken open. Ryan had given the order to stay away from them. If any nerve gas got released, the breeze blowing by them would have blown the gas cloud farther down the tunnel, killing them, as well as the others.

Mildred nodded. "Somebody in here was set up to take out this site. Maybe with all the tracking communications gear we've seen, it was part of the SDI."

"SDI?" Jak repeated.

"Strategic Defense Initiative," Ryan supplied. "Supposed to give the United States a chance to save the world in case the nukes were launched."

"Didn't work," Jak said.

"No." Ryan folded the letter and left it back with the dead man. He liked to read journals when he found them, and manuals, just to get an idea of what life had to have been like during the time before skydark. This was personal, and it belonged with the man. If there had been information in it, he would have kept it.

"Hot pipe!" Dean called up ahead. "I see light at the end of the tunnel."

"Ease up," Ryan called, moving forward across the slick ground. "Don't roam too far ahead." He followed the rising grade of the tunnel, his vision blocked ahead by the tunnel bending back down to level off again.

Dean stood at the top of the incline, his Browning in his fist and gray wisps of his breath dancing around his head.

Ryan went up the incline gingerly. The cracked ice made it easier going than the smooth ice would have been, but if the wrong piece was stepped on, a man would go back down the incline in a hurry. He noticed the sound when he was near the top, recognizing it at once as the crash and boom of surf.

The breeze thickened with the salt scent, and it became even colder. The wet handkerchief stuck to flesh where it touched Ryan's lips. His eye opened wide as he took in the scene, seeing but not believing.

The access tunnel leading to the redoubt had been sheared off. Not by an explosion, Ryan saw, but by a twisting elemental force. The tunnel now opened up on a peak of dirty white ice, pointing like an open throat toward the abominable orange and purple of the nuke-dust-filled sky.

The light coming from the sun barely visible through the heavy clouding was a jaundiced yellow. Ryan didn't think anyone around this place had ever seen a blue sky, which was still some days rare even in Deathlands.

And he knew they weren't in Deathlands anymore. No place he had been to looked anything like what he saw before him.

Sixty feet and maybe more below him, an emerald

green ocean lapped at the bottom of the shelf they found themselves on. There was no indication of land mixed in with the accumulated snow and fresh layers of ice. Out before him, scattered across the wide expanse of the sea, were hundreds of ice floes. Nearly all of them were smaller than the one they were encased in.

"Jesus H. Christ!" Mildred said, stepping up beside Ryan to look out over the ocean. "We're in a damn ice cube floating in the middle of the goddamn ocean!"

And that, Ryan figured, summed it up about the best.

Chapter Twenty-Three

For as long as he could, Ryan stood out on the lip of the access tunnel where the door had been sheared away trying to see a way clear of the situation. The companions had been in a lot of hard places, but nothing like the present predicament.

"How do you think it happened, Dad?" Dean asked. His teeth chattered from the cold.

"You should go on back inside," Ryan said. "You're going to catch your death if you keep standing out here."

"I'll go back in when you go back in," Dean said stubbornly.

For a moment the boy's refusal to do what he asked touched a raw nerve in Ryan. He felt his jaw twitch and turn hard. Then he made himself remember it was the situation he was mad at, not Dean.

The wind was worse in the open, whipping around the huge glacier with the intensity of a possessed thing. Mildred and Krysty had taken shelter inside the tunnel again.

Ryan let out a tense breath, watching the long streamer of his gray breath spin away from him. His face felt numb all over, not just the nerve-deadened spots. "I guess we're somewhere up near the Arctic Circle," he told Dean. "Only two places that I read about have glaciers as part of their natural environment.''

"The Arctic and the Antarctic," Dean said.

Ryan nodded at his son. "Guess you learned a lot at Brody's school."

"I tried. Lot of learning to do, Dad."

"I know. It's something a real man doesn't ever give up on."

"Trader teach you that?"

"Yeah. Him, and a few other real men I've had the chance to meet over the years." Ryan shifted the conversation back to the glacier. Below the drop-off, three white birds with wingspreads that must have been near ten feet across circled and heeled, riding out the rough winds. Their thin cries echoed back up to Ryan. Now and again one of them would dive below the water and come back up with a fish jumping in its beak.

"Back before skydark, when the Americans were up against the Russians, they had a lot of their armament invested in submarines. Russians ran the most and the biggest, according to the books I read, and the Americans kept track of them through satellites up in space and sensors along the ocean floor."

"Like some of the comps we saw back in the redoubt?" Dean asked.

"Mebbe." Ryan shrugged. "At this point I can only guess. The thing is, one of the most watched areas where the Americans searched for the Russian subs was the Lantic Ocean."

"Near here?"

"Yeah."

"So they put a redoubt here, watching over things. Then what?"

"Then skydark," Ryan said. "Earthquakes, tidal waves and lots of cold. The Arctic Circle was mostly ice anyway. When the nuke dust shut out the sun for all those years, mebbe nobody knows how much of the world turned to ice up here. Know for a fact that a lot of England is under water now." He glanced down at the iceberg. "Figures that the redoubt mebbe goes through all of this iceberg, helps hold it together."

"Like a skeleton," Dean said.

"Yeah. Like a skeleton."

"Only it's moving now. And we're moving with it."

Ryan nodded. He touched his upper lip with a finger, finding it completely numb.

"Mebbe we'll drift in someplace," Dean said hopefully.

The words were barely out of his mouth when one of the glaciers in the distance cracked with the sound of a cannon shot. Ryan watched as a huge chunk of the original glacier fell away and dropped into the ocean with a splash that sent a wave of water up dozens of feet.

"Don't know if we're going to last that long," Ryan said quietly. "Appears as if we have a time problem."

"IT IS CALLED calving," Doc said.

Ryan looked at the old man in disbelief, knowing

all the other companions were doing the same thing. Even Albert was regarding Doc as if he were something that had turned up unexpected under a rock.

"The process of an iceberg splitting off a smaller iceberg," Doc explained. "It's called calving."

"Doesn't matter what it's called," Ryan said. "We can't afford to be here when this one goes."

They were all gathered back in the mat-trans unit.

"Mebbe the redoubt will be strong enough to hold it together," Albert said. He sat shivering. Of them all, the dwarf had the least amount of body heat to waste, and was ill dressed for the weather.

"If those quakes are any indication," J.B. said, "that isn't going to be true."

"So what's the plan, lover?" Krysty asked.

"We continue mapping out this redoubt," Ryan replied. "Mebbe we get some heat in here, and we'll have a base of operations."

"That's going to happen," the Armorer said. He stood at the open face of an environmental-control comp. Jagged ice stood out around it where he had chopped his way through. "With all the damage done to the redoubt, the systems automatically went into conservative mode. Getting the doors closed again allowed me to access the relays. Got a new problem, though."

"What?" Mildred asked. "I'm ready to be warm again, John."

The Armorer glanced around the room. "Once this ice starts melting, we're going to have water everywhere."

"Then we'll clear as much of it as we can," Ryan said.

"Found a fire ax over here," J.B. said. "But if you use it, you're going to have to be careful with the comps. Don't know if I can fix the mat-trans unit again, but we don't need to be making things any worse."

Ryan took up the fire ax and walked to the corner farthest away from the comps and the gateway. "Start here," he said. "I'll bust ice loose for a while and the rest of you carry it into the next room. We get it clear, I'll expect to feel some of that heat." He swung the ax, and sheets of ice crashed to the floor.

IT TOOK slightly better than two hours to clear the room. Everybody took turns with the fire ax and the hand ax J.B. had in his kit. And everybody carried the ice away.

After a little while, Albert joined in, and proved to have a fine and deep singing voice that no one expected.

Once the room was clear of ice debris and the floor was scraped, J.B. switched on the environmental-controls override. "Only problem's going to be if the vents and fans are clogged up somewhere down the line," he said.

Ryan stood with the others, listening to the machinery gasp and wheeze to life. Somewhere down at the deep end of the duct work, metal beat against a hard, unyielding surface for a while. Then there was an explosion of noise, and the beating sound disappeared.

Only a thin trickle of heat came out of the floor vents. It was a lot weaker than Ryan figured the designers had intended, and not nearly as effective as the systems installers planned. Still, it was warm air and it was welcome.

They huddled around the main blowing unit against one wall opposite the comp stations. Gradually the room warmed, coming up to a degree of comfortability. The lights also brightened.

The main door leading to the access tunnel wasn't quite flush, but J.B. had made it work. However, gusts of cold wind were allowed in.

Dean fell asleep with his back to the wall, his hands held out before him to soak up the warm air coming through the vent.

Ryan was feeling the fatigue himself. He glanced at J.B. "Situation we're in is pretty bad, but we're not going to get anywhere without sleep."

"Been over thirty hours since we got any," J.B. said. "Except for that near coma the jump provided us."

Doc stretched and yawned. "If you are suggesting that we get some, my dear Ryan, then I heartily accept the decision."

"Me, too," Mildred said.

"Should we post a guard?" Krysty asked.

Ryan shook his head. "I think we can be pretty certain that we're all that's left alive inside this redoubt. And the sec doors are wedged pretty tight. We should be just fine."

He took time to get Dean settled proper, remembering the Trader's words in the jump dream. It made matters worse thinking about his son going down into the ocean when the iceberg fragmented.

He joined Krysty, stretching out beside her so they could share the warmth between them. The environmental controls had made a difference, but the room still had a long way to go before it got comfortably heated. Still, they were no longer in danger of freezing to death if they slept.

"Something on mind," Jak called from the corner.

"What?" Ryan asked.

"Warm up redoubt, iceberg melt faster?"

"The lad has a point," Doc said.

"And we're all out of choices," Ryan answered. And he didn't remember a single thing after that.

"THIS REDOUBT ISN'T as big as a lot of them we've been to," J.B. said. The Armorer sat in the corner, his fedora cocked back on his head while he worked a pencil over a ragged spiral-bound notebook.

Ryan blinked sleep out of his eye. "How long you been up?"

"Twenty, thirty minutes." J.B. had a fresh bandage on his side where he had been hit by the bullets during the fight back in Hazard. A med-kit had been in the room under all the ice, as well.

"Been outside?" Ryan sat up, disentangling himself from Krysty's arms. Her sentient hair lay protectively over her face.

"Nope."

"Find a map?"

"You could call it that." The Armorer kept working on the notebook with his stub of a pencil. "Reread a lot of those electrical blueprints this morning when my head seemed clearer. Was working too late to be sharp yesterday."

"A man working with not enough sleep is a man aiming on taking a dirt nap," Ryan said, remembering the Trader's words.

"Know it. That's why I gave the blueprints another go this morning. I think I've got a pretty good idea of where everything is and what it might be."

Ryan pushed up from the cold floor and joined the Armorer. Even with the heat on, a chill remained in the room. "Tell me."

J.B. tapped the drawing as he spoke. "This isn't scale. You're getting my best guess."

"It'll do."

"You got the room here with the mat-trans in it." The pencil hit the center of the page near the top. "Then you got the shaft you explored yesterday."

Ryan knew "yesterday" was a relative term. They had slept, so a "day" had passed by.

"The big chem lab's off that," J.B. went on. "Storerooms off the shaft. Mostly stuff for containing the nerve gas in case of an accident."

That explained the plastic suits with oxygen tanks Jak had found on some of the corpses frozen in the corridor. But the explosion had come too soon, too unexpectedly for it to be much good.

"And that takes you to the entrance you say was torn off," J.B. said. "Going back the other way, things appear to be a bit more hopeful. From what I can decipher, looks to be an armory and galley below, a warehouse-sized storeroom and mebbe what looks like a dock.''

"A dock? What kind of wags?" Ryan asked.

"Not wags," J.B. said. "Paperwork I found let on like it might be boats. Mebbe even a small sub. Won't know until we go look.''

"Then we'd better get it done. What about the mat-trans?''

"Going to have to take it apart," J.B. replied. "Mebbe I'll know more after I do that.''

"Then you'll stay here," Ryan said. "The rest of us will take a look at the rest of the redoubt.''

J.B. cleaned his glasses. "Probably going to be cold. Doubt if that heat ventilator is working throughout the whole redoubt.''

"If we're lucky," Ryan said, "the cold will be the worst of it.''

"LIKE WALKING in a tomb down here, lover.''

Ryan flicked the rechargeable electric hand lantern over the frozen floor ahead of him. Broken chunks of ice littered the corridor and became hazardous to every step. He had fallen himself nearly a half-dozen times, as had Krysty.

An arm stuck up from the frozen floor. The thumb and two fingers had snapped off some time in the past. Ryan guessed that falling ice had done the damage, but the owner of the hand was long past caring.

Not far from the gateway, the main corridor had

branched out in five directions. Ryan had split up the companions to cover ground more quickly. Mildred had gone with Jak and Dean, and Albert kept company with Doc.

The first corridor Ryan had chosen to explore had ended abruptly. The iceberg had swelled sometime in the past, probably battling against the interior heat of the redoubt before the environmental systems went into hibernation, then refrozen as the nuclear winter settled in. The second freezing had broken through the corridor and closed it down. The signs on the hallway leading to it mentioned only that barracks had been in that direction.

Ryan hoped it was so. That left the dock and the warehouse open to scavenging.

The iceberg quivered again, getting set for another big quake. Ryan had learned to recognize the signs. Krysty pressed up against the wall and hunkered down. Ryan followed suit, protecting his head with his arms. This time the quake lasted for nearly three minutes by his chron before subsiding. And that was followed immediately by the vertigo and disorientation Doc attributed to the iceberg redefining its position in the water.

The old man had let them know that somewhere in the vicinity of nine-tenths of an iceberg was beneath the water surface at all times. But when it calved, sometimes the biggest portion came from the bottom, depending on the fissures the melting ice followed. When it did, the remaining mother iceberg shrank lower into the sea.

And that, Doc had went on to say, wasn't taking

into account all the extra tonnage of the redoubt carried in the bowels of the particular iceberg they were floating on. Even more of it might be below the ocean level, which would create a tendency for the calving process to take place even more below the surface.

They were working on borrowed time.

It would have been better had the mat-trans unit not been functioning so their jump would have kicked them onto the next station.

When the quake finally subsided and the iceberg had renegotiated its equilibrium in the ocean to wipe away most of the feelings of vertigo, Ryan stood. He shone the electric glow of the hand lantern down the corridor, looking over the accumulation of new ice pieces.

"One of the worst," Krysty commented.

"I know. But mebbe it did some good. Look." Ryan played the lantern over the sign painted on the green wall in flat black paint: Docking Area.

The words gave Ryan a flash of hope that he nurtured in spite of their grim surroundings. He followed the arrows, ignoring the other listings of med facility, security office and filing rooms.

RYAN PLAYED the lantern's light over the elevator doors at the end of the corridor they were following. They were shut tight, which offered some hope, and the level-indicator lights flickered across the top, even more hopeful.

"Elevator's right where J.B. said it would be," Krysty said. The Armorer hadn't had the precise measurements, but he'd let them know how the corridor would shake out.

"If we get lucky," Ryan growled, "it'll still work." He stepped over to the control panel and put his palm over the activation plate. He unconsciously held his breath for a moment, wondering if the lingering comp systems were going to reject him because his palm print wasn't in its data banks. Some of the plates were programmed to react like that. Still others were boobied in some fashion.

But it pulsed amber, then turned green.

The elevator doors squealed as the servos surged into motion for probably the first time in a hundred years. When they settled back into their respective housings, no elevator cage was in view.

A harsh grinding continued.

Ryan watched vibrations of the huge tractor belt responsible for bringing the cage up as the pulling engine tried to raise it. With a harsh snap, it broke in two. The broken end whipped through the drum at the top, then fell back down into the elevator shaft.

Leaning in through the doors cautiously, Ryan directed the lantern down. The white beam knifed down through the darkness but didn't touch bottom.

"The cage didn't try to come up at all," Krysty said.

Ryan nodded. "Can't see the bottom."

"J.B. said it would probably be down there a ways."

Ryan shone his light around the room, then spotted a door marked Stairs. Ice sealed the door, but it wasn't as thick as some of the places they had been. He led the way through the door and started down the stairwell. He counted the landings as they went down, spiraling around and around. With the constant circuitous motion, he felt more vertigo than normal.

"You can feel the iceberg floating down here," Krysty said.

Ryan nodded, understanding what was upsetting his stomach. The motion of going down the stairs, coupled with the iceberg's natural buoyancy, was too much. It didn't last much longer, though.

Fourteen floors down, counting two landings per floor, they came to an end of it. Not the stairway shaft, but of how far they could go.

Ryan played his lantern beam over the black water sloshing across the stairway shaft. He had no way of knowing how much farther it went down. The fact remained that they couldn't.

"The water level inside the redoubt must be rising, lover," Krysty said in a low voice. "Otherwise all that water would be frozen."

"Or," Ryan replied, "it could be a degree or two just above freezing, just enough to start the iceberg melting a little faster."

Either way, it wasn't good.

Chapter Twenty-Four

J.B. laid the circuit boards on the table Jak and Dean had brought up from one of the storerooms they had successfully broken into. It was a long way from making the gateway room homey, but with the heat working a little better, the addition of the chairs gave the companions momentary respite that they weren't deep in a sinking iceberg. "These are the problem," the Armorer said. "Boards are shorted out."

"Can't you simply fix them, John Barrymore?" Doc asked.

"Mebbe, but this is precise work we're talking about, Doc. And if I get it wrong, mebbe we all just go out like a puff of smoke instead of getting on to the next gateway."

"What do you need?" Ryan asked.

"Access to an electronics shop," J.B. answered. "Got to have the right kind of soldering metals, magnification lenses so I can get a good look at what I'm doing. Robot arm with a laser is what would work best."

"Don't they have an electronics room in the re-doubt?" Albert asked. "Seems like they'd have one."

"They do," Ryan said. "From the blueprints J.B.

ciphered out, the electronics lab is down there somewhere around the docking bay.''

"Oh."

"Leaves us one choice," Ryan said.

J.B. nodded. "Go up top and take a look around."

"And if all you find is ice and snow?" the dwarf asked.

"Don't know that's true until we go look," Ryan said. "You start counting off possibilities before you go see what you can do, you might as well stay home and put a bullet in your brain. I'm not ready to do that yet."

IT WAS ONE HUNDRED feet to the top of the iceberg. Jak went up first, setting pitons they had found in one of the open storerooms.

The albino drove them deep and fast into the hard ice, having no problem at all to get them to seat. The white birds—Doc called them albatrosses and said they were birds with a lot of bad luck assigned to them—screamed at one another and took turns diving at Jak and Ryan. The cool green of the killer-cold ocean waited below for the slightest misstep.

Ryan wore the handkerchief around his lower face again, partly to keep out the water and partly to keep warm. The storerooms had also yielded new socks and underwear, all of them thermal lined. There hadn't been much in Albert's size, but the dwarf had made do.

Jak knew what he was doing when he set the pitons. The redoubt had also contained an enormous amount of rope. Between the pitons and the rope,

Ryan knew he and the teenager were crafting a stairway that the others could follow safely.

"Ready," Jak called down.

"Go," Ryan said, and dug into his position.

The albino removed one of his safety harnesses and latched it to the new piton he had in place. He pulled himself up and tied on to the new one, then reached for another piton.

Ryan hung on, feeling the wind pull at him with icy claws.

IT TOOK MORE THAN two hours for all of them to reach the summit of the iceberg.

Ryan stared out over the uneven terrain at the top. During the long climb, he had imagined several different ways that it might have looked. Seeing it still seemed a little stunning.

The top of the glacier was made up of a number of plateaus. Several of them held jagged edges, showing how the frozen surface had shaped then been reshaped by the elements. It was a nightmare rendered in cold white edges, stretching out as far as his eye could see.

"Dark night," J.B. yelled to be heard above the crash of surf below and the howling wind above. "All I've seen in this life, Ryan, and I've never seen anything like this."

Ryan swiveled from their lofty perch, taking in the various icebergs surrounding them. He'd taken a compass reading again at the mouth of the access tunnel, and it had showed that their iceberg was facing eight degrees farther south than it had previously.

"Looks like herd of icebergs," Jak commented. With the cold making his pale face even more white, his ruby eyes stood out like blood spots.

"And all headed south for the winter," Mildred said.

As they watched, three of the icebergs went completely to pieces, breaking and shattering in small white storms that left hardly anything visible above the ocean's surface. Their own iceberg shook and shivered, as well.

"You have to wonder where all those pieces of ice come from," Krysty said. "Makes me curious about what it must have looked like during the fiercest part of the cold after the nuclear winter."

"Probably like nothing you'd ever want to see," Dean said quietly. "I got no curiosity about seeing it. Be glad when we get off this one."

"I've been small all my life," Albert said, "but seeing this, going through that gateway like you people call it, makes me feel real small."

"We're all small when you get right down to it," Ryan stated. "It's up to a person how big of a footprint they want to leave when they step out of this life. That's what Trader always said." He shook himself, then resettled his gear over his body. "Let's move out. Jak, you and me are going to run point. Dean, you're walking drag with J.B., and make sure you don't lose sight of him and he doesn't lose sight of you."

"Right, Dad."

"Mildred, Krysty, you two are walking the middle, kind of loose wing positions. Not going to need to get spread out too far because we're going to keep this narrow. Doc, you and Albert are next."

"I have only one small question, my dear Ryan," the old man said. The wind blew his silvered lock over his shoulders where they were free of the muffler around his lower face.

"What?" Ryan asked irritably. He didn't have time for Doc's usual addle-brainedness with the iceberg sinking beneath them.

"How do you propose we find our way back to this place?" Doc asked.

"Got the compass," Ryan said.

"And with the shifting this deep-sea diamond in the rough is doing," Doc said, "I do not think you can count on the readings you are going to get from that compass."

"Doc's right," J.B. agreed. "If we get enough of a drift, even the minisextant isn't going to be much use. Especially if we get in a hurry."

"Fireblast," Ryan growled, looking out at the white expanse of broken terrain before him. "It's one bastard big rock, but how lost can we get?"

RYAN KEPT THEM moving with the ocean always to the right. If nothing else, they would walk in a giant circle. The problem would be to effectively search the center of the ice mass.

Snow was a problem, too. Piles of it covered the surface, making it necessary to test footing before stepping down through it. Only Jak's cat-quick reflexes saved him from dropping through a fissure in the iceberg that was thirty feet deep.

After an hour of moving through the cold and the snow, Ryan called a break. They huddled in a little group on the lee side of a massive upthrust of ice that shielded them from most of the wind. They ate double helpings of the self-heats they carried with them from the redoubt. All of them knew the dangers of exposure, and knew that they were burning extra calories simply by being out in the cold.

Even Ryan, as hardened as he was to the harsh life in Deathlands, couldn't help feeling a little doubtful about their chances.

"You're thinking too hard, lover," Krysty said.

Apart in their conversation from the rest of the companions, Ryan nodded. "Can't help thinking this is a fuck-all place to be."

"There's a way, lover." Krysty touched his face with her gloved hand, and he hated it that the cold had robbed him of the sensation. But the gesture meant a lot. "Over, under or around. There's always a way. You taught me that."

"We'll get it done," Ryan said. "We haven't ever been stopped before."

Then, with a clear, unmistakable intensity, a gunshot rolled over the companions.

RYAN TOOK THE LEAD, matching himself with Jak. He stayed low to the terrain, feeling the added moisture of his breath starting to cake up the handkerchief around his lower face. He held the Steyr at the ready in both hands, but kept the sweatshirt he'd taken from the clothing bins in the redoubt wrapped around the rifle to keep the action from freezing.

Jak paced him, twenty yards away, a pale ghost running against the snow-covered backdrop.

More gunshots echoed over them, coming faster now. Somewhere up ahead, serious gunplay was being dealt out.

Ryan felt more hopeful about the situation. J.B.'s minisextant had revealed they were in the Arctic Circle, somewhere below Greenland, if that place still yet existed. But the population density of the area preskydark hadn't been heavy. Doc had said that a few shipping lines used the routes during the warm seasons of the year.

But blasters meant men, and men usually meant some way of surviving. He was even further encouraged by the sounds of running engines. Images of boats filled his mind, and he figured he'd never really thought about how good a boat could look until he was thinking about them at that moment.

The land rose up before Ryan, but it was so white and so like the rest of the terrain that he couldn't tell the difference until he noticed that his angle to the ground had changed. His calf muscles ached from the increased fatigue, the cold and running uphill.

Then he cleared the edge, scanning it tight against the orange skyline for just a moment. The iceberg dropped away below him, cutting inward in a bowl-shaped depression from the shoreline.

Nearly forty people scrambled for cover below, dodging bullets fired at them from eight men ringed around them. The engine noises came from two small airwags that glided over them like giant hornets.

The airwags weren't true planes. Ryan had seen pics of those before. These were little more than seats with wings and a pusher-prop behind. The wings were nearly three times the length of a man, though the body of the plane might have been barely as long as a man was tall. Trapped in the bowl-shaped depression, the engines sounded loud, popping and snarling.

The forty people running for their lives didn't have weapons except for bows, arrows and spears. They dressed in furs and homespun clothing. Children ran with the adults, crying out in loud voices.

The gunners used full-scale assault weapons and moved in a definite military pattern. Luckily they seemed to be selective in their targets. Otherwise, every person down there would have been dead.

At another time, in another place, Ryan might not have been so quick to get involved. He'd seen massacres before, had taken part in some of them. A man wanting to keep his head on his shoulders where it belonged also kept his nose where it belonged. That had been one of the Trader's earliest remembered sayings.

But the companions were trapped on the iceberg, which was definitely not long for the world. The gunners had assault weapons and obviously a purpose for being there, but Ryan had to ask himself who would willingly stay on a sinking iceberg.

The other people, dressed in their furs and their

homespun clothing, gave him the impression of being native to the area. And there was no better source of information than a local.

One of the fur-clad men rose from behind a boulder, an arrow fitted to his string. He loosed it, and it crossed the distance to their attackers, catching the target in the chest. Before the bowman could get back to cover, a short burst blasted through his head.

Ryan settled in behind the Steyr, bracing it on the ground and easing the barrel past the ledge. He knew he would have only a few seconds' surprise working on his side before the gunners knew he was among them. He sighted on the middle of his targets, not going for a head shot because the chances were so slim. Then he let out half a breath, squeezed the trigger, then squeezed off a second round.

The heavy 7.62 mm bullets skated through the air, not affected by the wind at all. Two of the gunners were going down when Ryan dropped the crosshairs on the third. He squeezed again, moving his head automatically from the telescopic lens. If he had possessed two eyes, moving onto his next target would have been simply a matter of shifting the emphasis of his vision to his other eye. With one, he had to force the shift.

He caught the third target low in the back, ripping out a wash of blood from the man's midsection as his stomach shredded. Ryan moved to a fourth target, catching the man shifting behind cover, trying to get out of the line of fire. Ryan's round caught him flat-footed and knocked him down.

With an ululating wail, three of the fur-clad warriors pushed themselves free and rushed the three surviving men on the ground. One of them went down, his face shot away.

The small airwags fought to gain altitude and come around. Both of them had light machine guns mounted on the front of their craft. One of them got a line on Ryan and cut loose with a roar of autofire.

The ice ledge in front of Ryan seemed to go to pieces, hammered by the machine-gun rounds. Giving up his position, Ryan rolled on his side to escape the barrage. He scrambled on hands and knees to get back to cover, then brought up the Steyr again.

By that time one of the airwags was almost on top of him, the machine gun mounted on the front of it chattering away.

The Steyr banged against Ryan's shoulder as he put a round through the pilot's head.

Out of control, the airwag slammed into the side of the ice cliff just below Ryan. It erupted into a huge ball of flame that twisted up over Ryan's head and scudded black smoke clouds into the air.

Ryan felt the heat wash over him as he chambered a round and sighted the Steyr back on the killing site. Two of the fur-clad men had overrun one of the two surviving men on the ground. The last ground gunner was making tracks, heading over the ridge.

Leading the man slightly, Ryan picked him off in midstride, sending him tumbling back down the grade. He searched grimly for the last airwag, seeing it fleeing the battle area and streaking away straight out to sea. Before it went far, one of the albatrosses swooped down at it, maybe merely coming in for a better look, and maybe to defend its chosen territory.

The pilot couldn't avoid the big bird. He tried to bank his craft, but the albatross pursued, running straight over his head into the pusher-prop. Feathers flew in all directions, and the sound of the engine popping died instantly, its last echoes gasping across the icy beach. The airwag dropped into the ocean and disappeared in a heartbeat.

"Gone," Jak said.

Ryan nodded, confirming the albino's statement. Still, he waited for a while in case they had both been wrong. It wasn't likely, and it didn't happen. He turned, knowing J.B. could see him. The Armorer had held his position with the others in case Jak and Ryan had been forced to abandon theirs. Ryan waved them up.

Then he stood and started down the steep side of the bowl-shaped depression, wondering whose fight he'd interrupted and which side he'd joined. More than anything, he hoped the fur-clad people had a way off the iceberg. He didn't relish the thought of being adrift somewhere in the Arctic Circle, but it beat the hell out of drowning.

Chapter Twenty-Five

Ryan kept the Steyr in both hands as he walked down the incline. Despite the help he had given them, the fur-clad people hadn't chosen to come out of hiding. The line of warriors shifted, coming on point to face him. Since there appeared to be only one of him, they were braver.

One of the warriors stood and approached Ryan. He carried an ice ax in his hands. Someone had altered the handle, though, adding a four-foot-long bone shank instead of the foot-long metal handle, increasing the weapon's reach.

Ryan halted just out of what he considered to be easy bow-and-arrow range.

Through the narrow face of his hood, the fur-clad warrior looked Indian. His features were dark, with marked cheekbones, his hair a raven's-wing black. He wore fur mittens that covered his hands but allowed him to use his ax freely.

The man spoke in a guttural language.

"Don't understand a word you're saying," Ryan said in a nonthreatening voice. He looked past the man and saw that despite his actions of gunning down their attackers, he had gained no new friends. That was okay, though. It proved that the crowd he was facing was a savvy lot.

Even as he stood there, several warriors were seeking out the men he had shot. They finished off those who survived with knives, and took the weapons, brandishing them and yelling in that same guttural language as the warrior who addressed Ryan.

"You speak English," the warrior said.

"Yes," Ryan replied. And from the look on the man's weathered face, he didn't know which of them was more surprised about the other's ability.

The warrior nodded. "You're Russian?"

"No."

"Then what?"

Ryan shrugged. "I'm from a place called Deathlands. Heard of it?"

The warrior shook his head.

"Had another name a long time ago," Ryan said. "Called itself the United States."

"American," the warrior stated.

"Guess so." Ryan didn't really consider himself anything but free. But when the companions had made a jump to Moscow, Ryan had been surprised to find how much patriotism remained in him for the old, dead country. "Those men were Russian?"

"Yeah."

"Who are you?" Ryan asked.

"My name's Harlan," the warrior said. "I'm chief of this tribe. Have you got boats?"

Ryan shook his head. "I was hoping you would have."

Harlan narrowed his eyes. "How did you get here?"

"That's a long story, Chief."

"Don't have time for a long story," the chief said. "As soon as Vitkin finds out his search-and-capture team is dead, he's going to come hunting."

THE ALLIANCE between the companions and the fur-clad people was uneasy. Ryan and his small group sat together, except for Doc and Mildred, who helped with the wounded. The med kits they had packed in the redoubt to carry them through their excursion exhausted quickly, but most of the Inuit were taken care of.

Ryan knew Chief Harlan didn't buy his story about having been part of a trading ship that had blown off course and went down only a short distance from the iceberg, but the Inuit leader didn't press the issue. Ryan didn't want to give up the gateway, or the redoubt, if he could help it.

Harlan's own story was that he and his tribe were trying to get some of their people back from the Russian Captain Gotfrid Vitkin after the chunk of glacier had split off from the main mass.

Ryan hadn't quite gotten used to the way the chief could slip from his native tongue into English so easily. Harlan said his ancestors had been part of a British science observatory in the Arctic Circle at the time of the nukecaust, and they'd been taken in by the Inuit. When everything froze over, there weren't many other places to go, so they'd become more Inuit than British.

"The quakes had gotten worse than usual in the area lately," Harlan said. "Still, no one expected all the ice masses to tear free the way they had. We tracked this iceberg for two days before we found the right one.''

''Where are your boats?'' Dean asked.

''Vitkin's sailors shot them up,'' Harlan answered. ''We got caught coming onto the iceberg less than an hour ago. Vitkin's got to be getting desperate.''

''Why?'' J.B. asked. ''If he's a captain, then he's got a ship.''

Harlan laughed without humor. ''He's got a ship, all right. But it's mired in the ice. Been there since skydark.''

The battle between the Russians and the Inuit had raged for decades, according to Harlan. They had started out trading back sixty years earlier when Harlan's wandering tribe had found the Russians.

''Vitkin has a ship?'' J.B. asked, pausing in the middle of stripping a piece of pemmican one of the Inuit women had passed out to the companions.

''Yeah,'' Harlan said, then added a Russian phrase. ''Means *Red Star of Glory* or something like that. After all these years, who cares, you know?'' He shrugged. ''Anyway, the story my ancestors handed down to me—and most things are stories around here, because paper and pencil is a luxury, not to mention extra weight you have to lug around—the Russians were some sort of strike team sent into the area to take out some secret base the Americans were supposed to have. Who knows if any of that is true?''

Ryan ate his pemmican, working around the salty taste of it, and didn't say anything.

"Vitkin's father's father or something like that, so the story goes, was the original captain of the ship," Harlan went on. "Supposed to have been some other ships, but they all got lost in a battle. Only thing that survived was the *Red Star of Glory*. And it's locked up in the ice."

"Vitkin has some of your people?" Krysty asked.

"Yeah. See, back in those days, you didn't find many Russian sailor women," the chief said. "Vitkin's ancestor, to keep up the population, started trading with the Inuit people—other tribes than ours—and traded a few guns for young women. Chiefs made the deals. Up here, a large tribe is a pain in the ass to take care of. You're always on the move, always looking for enough food to get you by."

"Seems to me," Albert said, "that the Russians would have the same problems. Did they trade for food?"

"A little. Stuff that they wanted. They had a lot of stores on ship, though. And the original Captain Vitkin didn't want to become dependent on the Inuit."

"Except for women," Dean said.

"Right. But after a while, he started raising his own women. Didn't want to lose the Russian bloodline, you see."

"How inbred are they?" Ryan asked. He had seen small villages so phobic they killed outlanders outright with no thought at all to their own gene pool, degenerating quickly in a matter of a few generations.

"Pretty badly," Doc said, approaching the group.

"Got a lot of stale genes," Mildred added. "Those dead guys I got a look at have mismatched arms and legs, cranial problems, cleft palates, no chins, and an assortment of other prime indicators that daddy's not been rutting far from the old homestead." She hunkered down and helped herself to the pemmican.

"That's what the latest Captain Vitkin was doing when he captured our people," Harlan said. "Trying to add to his bloodstock. After his father started killing some of the Inuit who came to trade with him, getting medicines and guns, everybody said fuck him, who needs it? They go out, pound a seal to death when it's asleep, had a new set of clothes, fat for their lanterns if they had or wanted them, and meat for a week. Russians were the ones who needed something."

"But he captured your people?" Ryan said.

Harlan grinned. "Sure. We let him."

"Why?" Krysty asked.

"Vitkin has guns," Harlan said. "With the ice breaking up the way it has, hunting and fishing areas among the Inuit are getting more tense. Man who has the most guns is going to get to hunt and fish. Everybody else is going to starve. Me, I intend to have a bigger tribe."

"And do what?" Ryan asked.

"Mebbe go south," Harlan said.

"Lot of ocean to cover."

"Vikings did it," the chief said confidently, "in really small boats."

"Then why let Vitkin capture your people?" Dean asked. "Seems stupe."

Ryan gave his son a glance, letting Dean know he had said more than was necessary.

Dean nodded.

"Actually it's a pretty smart thing to do," Harlan said. "Vitkin's numbers aboard the ship have gotten low. They're having a lot of stillborn lately because their gene pool is so messed up. But the Russian sailors are lazy. They get our women on the ship, they have sex with them, hope they turn up pregnant and use them as slaves to cook and clean."

"You sent those girls into that?" Doc asked in an incredulous voice.

"That's cruel," Mildred said.

Harlan looked defensive, as if afraid he were going to lose the goodwill of his new friends. "I asked for volunteers. I had four girls who said they would go. No pressure from me. Sex is sex. Enjoyed sex a time or two with a couple of them myself. You've got to have something to do when it's too cold to go out and do anything else. Hated to see them go."

Ryan didn't like the idea, but he saw the logic in it.

"And they were trading off a few months of discomfort against a training that would make them valuable," Harlan went on.

"As maids and gaudy sluts?" Mildred asked.

"I don't know about gaudy sluts," Harlan said.

"A girl who sells sex for money," Mildred elaborated.

"No." Harlan waved the accusation away.

"Cooking and cleaning aren't the only things the girls get trained on. Vitkin also puts them to work making reloads for their weapons and doing some repair work on the guns." His eyes widened. "Do you know how much those girls will be in demand when they get away from the Russians?"

"Why hasn't anyone ever done it before?" Ryan asked.

Harlan swiveled his gaze to the one-eyed man. "Hell, they have. You think I thought of this all on my own? A lot of Inuit tribes who have chiefs like me have thought of this. I bet there's nine tribes I know of right now who've benefited from their girls getting on the Russian ship, then escaping and bringing back the knowledge they learned. This is just business. Why do you think the Russians try to hang on to their own gene pool so long? They have sex the second and third generations because the kids generally won't try to escape the ship. Soon as they're born and up and around, the Russians kill the mother. Or the mother escapes and leaves them there because it's too hard to escape carrying a baby."

"But the more the Inuit learn from the Russians," Mildred said, "the less reason they have to go back."

Harlan smiled and nodded like a teacher who had just gotten the correct answer to a difficult question from the brightest of his students. "Exactly. Got a tribe who sent a few girls in to learn the hydroponics procedure the Russians developed on the ship, got two girls back, which is a pretty good return. That was twenty years ago. Now they're set up in a ville on a coastline where they can reach the dirt, put in some of the seeds the Russians got from gutting the birds in the area and raise a few vegetables that hadn't been seen in this area before. Other tribes work themselves to death finding things to trade them.''

''The Russians had a hydroponics farm set up on the ship?'' J.B. asked.

''No,'' Harlan answered. ''They set one up after they found out how trapped they were.''

''A goodly number of the sailors for the Russians at the time,'' Doc put in, ''were men taken from the collective farms. They were conscripted by the government to learn the navy after learning how to farm in bleak conditions sometimes not too unlike what we're seeing here. It makes sense that some of the crew would be able to put a hydroponics farm together.''

''How long have your girls been on board the ship?'' Ryan asked.

''Three months, give or take a couple weeks,'' Harlan replied. ''The plan was to leave them there for three months. They got ways of keeping themselves from getting pregnant too easy. Six months, they would have learned a lot of things. Then this quake hit and set this iceberg loose. The tribes, we all saw it coming. Just figured we had more time.''

''How many Russians do you think there are?'' Ryan asked.

''Able and willing to fight us?''

''Yeah.''

"Twenty, maybe as many as forty."

Ryan looked at J.B., turning the numbers around in his head. "What do you think?"

"If Harlan's people join in," the Armorer said, "it puts us closer to even. We wait until dark, give them time to bed down, mebbe it'll get a little easier if we can put a boarding party onto the ship and reduce the numbers before all hell breaks loose."

Ryan nodded, then looked around at the rest of the group, waiting.

Everyone was in favor of throwing their lot in with the Inuit and taking the Russian ship. "We don't really have a choice if we want to get off this iceberg, lover," Krysty said.

In the distance another cannon burst of cracking ice sounded. The glacier shivered, the ground actually seeming to bob beneath their feet.

"Wow!" Harlan exclaimed. "That was a big one."

Ryan turned back to the chief. "Let's go take a look at that ship."

Chapter Twenty-Six

"Russian frigate," J.B. said. "Probably the Krivak-class type II. The IIIs had helicopter additions. And the IIs came out with the four-inch blasters aft that you see covered over by the tarp."

Ryan scanned the big ship from stem to stern with his field glasses. He noted some movement on her decks. Evidently Captain Vitkin had gotten disturbed about his search-and-capture team's failure to reappear and had put out extra guards.

Ice climbed more than halfway up the sides of the big ship. There were also places that looked like they had been cleared of ice that threatened to climb up on the decks. As Ryan shifted his field glasses to the frigate's prow, he saw a four-man crew working on roped scaffolding with axs and sledges to break the ice free there. Rust had settled into the ship like rad cancer, starting to eat holes through the plate steel. In places, cut metal had been riveted over what Ryan had to assume were holes that went all the way through.

"Been cannibalizing their own ship to hold the outer hull together," J.B. said. "You take a close look at the plates that have been placed, you can see where a welding torch has cut through them."

Ryan nodded. He had noticed the same thing.

As had the dead Russians they had left behind at the firefight, the sailors aboard the ship wore uniforms. They also carried blasters.

Tarps covered the big blasters on the deck, drawing Ryan's attention.

"Got cannon and heavy machine blasters on the decks," he said.

The Armorer nodded. "Saw them. With those tarps over them, you have to think they're taking care of them for a reason."

"Harlan," Ryan called.

"Yeah," the Inuit chief responded.

"The deck blasters work?"

"Blasters?"

"Guns."

"They did twelve years ago or thereabouts," Harlan answered. "That was the last time anybody tried to take the ship by force. Those heavy-cal machine guns chewed up every warrior caught out in the open."

"They attack by day or night?"

"By night. Are you kidding?"

"And the Russians turned them back?" J.B. asked.

"They got goggles that let them see at night," Harlan replied.

"And you hoped to pull off a night time attack against them?" Ryan said.

"Yeah. Seven years ago, the Russians got a virus that killed off a lot of them. I know about it because some of the tribes they traded with were offered guns in exchange for cures."

"Did they give them a cure?" Ryan asked.

"No. Everybody hoped the Russians would die down to a handful. It would be easier to take the ship. But they brought up every evil-tasting concoction that the Inuit tribes could think up for nearly five months. Nobody ever passes up a chance to get guns from those people."

"Why didn't the Russians leave the ship?" Krysty asked.

"The first few years, according to the legends I've been handed down and told to keep track of," Harlan said, "they tried to chop their way out of the ice. Even tried blasting their way out with the big deck guns. Nothing doing. Had more ice freeze up overnight than they could blast if they fired all day long. So they stayed put, protecting secrets or some such nonsense. The fact was, none of them were going to be able to survive the nuclear winter at the time, nor really know which direction to go. Compasses were screwed up for a long time. Then they had an explosion in the engine room. Blew out part of the keel. They tried to fix it but couldn't. Only thing keeping them afloat is that ice out there. If this iceberg breaks up, even if it cracks somehow around that frigate, that ship's going to sink."

"Do they know the iceberg's going down?" Mildred asked.

"Did you stop to ask any of those guys back there?" Harlan asked.

Mildred made a face but shook her head.

"Neither did I. But they shot up our boats like they didn't have a worry in the world. Maybe they're just too stupid to know, and maybe they're going to make use of some of those lifeboats they got on board.''

"Hot pipe, Dad!" Dean said. "If they've got lifeboats, we might be able to get one and not have to worry about fixing the—''

Ryan froze his son's last few words with a stony stare. "That's right, Dean. A lifeboat's what we're going to aim for.''

But he knew Harlan hadn't missed the exchange.

Ryan turned his attention to Harlan. "I want you to keep your people back out of sight. Two of us are going to go forward for a look, get the probable Russian numbers and get ready to go in at night.''

Harlan nodded.

"Vitkin's probably going to expect something, but if we can get a small team on board quietly, we can cut the numbers down some. Mebbe whittle the odds in our favor. First time things go ballistic on board, the team there will dig in and try to hold the fort while the rest of you come running.''

"That's pretty much how I figured it," Harlan said. "When we take the ship, you're welcome to any boats or weapons you can carry.''

Ryan gave the man a hard glare. "No, friend, *you're* welcome. Because I don't think you people would have a snowball's chance in hell against those Russians without us." And it was important to make that statement, because he didn't want Harlan or any of the other Inuit to get the idea they would be better off going it alone.

"Sure," Harlan replied. "No reason to be so hard-assed about it."

"I've got every reason," Ryan said. "So do you. I'm just laying the ace on the line so everybody can see it. Won't stop at just sending Russians on the last train for the coast if it's got to be done. You need to know that."

RYAN SHIVERED as he crawled toward the frigate. It was bad enough the sun had gone down nearly an hour earlier and the full chill of the Arctic night had settled in over the iceberg. The wind whipped away even more warmth.

But the thing that hurt most of all was the snow he had packed around his body. Doc had come up with the idea, dipping somewhere into his tangle trove of memories. Using spare furs and blankets, sinew and bone needles, they had stitched up bulky suits to wear over their outer clothes. Then they had filled the gap in between the extra furs and their clothes with snow and ice chips.

If the Russians were using thermal imaging as J.B. figured, the snow and ice packing would reduce the escaping heat signature of their bodies. And if they were using night-vision goggles, the white polar-bear fur they wore would make them harder to be seen against the terrain.

He paused for a moment, trying to make little distances so a guard wouldn't be as likely to notice the change. Glancing over to his left, he barely spotted Jak and J.B., clambering along in the thick suits, as well.

Fifty yards passed in virtual silence. The ship grew bigger against the terrain. A hundred yards farther on, the ship became the skyline in front of Ryan. The moon sat in the sky behind it, only a quarter full.

When he reached the ship's shadow straddling the frozen ground less than forty yards from his goal, Ryan felt like he was crawling inside the coldest spot he had ever entered.

Voices reached him, speaking in Russian.

He lay still on the ground, trying not to shiver too much. The voices drifted over his head, then finally drifted away. When he looked up again, he saw Jak crawling up the icy incline to reach the starboard side of the ship.

Ryan crept along, as well. With the cold wind whipping, the Russian guards weren't as enamored of doing the sentry duty as they might have been at some other time.

He pushed himself up silently, then grabbed the railing in a gloved hand. He eased up and took a look, spotting a guard poking his head around the corner. Going still again, he waited, feeling his body rebel against the seeping cold that ate in from the big fur suit.

When the guard looked away, he hauled himself aboard. Before he could take more than a couple steps, another quake rocked the iceberg. Earsplitting cracks sounded off in the distance, then the iceberg twisted sickeningly again.

Ryan held on to the railing, his feet sliding across the fresh ice that had frozen on the decks. He hung on to the fur-wrapped Steyr grimly, working to keep it from banging against the railing. He didn't really think it would be heard above the grinding that sounded deep within the ice around the frigate, but didn't want to take the chance all the same.

Metal screamed below from the abuse it was taking as the ice shifted. One of the lifeboats in its moorings beside Ryan squealed as the chains shifted.

Then the quake was over, although the vibrations continued running the four-hundred-foot length of the frigate.

After stripping out of the bulky fur suit packed with snow and ice, Ryan moved toward the guard he had spotted, staying in close to the superstructure. He slid the panga free and shouldered the Steyr.

The man coughed in front of him, and Ryan saw the puffs of gray breath slip around the corner. The one-eyed warrior slid forward, staying behind the corner.

The man had his back to Ryan, sipping from a cup held in both his hands. Ryan slipped an arm around the man's face, jamming it tight up against the man's mouth so he couldn't scream. Then he yanked the panga's cruel blade across the Russian's throat. The cup dropped to the deck, spilling its contents across the ice and causing gray steam to rise.

Blood spurted as carotoid and windpipe were severed. Holding on to the man to keep him from running, Ryan felt the life leave the man.

He waited, making sure no one saw him, then threw the body over the side onto the ice. The sound of it hitting was muffled by the bulky clothes the corpse wore.

Ryan went on, the panga bare in his hands. The second man saw him and had enough time to attempt to raise his pistol, then the one-eyed man was on him. Ryan drove the man back with his weight, clapping a gloved hand over the sailor's mouth. He stabbed the panga deep into the man's throat, then angled it up so it went into the Russian's brain.

Dragging the body, Ryan stashed it under one of the tarps covering the deck-mounted machine guns.

A shadow drifted in front of him, coming from the other side of the ship. Moonlight splintered off of J.B.'s glasses as the Armorer turned to face Ryan.

J.B. held up three fingers, then closed them, signaling that he'd met three Russians along the way and none of them were part of the problem anymore.

Ryan showed him two fingers, then turned a hand up, letting the Armorer know that he hadn't completely recced the stern section of the frigate yet.

The stern section of the frigate had two levels. The back dropped down eight feet or more, Ryan couldn't tell exactly because of the shadows, and companionways on either side that led down. A second set of blasters was below the first, also covered by a tarp.

Footsteps came toward Ryan, sending him into hiding behind the steps after waving a warning to J.B. He remained still, hoping the shadows beneath the companionway would be enough to hide him.

The Russian sailor's eyes had to have been bad, or he was one of the really inbred ones. He looked short and skinny, almost like a mutie because his face was a set of mismatched angles. He started up the companionway without a second thought.

Ryan fell in behind him, wrapping a big hand around his throat to squeeze off any chance of the sailor crying out. Then slipped the panga between the man's third and fourth ribs, driving the long blade into the heart beneath.

The man gave a series of convulsive jerks, flailing back at Ryan with both hands. It took him less than a minute to fight through what remained of his life.

Ryan wiped off the blade, then left the corpse lying out of sight beneath the steps. He continued on, matching his stride with J.B.'s. He found a final man at the very back of the stern, pressed up against the railing and looking out against the stark whiteness of the iceberg that was carrying them all to their doom.

He ate slowly and methodically from a small cup of what smelled to Ryan like soup broth with a fish-and-potato base. He leaned against the storage wall of the abovedecks room, taking shelter from the wind.

Ryan moved in behind him.

The sailor had to have sensed something, because Ryan knew there was nothing for the man to have heard. The guy turned dropping one hand to the blaster holstered on his hip.

Ryan buttstroked him with the Steyr, the stock making a dull crunch against the Russian's head. He moaned weakly as he fell, letting Ryan know he wasn't dead.

The one-eyed man knelt, slipping the blaster away from the man and pressing the panga against his naked throat. "Talk quietly or you die."

The man remained still. The moonlight played over his waxy features, showing the knots of bone swelling up from his forehead, and the unevenness of his face, one cheek higher than the other. His nose had an extra hole in it, just to the side of the right that made a whistling noise as he breathed hard.

"Do you understand English?" Ryan demanded in a harsh whisper.

"*Da,*" the man replied.

"Do you know what an electronics lab is?"

"*Da,*" the man said.

"Where is it?" Ryan asked.

The mismatched hazel eyes blinked in perplexity. "*Da?*"

"The electronics lab," Ryan repeated.

"I found it," J.B. said from beside Ryan. "Guy I questioned on the other side said it was amidships. Door on the port side will take you into it."

"Get there," Ryan ordered. "See if you can repair that circuit board."

The Armorer nodded and slipped away.

"*Da?*" the Russian said. Only a low level of intelligence flickered in his gaze. His voice rose in a wail at the end before Ryan slashed his throat.

A harsh question ripped from a man farther up on the superstructure.

Ryan took shelter against the wall beside him an instant before a bullet ricocheted off the deck in a haze of yellow sparks. He unfurled the Steyr from the fur covering and brought it to his shoulder in one smooth movement. Autofire raked the deck, searching for him, coming closer.

Then he had the Russian sailor in his sights. His finger curled over the trigger and pulled. The Steyr bounced against his shoulder. The heavy 7.62 mm bullet struck its target, driving the man back and off the superstructure by the radar dish and sent a corpse crashing to the deck.

Ryan ran forward, climbing up the companionway at a dead run. His foot nearly slipped out from under him on an ice patch as he pushed himself to the upper deck. He passed the first ladder built into the superstructure, then took the ladder attached to the wall to the right at the side of the lifeboat he'd spotted earlier. He scrambled up the ladder as Russian sailors bolted from inside the ship.

He climbed up another ladder to his left, heading for a higher deck near one of the radar dishes. It wasn't the forward vantage point on the main section of the superstructure where the antennae were clustered, but it gave him a view over much of the stern decks. Jak would have to control as much of the forward decks as he could.

The cold didn't touch him anymore as he lifted the Steyr. He focused on the telescopic sights, finding the first of his targets. His finger caressed the trigger, blowing the Russian's head apart.

J.B. HESITATED only a second when the blasterfire erupted before twisting the handle on the door to the electronics room. The Armorer knew Jak and Ryan were going to be hard up against it, but none of them had a chance if the circuit boards weren't repaired.

He went through the door with the Uzi held at waist level.

A question erupted in Russian from one of the two men standing beside a metal lathe. The room was filled with the sound of grinding. Harlan had stated that the solar-powered batteries that powered much of the frigate remained intact, and that most of the electronics and propulsion systems were also intact.

J.B. had pretty much figured that after seeing the remains of the makeshift airwag back where Ryan and Jak had hooked up with the Inuit. The airway had been cobbled together from motors on different pieces of the frigate's equipment, and shaped in a machinist's shop.

He brought up the Uzi and loosed a snarling burst that caught both Russians as they went for their blasters. The room was lit by electric lights, though there were only about one-third the normal number. J.B. figured they were trying to conserve on the number of bulbs they had.

Unfortunately the bullets also ripped into a control panel, starting an electrical fire.

Spotting the red fire extinguisher on the wall, J.B. crossed the room and grabbed it. He pulled the pin and shook it up, then squeezed the trigger. Instead of a blast of chem-suppressor hosing the fire, a little fart of powder jumped at the fire. It did nothing to slow the blaze down. Smoke pooled against the top of the room.

J.B. tossed aside the fire extinguisher and scanned the room, listening to the crash of blasterfire outside the door pick up the pace. He moved at a jog, going deeper into the room.

The comp-assisted solder system was next to a diagnostics tester.

The Armorer switched on the machine. While he waited for the soldering points to warm to the prescribed temperature, he took the mat-trans circuit boards from inside his shirt where he had kept them over his heart. He had figured that his heart would be the last place he would get hit by a bullet and live to regret losing the circuit boards.

He placed the circuit boards on the soldering surface, locking them down with wing nuts specially designed to hold delicate electronics. The soldering iron already glowed red, and wisps of smoke eddied up from the tip as impurities burned off.

The smoke it made, though, was nothing like the smoke coming from the fire starting to ravage the electronics workshop.

Resolutely J.B. leaned in over the comp and used the joystick to start laying in the lines of solder to repair the circuit boards. The comp setup and program were similar to ones he had worked with when the Trader had needed serious work done on communications or munitions systems.

He watched the thin beads of silver solder fit neatly into place.

Then a quiver shook the ship, even stronger than the one that had hit it before. Instinctively he lifted the soldering point from the circuit board's surface to wait until the quiver was over.

But it lasted longer than the previous one.

And this time J.B. felt himself go weightless for a moment as the frigate slipped in the embrace of the iceberg. Ice crushed against the walls outside, and the skidding sounds let him know they were rising.

The Armorer looked through one of the windows near the workstation, not surprised at all to see the broken edge of the ice that had been chopped away from the ship suddenly rise three feet above the railing.

Whatever ice remained below the ship, it was no longer strong enough to support the frigate's weight.

The ship was sinking.

Chapter Twenty-Seven

"The ship's going down!"

Krysty watched as Harlan's shout became a reality. The Russian frigate wallowed like a dying animal in the ice trough. Even from a distance, she could hear the splintering of ice around the vessel. "Gaia, protect Ryan," she prayed quietly.

"We've got to go," Dean said from beside her. He pushed himself up from hiding.

"Wait!" Krysty's sharp command froze him into place.

A pained look filled the boy's face.

"We're going," Krysty said, "but we're going to do this just the way Ryan would. If we go rushing in there like chickens with our heads chopped off, you know what's going to be on the lunch menu."

Dean nodded.

"Harlan!" Krysty yelled over the thunder of the breaking ice.

"Yeah," the Inuit chieftain called back.

"Are your people ready?"

"That ship's going down."

"It isn't down yet," Krysty said.

Abruptly the iceberg stopped quivering, and the frigate stopped its plunge.

"Okay," Harlan said, his gaze locked to the ship

that barely remained above the rim of ice that had
been chopped around it. "But if it goes—"

"If it goes, you're going down with this iceberg,"
Krysty reminded him.

"I guess we're in it as deep as you are."

"Whether we save Ryan and the others," Krysty
declared, "those lifeboats aboard the frigate are all
the hope you have left of getting off this iceberg."

Harlan nodded, turning and speaking quickly to
his little band of warriors. None of them seemed
happy about the prospect. "Whenever you're
ready."

Krysty looked at Doc, Mildred and Albert.

"Lead on," Mildred said.

"'Damn the torpedoes—full speed ahead,'" Doc
shouted, waving his sword stick toward the foundering frigate.

Krysty pushed up from cover and started for the
ship. Her friends followed her, flanked by the Inuit.

RYAN BLASTED the Steyr empty. Having no chance
to reload, he cleared leather with the SIG-Sauer and
started to fire again. He had put three of the Russians
down with the long blaster, but there appeared
plenty of them left.

Footsteps rung on metal at his side, slightly behind him. Only his combat senses honed over years
of living in the Deathlands and dozens of battles
fought while with War Wag One allowed him to sort
that new, more threatening sound out from the noise
of battle all around him.

He spun, leveling the 9 mm at the end of his arm.

A face, malformed and demonic in intensity, appeared at the top of the stair, followed almost immediately by a rifle barrel.

Ryan fired from less than six feet away. The hollowpoint blasted through the sailor's head, emptying his brainpan in a scarlet rush. The corpse clung stubbornly to the ladder for a moment, then finally lost the fight against gravity.

Even as he was pulling back into position, Ryan's eye caught a flicker of movement arcing through the air. He tracked it, bringing up the SIG-Sauer, then recognized it as an implo gren.

"Fireblast!" He threw himself behind the support struts for the antenna overhead and curled into the protection as much as he could.

The implo gren went up in a thunderclap of noise and a white-hot flash of light.

Partially deafened from the concussion, Ryan forced himself to a standing position. He peered over the railing and took a two-handed grip on the 9 mm blaster as a man broke cover. He led the Russian sailor slightly, then squeezed the trigger and put two rounds through the man's lungs.

The sailor dropped to the deck, then tried to get back to his feet.

Knowing the man was already dead where he was, Ryan moved on, seeking more targets. He fired the blaster dry, then took cover again briefly to change magazines. He tripped the slide release, stripping the top round and feeding it into the breech.

Movement across from him, skylined against the

moon hanging against the sable sky, alerted him to the fact that another Russian had climbed to a threatening position. A fully automatic weapon kicked to life, blistering the deck and the railing with sparks.

Ryan rolled left and brought up the SIG-Sauer. Partially covered by the superstructure, he blasted at the gunner. The first four rounds clipped metal all around the sailor before the fifth one bounced from the railing and cut through the man's crotch.

With a shrill scream, the gunman dropped his weapon, sank to his knees and tried to hold his groin with both hands. Even in the dim moonlight, Ryan saw the dark black blood come spilling through.

Then he noticed motion to the left and thought the rest of the companions and the Inuit were closing on the frigate as arranged. A barrage of muzzle-flashes split the night, giving further weight to his impression.

Then he noticed they were approaching from the starboard side of the vessel, not the port side. A closer look while under cover showed him that the newly arriving group was twice the size of Harlan's tribe.

Arrows pelted the frigate, letting Ryan know it was another Inuit tribe even before he got a clear look at the leaders.

Then the frigate slipped through the ice, dropping another few feet.

"SOMEONE ELSE IS attacking the frigate!" Doc shouted.

Krysty laid down a covering fire with her .38,

blasting away at the small knot of Russians grouped around the superstructure where she had last seen Ryan. She glanced across the frigate—it was so low in the ice that she could see the iceberg's terrain on the other side of it.

"It's Dichali's tribe," Harlan said. "The old bastard must have figured on making a last attempt on the Russians himself." He reloaded the weapon he'd taken from one of the dead men earlier.

"Are you friends with him?" Krysty asked.

"Hell no. Dichali would cut his own mother's throat if she couldn't look after herself. He'll try to kill us just to keep us from getting anything from the ship."

Krysty reloaded her pistol, staring into the distance. Dichali's tribe had nearly three times the number of warriors as Harlan's.

Ryan, J.B. and Jak were caught in the cross fire.

"The boats," she said. "If your people don't get them before that ship goes down, you're all dead."

"And you're not?" Harlan demanded.

Krysty gave him a hard stare. "Better be a lot of boats." She pushed up and closed the distance to the frigate.

LOOKING AT THE LAST BEAD of solder he had just finished putting down, J.B. knew it was as close as he was going to be able to manage to getting the circuit boards back to original form. He switched off the soldering iron and shoved the robot arm out of the way.

Before he could pick up the circuit boards, the

frigate listed hard to starboard. He crashed up against the table, bruising his injured ribs. Pain almost claimed him, sucking his senses down into a black void.

He made himself breathe, made himself see through the swirling black comets in his vision. Then he became aware of a liquid roar that rushed into the room. The acrid smoke from the electrical fire had already burned his lungs and seared his eyes.

Glancing to the left, he saw water rush into the ship through a tear in the side. Evidently the frigate had been torqued by the ice and broken in two.

With the way it was taking on water, J.B. knew the ship's life expectancy above the ocean could only be measured in minutes now. He unfastened the wing nuts and picked up the circuit boards as water swirled over his feet. He felt the freezing intensity of it at once, feeling his feet almost go numb.

He wrapped the circuit boards in the bubbled plastic he had found at the redoubt, then put them back close to his heart. The Uzi in his hands, he made his way to the door, sloshing through the seawater.

Outside he caught a Russian sailor flat-footed as he tried to sneak up on Ryan's position above. He cut a blistering figure eight with the weapon and blew the man backward. He raised his voice. "Ryan!"

"Yeah."

"We're done."

"Got a new problem."

As J.B. listened, he realized there was entirely too much blasterfire, even when he added in Harlan's people. "Coming up."

"Come ahead, but watch your ass."

The Armorer climbed the ladder rapidly, letting the Uzi hang by its strap. As he crested the top, he saw the approaching army of Inuit. "This is a bad place to be right now."

"Without a doubt," Ryan agreed. "You got the circuit boards fixed?"

"Won't know until we try to do the jump."

"Then let's see if we can cut and run from here." Ryan blasted another Russian on the deck. "I've got a feeling those men coming up aren't going to call it quits early."

J.B. looked down on the starboard side, seeing the depth-charge launcher below. The approaching Inuit were about two hundred yards away. "Mebbe I can do something about them." He crossed to the starboard side and clambered down.

Ryan provided covering fire instinctively.

The Armorer hoped the frigate's fire controls were still on. He checked over the depth-charge launcher and found the operations panel. He activated it, watching as the launcher shot the explosive drums over the side.

The barrels arched in the air, sailing fifty yards up and nearly that far out. They came crashing down against the ice, throwing up chips and snow in a crystalline haze on impact.

They didn't explode.

The ranks of the Inuit from the second tribe pulled

back at first, afraid of getting hit by the barrels even
if they didn't recognize what they were.

J.B. pulled up the Uzi and slipped in a fresh magazine. He stood beside the depth-charge launcher as
it continued to cycle through its twenty-five-drum
supply. Then he opened up with the subgun, target-
ing the depth charges.

He had no idea what the preset depths were on
the drums, but they exploded just fine when they
were hit with the bullets. He even caught some of
them in the air, sending flames and debris shooting
in all directions. Shrapnel dug into the ice and shat-
tered against the steel hide of the frigate.

Then he climbed back up to rejoin Ryan.

The one-eyed man sighted through the Steyr's telescopic lens and set off some of the other barrels
that J.B. hadn't hit.

"Time to leave," Ryan growled.

BELOW, KRYSTY REACHED the lifeboat's release
switches as a fresh shudder ran through the Russian
frigate. The big boat came down, slamming hard
against the packed ice. With the deck tilted, the lifeboat didn't touch the ship at all.

"Get the boat," Krysty told Harlan.

The Inuit chief yelled at some of his warriors,
motioning them over. They got behind the boat and
managed to push it quite easily across the frozen
surface. The rounded keel was a natural runner
across the ice.

Mildred stood nearby, her ZKR 551 pistol in her

hands, blasting methodically at any Russians that became available.

Krysty scanned the ship, tense with worry, wondering where Ryan was. She went forward, climbing onto the ship. She felt it shivering, sinking, but couldn't just stand by and watch it.

Then she felt hands close around her waist from behind. At first she thought it might be Ryan. But when she turned, the lean face definitely wasn't that of her lover.

The man raised a pistol into her throat. "You will please refrain from screaming," he said.

In the confusion swirling around the lifeboat below, she knew no one saw the man take her.

"ICEBERG'S SINKING, TOO," J.B. said. "Explosions and the weight of the ship are too much for it." The dull, roaring echoes of the depth charges continued to roll across the icescape.

Ryan looked down at the black water swirling up out of the dark fissure as they climbed down on the port side of the frigate. "If the whole iceberg goes, we lose the mat-trans unit and possibly our way back to Deathlands."

"Can't be helped," the Armorer said pragmatically. "It'll be there, or it won't."

"Ryan, J.B."

Ryan turned, spotting Jak farther up the crooked deck.

"Found another boat. But need help."

"What kind of boat?" Ryan asked.

"Has motor," Jak said. "Mebbe faster than life-boats."

Ryan and J.B. followed the albino.

"Ryan!"

The one-eyed man glanced down over the side of the ship, spotting Albert. "What?"

"Krysty's missing. One of Harlan's people said she got taken back into the ship. There." The dwarf pointed toward one of the open doors ahead of Ryan.

"Get her," J.B. said. "Me and Jak will see to the boat."

Ryan unlimbered the SIG-Sauer and entered the door. The corridor ran straight and narrow before him. The creak of tortured metal was loud. The frigate shivered again. He plunged around the corner, looking for Krysty. The lights in the vessel were starting to fail as the power centers went out. The frigate was dying.

"Krysty!" he yelled.

"Here, lover," she said in a strained voice.

"Turn slowly," a man commanded.

Ryan turned.

"Drop your weapon."

Ryan lowered the SIG-Sauer to his side, keeping it in his fist. He saw Krysty in front of him, the mustached man standing just behind her, the corridor of flickering lights extending behind him. The little black pistol in the man's hand looked quite capable of blowing her head off.

"To the ground."

"No," Ryan said in a quiet, deathly voice. "If

you wanted her chilled, she'd already be chilled. Means you realize it's only to your advantage that you keep her alive. I'd like to keep you thinking that. If I put my blaster down, mebbe you get too brave, do something stupe. I keep mine, keeps you honest. Gives us common ground."

"I'll take her head off," the Russian sailor said.

Ryan spotted the gold braid on his shoulders. "Captain Vitkin, isn't it?"

"Da."

"You're in command of this situation. Up to you how you handle it, but if you chill her, I chill you next. That's a damn promise. Right now I'm in a position to give you something you want. Otherwise you wouldn't be asking."

"I'm not asking. I'm demanding."

"Sure." Ryan faced the man, reading his features, reading the fear in the man over dying. "But going down in this ship, that's not a fate I'd want to wish on any man. You hurt her, I'll shoot you in the legs, let you see if you can float free somehow. Don't think you can manage it, but mebbe. Guess we'll see."

"I want a boat."

"Get out there soon enough, mebbe you'll find one. I'm not bringing you one."

"You have to."

"No," Ryan said calmly, "I don't. You should have just taken your chances, not grabbed the woman. Same as every other mother's son out here. Right now I'm wondering if that steel bulkhead behind you will ricochet a bullet into your back."

With an inarticulate cry of rage, the Russian frigate captain pulled the trigger.

Only Krysty wasn't there when the bullet cut through the air.

Applying pressure at the proper point, she snapped his gun arm with ease, pushing it away from her. She rotated the arm again, snapping the wrist, as well.

The Russian screamed in pain.

Ryan shot him through the mouth, dropping him in his tracks as his brain and his spinal cord emptied out the big hole in the back of his head and neck.

Water ran into the corridor from outside. "Got to go," Ryan told Krysty as the frigate dropped through the ice again.

Together they ran outside. Glancing over the side of the frigate, Ryan saw that the water had risen over the top of the iceberg, looking three and four feet deep in places. The deck tilted again as the stern dropped more deeply into the water.

"Ryan!" Mildred called.

Swiveling his head, Ryan saw the rest of the companions and Albert in a black rubber raft below them. He helped Krysty scramble through the railing and drop into the boat, then followed her.

It was impossible to stand in the rubber boat and hard to hear over the throb of the powerful outboard motor mounted at the rear.

"Hot pipe, Dad!" Dean said. "Isn't this a great boat?"

"Raft, son," Ryan replied. "And it might be great right now, but for crossing the ocean, I'd rather have one of those lifeboats Harlan and his people have.''

''Never be able to get back to the mat-trans unit in time with one of those,'' J.B. said. ''This raft gives us the best chance for that.''

''There's no guarantee that the access tunnel will be above the waterline when we get there,'' Mildred cautioned.

Ryan looked across the black water drinking down the iceberg as the Armorer steered them away from the sinking frigate. Harlan and his Inuit tribe had boarded the lifeboat. The quarters were close, but they all fit. He didn't know if the man had found the girls he'd come after.

''Got two choices,'' Ryan said. ''We trust the Inuit and see what kind of shake we get with them, or we go back to the redoubt and see if it's still above the ocean level. I don't like the idea of trying to stick it out here if the redoubt could be open. This is far away from the places we know. Don't know who's who out here, or even how to live off the land properly.''

In the end, there was no choice at all. Not if they were going to maintain control over their future.

J.B. steered the little raft around, then opened up the engine, streaking for the edge of the iceberg so they could sweep around it and follow it back to the access tunnel.

The frigate sank without a trace, leaving only corpses in its wake. The lifeboat of Inuit disappeared into the gray clouds left over from the depth-charge blasts.

Chapter Twenty-Eight

When the companions arrived, the ocean was less than four feet below the lip of the access tunnel, and rising. Ryan played his lantern over it, the light very weak and orange now that the battery had almost depleted itself. The wind whipped the waves to splash over the lip in a salty spray.

"We all know the tunnel bends down a little farther on," J.B. said. "Means the gateway and those rooms are already below the ocean. Going to take on water bastard quick when it starts."

"Water level rising," Jak commented. "Went up couple inches while sit here."

"The time to go," Ryan stated, "is now or never."

"We have the same choices as before, lover," Krysty said. "Except that now we have no clue where Harlan and the Inuit are."

"And this little bastard boat is no place to be out on this ocean," Albert said. "Leaves us no choice at all."

"Pull us in close, J.B.," Ryan directed.

Even as the rubber raft bulled into the ice, everyone saw that there was little more than three feet remaining before the access tunnel started taking on a flood of water.

Ryan leaped from the raft onto the lip, followed by Jak. They helped the others to climb onto the slick ice. "Shed any extra gear," he ordered. "Keep your main weapons, some self-heats and ring-pulls. Everything else goes. It'll only slow you when you run." He flicked a glance at Albert. "You've got short legs, and that can't be helped."

The dwarf nodded, but Ryan could see the fear in him. "There's no place for me here. Little man like me draws attackers. You know that. At least you people have treated me decent. Reckon if I make it, that'll stay the same."

Ryan nodded, then glanced at Doc as Jak led them farther into the tunnel, stepping the pace up to a run. "You can't help him, Doc. Not unless you want to piss your life away."

"I know, my dear Ryan. I can only pray that he is there to meet us."

"Best thing you can do is be safe yourself. Be able to help him better then, if it's to be done at all."

"I know."

The lights along the corridor still operated. There was, however, barely enough light to see by, and the ice and water trickling over it made footing treacherous. All of them fell several times.

And the distance between the companions and Albert grew greater. The little man tried valiantly, but nature's pranks had also stacked a final joker in the deck for his race against the clock. He couldn't keep up the same pace as the others.

Jak reached the mat-trans unit first, followed by

Dean. With only a look shared between them at the outset, J.B. had run well ahead of Mildred. He still had to put the repaired circuit boards into place. Doc paced Mildred, his long legs barely managing to keep up with her quicker strides. Krysty sprinted beside Ryan, pacing him easily.

They slipped and fell, getting separated at times, but always returning to each other's side.

Ryan looked back when he dared at the small figure of the dwarf now nearly a hundred yards back. Behind Albert, he heard the roar of the surf. The trickle of water across the corridor floor grew stronger and faster, a full inch deep now.

By the time they reached the mat-trans unit right after Doc and Mildred, J.B. was just battening the cover back into place.

"Circuit boards are there," the Armorer said. "Remains to be seen if they work." He joined Jak and Dean inside the gateway.

Ryan waited until Mildred, Doc and Krysty entered the mat-trans unit, then stood in the door. His position assured that it would be his decision to wait for Albert or leave the dwarf behind. To set the gateway into motion, all he had to do was close the door.

Through the open door, he could look up the corridor leading to the access tunnel. He stared hard, searching for Albert. But he heard the crash of the water first, then the dwarf's screams of fear.

Albert was still fifty yards out when the wall of water overtook him from behind. His legs buckled and he went down, sliding across the icy floor. Miraculously he forced himself to his feet, making another attempt to reach his goal.

It might have taken him nine or ten seconds to cover the last bit of the distance.

Ryan knew that the second wall of water was going to give the dwarf maybe three seconds at the most. The race was over even though it hadn't finished.

"Wait," Doc begged.

"Can't," Ryan said hoarsely. "If I do, mebbe I'll chill us all. Little man did his best. He's not going to make it." He pulled the door shut, activating the jump sequence. "Mebbe I waited too long now. That water hits the gateway as hard as it's going to, mebbe it'll rip it right out of the floor."

But it didn't, withstanding the battering force of the wave. The outside room filled with water immediately.

Ryan took his seat on the floor, listening to the roar of the water slam against the mat-trans unit as the metal plates on the ceiling and floor began to glow. The familiar gray mist began to fill the chamber, unknotting the worry in his stomach.

He coiled his hand in Krysty's as the jump began, holding on to her.

Albert, slammed into the armaglass walls for just an instant. The dwarf had his mouth open, trying to scream in wild-eyed terror, giant bubbles emerging as his lungs emptied, frozen for that brief flicker of time like a nightmare. His legs kicked violently, and he tried to claw his way into the chamber. He hung on for a while, fighting against the surging current rushing by to fill the lower regions of the redoubt.

Then he was gone.

"Alas, poor Albert," Doc said, his voice strangely calm, indicating that he had slipped back into dementia with the horror of it all. "I fear he is too deep in the brine this time."

Ryan let go of his senses as the jump pulled at him, then closed his eye.

James Axler

OUTLANDERS™

DOOMSTAR RELIC

Kane and his companions find themselves pitted against an ambitious rebel named Barch, who finds a way to activate a long-silent computer security network and use it to assassinate the local baron. Barch plans to use the security system to take over the ville, but he doesn't realize he is starting a Doomsday program that could destroy the world.

Kane and friends must stop Barch, the virtual assassin and the Doomsday program to preserve the future....

One man's quest for power unleashes a cataclysm in America's wastelands.

The Camorra takes on the Mafia on America's streets....

DON PENDLETON's

MACK BOLAN®

BLOOD FEUD

A blood feud erupts between the Camorra and the Mafia, as Antonio Scarlotti takes the Camorra clan into a new era by killing his father. Soon a series of hits against top American Mafia men shocks the country, as families and innocent bystanders are brought into the fray. Brognola entrusts Bolan with the mission of shutting down this turf war and stopping the driving force behind it.

Available in August 1998 at your favorite retail outlet.

A powerful cult leader triggers a countdown to terror....

STONY MAN™ 36

STRANGLEHOLD

Trouble is brewing in the Land of the Rising Sun as a powerful cult leader has assembled a fanatically dedicated following, ready to do his bidding and deliver his gospel of death on the rest of the world.

It's up to the counterterrorist commandos of Stony Man Farm to act quickly to keep the world safe from this displaced doctrine.

Available in September 1998 at your favorite retail outlet.

Sinanju software?

THE Destroyer™

#112 Brain Storm
The Fatherland Files Book 1

Created by
WARREN MURPHY
and RICHARD SAPIR

Ordinary bank robbery turns into larceny of the highest order as the very secrets of CURE (and the minds of its members) are stolen and laid bare on a computer disk. It's up to Remo and Chiun to find a way to restore CURE's abilities while there's still time.

The first in The Fatherland Files, a miniseries based on a secret fascist organization's attempts to regain the glory of the Third Reich.

Look for it in August 1998 wherever Gold Eagle books are sold.

Don't miss out on the action in these titles featuring THE EXECUTIONER®, STONY MAN™ and SUPERBOLAN®!

The American Trilogy

#64222	PATRIOT GAMBIT	$3.75 U.S.	☐
		$4.25 CAN.	☐
#64223	HOUR OF CONFLICT	$3.75 U.S.	☐
		$4.25 CAN.	☐
#64224	CALL TO ARMS	$3.75 U.S.	☐
		$4.25 CAN.	☐

Stony Man™

#61910	FLASHBACK	$5.50 U.S.	☐
		$6.50 CAN.	☐
#61911	ASIAN STORM	$5.50 U.S.	☐
		$6.50 CAN.	☐
#61912	BLOOD STAR	$5.50 U.S.	☐
		$6.50 CAN.	☐

SuperBolan®

#61452	DAY OF THE VULTURE	$5.50 U.S.	☐
		$6.50 CAN.	☐
#61453	FLAMES OF WRATH	$5.50 U.S.	☐
		$6.50 CAN.	☐
#61454	HIGH AGGRESSION	$5.50 U.S.	☐
		$6.50 CAN.	☐

(limited quantities available on certain titles)

TOTAL AMOUNT	$
POSTAGE & HANDLING	$
($1.00 for one book, 50¢ for each additional)	
APPLICABLE TAXES*	$ _____
TOTAL PAYABLE	$ _____
(check or money order—please do not send cash)	

To order, complete this form and send it, along with a check or money order for the total above, payable to Gold Eagle Books, to: **In the U.S.:** 3010 Walden Avenue, P.O. Box 9077, Buffalo, NY 14269-9077; **In Canada:** P.O. Box 636, Fort Erie, Ontario, L2A 5X3.

Name: _____

Address: _____ City: _____

State/Prov.: _____ Zip/Postal Code: _____

*New York residents remit applicable sales taxes.
Canadian residents remit applicable GST and provincial taxes.

GEBACK19

Journey back to the future with these classic

titles!

#62535	BITTER FRUIT	$5.50 U.S.	☐
		$6.50 CAN.	☐
#62536	SKYDARK	$5.50 U.S.	☐
		$6.50 CAN.	☐
#62537	DEMONS OF EDEN	$5.50 U.S.	☐
		$6.50 CAN.	☐
#62538	THE MARS ARENA	$5.50 U.S.	☐
		$6.50 CAN.	☐
#62539	WATERSLEEP	$5.50 U.S.	☐
		$6.50 CAN.	☐

(limited quantities available on certain titles)

TOTAL AMOUNT	$
POSTAGE & HANDLING	$
($1.00 for one book, 50¢ for each additional)	
APPLICABLE TAXES*	$ _____
TOTAL PAYABLE	$ _____
(check or money order—please do not send cash)	

To order, complete this form and send it, along with a check or money order for the total above, payable to Gold Eagle Books, to: **In the U.S.:** 3010 Walden Avenue, P.O. Box 9077, Buffalo, NY 14269-9077; **In Canada:** P.O. Box 636, Fort Erie, Ontario, L2A 5X3.

Name: _____

Address: _____ City: _____

State/Prov.: _____ Zip/Postal Code: _____

*New York residents remit applicable sales taxes.
Canadian residents remit applicable GST and provincial taxes.

GDLBACK1

GOLD
EAGLE ®